THE CENTER
OF EVERYTHING

The
Center of
Everything

A NOVEL

Jamie Harrison

COUNTERPOINT
Berkeley, California

The Center of Everything

Copyright © 2021 by Jamie Harrison
First hardcover edition: 2021

Library of Congress Cataloging-in-Publication Data
Names: Harrison, Jamie, 1960– author.
Title: The center of everything : a novel / Jamie Harrison.
Description: First hardcover edition. | Berkeley, California : Counterpoint, 2020.
Identifiers: LCCN 2019040742 | ISBN 9781640092341 (hardcover) |
ISBN 9781640092358 (ebook)
Classification: LCC PS3558.A6712 C46 2020 | DDC 813/.54—dc23
LC record available at https://lccn.loc.gov/2019040742

Jacket design by Nicole Caputo
Book design by Jordan Koluch
Family tree illustration by Lena Moses-Schmitt

COUNTERPOINT
2560 Ninth Street, Suite 318
Berkeley, CA 94710
www.counterpointpress.com

Printed in the United States of America

1 3 5 7 9 10 8 6 4 2

For Will and John

This beautiful sound. Like you're thrown a plum and an orchard comes back at you.

RICHARD FLANAGAN, *The Narrow Road to the Deep North*

. . . the thing I came for:
the wreck and not the story of the wreck
the thing itself and not the myth

ADRIENNE RICH, "Diving into the Wreck"

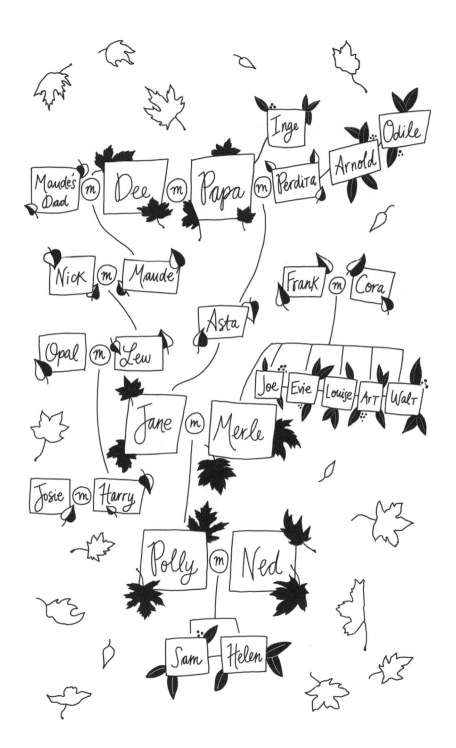

CONTENTS

Part One

Part Two

Part Three

Part
One

1

Sunday, June 30, 2002

When Polly was a child, and thought like a child, the world was a fluid place. People came and went and never looked the same from month to month or year to year. They shifted bodies and voices—a family friend shaved a beard, a great-aunt shriveled into illness, a doctor grew taller—and it would take time to find them, to recognize them.

Polly studied faces, she wondered, she undid the disguise. But sometimes people she loved disappeared entirely, curling off like smoke. Her father, Merle, told her that her mind was like a forest, and the trees inside were her people, each leaf or needle a memory. Her mother, Jane, said that memories were the way a person tried to turn a life into a story, and Papa, Polly's great-grandfather, said that there was a story about everything. He would tell them something long and strange to explain the existence of tigers or caves or trees, but then he'd say, Well, the Greeks said the same thing, or the Finns; the Athabascans, the Etruscans, the Utes. Days were an Aztec snake swallowing its tail, water came from a Celtic goddess's eyes, thunder was a deadly fart from a Bantu in the sky. There was nothing new under the sun, but nothing truly repeated. Papa would row down a stretch of the Sound and back at high tide, proving his point, slipping home before it was too late to recognize home, but the water and light and noises of the world they'd left were different than the one they returned to, except for his humming, the splash of the oars, the fact of his presence.

Lately, Polly thought her mind was a river, constantly scouring and pooling, constantly disappearing, filling with details that glinted and vanished. Even as an adult, every small thing meant a little too much to her, but these days she couldn't go on like that, because though the world had become as strange as it had been when she was a child, she could no longer indulge it. She needed to buckle down, accept some objective reality.

On June 30, a Sunday morning, Polly Schuster and her mother, Jane, were having a carefully worded argument in Livingston, Montana. Polly had smacked her head in a bicycle accident a few months earlier, and during a bumpy recovery, a long period of confusion and doubt, she'd begun to point out all sorts of things she could still remember clearly: arcane facts from college Russian history courses, lines from *Othello*, houses and funerals and train rides from early childhood.

"These aren't true memories," said Jane, reaching into the back seat to fix her granddaughter Helen's twisted car-seat strap. Polly was backing the car out of the garage; they were off to do errands. "They're photographs you've turned into memories. Ninety percent of childhood memories are pulled from photographs."

No one believed Polly about anything, and it was wearing her down. As she craned to check behind the car, she saw the alley rabbit by a neighbor's gate, and the alley rabbit—clear-eyed, dusty gravel-gray fur, brain the size of a chickpea—watched back, sweetly framed by new green grass. Fritz, a black-and-tan mutt, saw the rabbit, too, and went on something close to a point, frozen with one paw up, tail straight. The old poodle watched, and

Jane's spaniel twisted on her lap, but the children in the back seat seemed oblivious. Sam was reading a comic, and Helen kicked her grubby sockless sneakers in time to a Clash song Polly was playing to annoy her mother.

One side effect of Polly's head injury was a tendency to lose her train of thought. Once she saw the rabbit, which had waited for them every morning that week like some furry Pythonesque talisman, she might as well have been another dog. But Jane would not give up the argument, which was really about what Sam and Helen would remember about a drowning that had happened two days earlier.

"All those photos we have out for Maude's party—you're turning them into memories," said Jane. "You've always been muzzy that way, but the head thing has made it harder to tell the difference."

Muzzy; was that a word? Polly and the rabbit held their stare, and here was the thing: Polly wanted to reach behind and set Fritz free, give him a little joy. He'd never manage to catch it, and maybe this was a game for the rabbit, too.

"It's possible that you remember that first apartment, or doing errands in the Village," said Jane, oblivious.

If they kept this up, Jane would be putting her daughter in a book. Polly thought she might as well give her something to write about. She was reaching back with her left hand for the door handle when a flash of light glinted through the trees, like a bright-plumed bird, a noisy parrot: the helicopter looking for their friend Ariel Delgado.

"Give me another example," said Jane. "And what are you doing with the back door? You need to concentrate on the car, honey. And Sam, put on your belt."

"Nothing," said Polly, bringing both hands to the wheel. This was the second time she'd driven in a month. In the rearview mirror, she watched Sam peacefully turn pages, Helen hug the spaniel now trampling her lap. Two women, two children, and three dogs in one car; a strange idea of fun. "Well," she said, while Sam fumbled with his belt. "Another example, then. The drowning."

"What do you mean?" said Jane.

"Not the one on Long Island. On Lake Michigan, with Rita and Tommy, when we were seven," said Polly. A long, idyllic day on the beach with the Wards, but then a drowning, a young woman pulled out of the water after an hour of being churned against a harbor break wall, like a forgotten sock in a dryer or more pointedly a pebble in a rock polisher. Polly remembered the picnic basket of fancy food the Wards had brought, the quilt Jane spread on the sand, the wind spout that ran across the water toward them and disappeared just before it struck. The children lay on their bellies in the wet sand, letting the waves tug at their feet, watching everyone talk and laugh until a woman ran toward them from the harbor, calling for help.

"Another photograph," said Jane abruptly. "Or Merle talking."

There might have been a snapshot of the group together that day, but they certainly didn't have a photo of the red-and-white body. Just a glimpse, but Polly could see the color, feel the water, hear the waves, hear the person who'd found the body scream. Which was only natural. Wouldn't anyone scream?

"Not the picnic or swimming," Polly said. "I remember the body."

It was the wrong word to say out loud. Helen was tracking everything now, watching Polly's face in the rearview mirror, and Sam gave up on the comic. He wouldn't look at the helicopter anymore but she knew he could hear it.

"What body?" he asked.

"Years ago," said Polly, putting the car in drive. "Put on your belt, now."

Fritz gave a low keen, still locked on the rabbit, which squared off to face the car directly. Polly put her foot on the brake and turned in her seat, once again judging the distance to the back door handle. Fritz was trampling Sam, but he only held his comic higher and gave his mother a small, evil smile. "He just wants to play with the rabbit," he said. "Aren't you going to let him?"

People told Polly that she had the nicest children in town.

Jane tapped her leg. "Don't do it."

Polly honked and accelerated and focused on the street ahead. Look twice at stops, brake, be patient. The rabbit vanished into some browning lilacs.

"Do you think I don't truly have a memory of the next summer, either, the man on the Sound?" asked Polly. "No cameras, that day."

"No," said Jane. "I'm sure you remember finding the man."

Muzzy: Polly had close-cropped hair and a scar on her scalp; Polly had thunked her head on the pavement. Polly was bouncing back, sharpening up, vigilant, and on her way to being perfectly fine. To that end, at a doctor's suggestion, she made at least one list each day, starting with everything she hadn't managed the day before. She'd always loved lists, and she despised the doctor, and so she now believed the tactic had been her own idea.

> *REMIND PEOPLE blue tape for dates on walk-in*
> *drop off food at restaurant*
> *clean house! hahaha!*
> *Maude party menu*
> *Mom's manuscript & tribute notes*
> *call Helga about edit on Andalusian cookbook—okay by Sept*
> *Drake's stuff*
> *PHOTOS*
> *family tree*
> *note to the Delgados? food to the Delgados?*

Polly could have combined some of these lines, but she was trying for a sense of accomplishment. She'd forgotten to include *errands* on the list, a lost opportunity for a satisfying deletion. When she added it to the top later, she would not realize that she'd written *errants*.

The new morning drill, before they'd set out in the car that morning, Jane phoning from across the yard to ask if she could come over: Did Polly want to start editing Jane's manuscript, just for practice? They could do something fun, or Jane could help with the kids, they could simply get ready for Maude. Or Jane could help Polly sort her projects, the great slipping piles of paper in the office, so that Polly could be ready to start working when she felt better.

A dizzying welter of shit, but it was meant to be face-saving, all around. If Jane didn't approach it this way, if she didn't dangle herself in multiple positions, Polly might act as if she didn't have time for her mother, or Polly might feel that Jane was making the obvious point that Polly's brain might be too damaged for much of anything.

Polly and her husband, Ned Berrigan, had moved to Livingston, Montana, fifteen years earlier from New York, and their two children—Sam, nine, and Helen, four—were born in the hospital six blocks from their frame house. Ned worked as an attorney for five years before they bought an old restaurant in the Elite Hotel, which they named Peake's after an old family friend, with a small inheritance. As she had in New York, Polly edited (mostly mysteries, scripts, and cookbooks) and helped on a few shifts. They acquired two dogs, a cat, and good friends. Polly had piles of second cousins in town, and now more family was visiting: her parents, Jane and Merle Schuster, had driven out from Michigan the week before, and would stay another month in the alley cottage next to Polly and Ned's house. They wanted to help; because of the accident, they thought Polly and her family needed help.

On a strange, warm day at the end of March, Polly had been riding her bicycle home from the restaurant when a car blew past a stop sign. It clipped her and sent her sideways, nothing like a horse fall, no midair time to think of how to handle it. Her head hit the pavement, but the first, larger feeling was the airless sucking and pain of her deflated chest, the fear that another car would come, rage at the person who got out of his car to scream at her.

The old man who'd hit her (twice, in emails to friends, she'd written *bit*) howled while witnesses waited with them for the police: Stupid girl, stupid girl, how dare you? He screamed harder when people insisted he was at fault. He was malign and narrow-faced; later, she learned he was the candy factory owner who lived on Yellowstone Street, collected old cars—he'd dented a Bentley on Polly's bike—and, according to Josie Wall, spent too much time watching children through his plate glass window. When the sheriff, Cyrus Merwin, arrived, Polly said she felt fine—look at her talk, look at her move, look at her not beating this frail mutant bloody for nearly killing her. Cy stalled for the paramedics, but as they arrived in the town's second-best ambulance, the radio went wild about an accident on the interstate. When the old man turned blue and collapsed into a heap, Cy forgot Polly.

She pushed her broken bike home with the police report crumpled in her shorts. If she thought at all, it was about whether the old shit would survive to buy her a new bike, and if her scraped legs—almost tan after a week of digging in the garden in the weird, balmy weather—would make a short skirt no longer an option for Josie's wedding to Polly's cousin Harry Swanberg that weekend. But before Polly let the bike drop in the grass in the front yard, she'd forgotten who was getting married, and she didn't wonder at the absence of her children or her husband or her dogs, all off at a friend's cabin at Mission Creek. She didn't remember she had kids or Ned or pets, even though the cat was following her around the house. She climbed into bed and slept. When Ned came home at 9:00 and tried to wake her, Polly said "sick," but she wasn't hot, and she wasn't fretful, and since she'd never done anything like this before he was worried but let it go. He put the children to bed and was asleep next to her within an hour. In the morning, when she wouldn't get up, he saw some blood on the pillow and found the police report in her shorts and took her to the hospital. They sent Polly by helicopter to Billings and thought of transferring her to Seattle, but the bleeding was minor, and the swelling abated quickly, and Polly seemed like herself within a couple of days.

And so she went home with a stitched scalp and waited to feel normal after Josie buzz-cut the rest of her hair. Jane and Merle flew from Michigan the day after the accident to sit in the hospital. Polly's three younger siblings, all in California, visited over the next few weeks. Jane and Merle talked of moving, saying they'd wanted to for years. Merle, who'd retired after thirty years of teaching high school biology, spent most of his time lulling Polly into playing card games.

At Easter, Polly overboiled eggs and spilled dye everywhere, but she worked on her attitude and was reassured by the idea that she'd always been a flake. She'd put a tray of something in the oven, sit down to work at the dining room table, remember she needed to move the sprinkler, and head outside. Once there—sometimes forgetting the sprinkler mission—she'd start looking at her plum tree for evidence of blossoms, and she'd keep doing this until the smoke detectors rang and smoke billowed through the windows she'd forgotten to shut. The worst moment of confusion came during her thirty-year-old sister Millie's visit, when Polly looked down at the child next to her on the hospital bed—Helen—and wondered how Millie could be in two places. The second worst came when Polly called Sam "Edmund," and everyone left the room in tears.

Polly painted half of her tiny study dark blue before losing interest. Sometimes she sat at intersections for minutes, and sometimes she power merged. She'd nearly backed over an elderly woman in the Costco parking lot in late May. Vinnie Susak, Ned's former law partner, gaped through the window at Peake's as Polly accelerated through a stop sign into oncoming traffic a week later. That was it for the car for a while.

Polly had ocular migraines for the first time in her life—jewel-like, kaleidoscope patterns that got in the way of reading but didn't hurt—and she'd watch the show spread from a hard diamond to a fractal whirligig. At other times, she'd drop into a dream, a film instead of a painting, memories moving in her brain like a current. During these spells—she liked the Victorian weirdness of the word better than seizures—she'd see wonderful or horrible things, true moments and others that couldn't possibly have happened. She fell off the end of the picnic table on May Day after a single glass of wine, having simply lost any sense of where her body was, but usually she'd just freeze in place. "Just give her a minute," said Ned, now used to watching his wife dream with her eyes open. Sometimes she could hear him say it, even if she couldn't speak. "She'll come right back."

No one anticipated any sort of brain cell death spiral; the doctors said these small, mostly peaceful pauses should become less frequent. Polly needed a few months to recover and should ideally avoid future impacts. Some glitches might persist, executive function issues. Her first impulse would no longer be her best.

Ned and Polly decided to let the manager at Peake's buy into the business and take on more responsibility, and Ned cut down on his own shifts. He and Polly came up with bits of the menu she could manage at home. Friends were oddly eager to stop by. Josie, who worked as a grant writer, taking the town through incremental improvements, claimed she needed help revising the local soup kitchen's fundraising materials, and said the incomprehensible pages Polly turned in were brilliant. Polly's cousin Harry badgered her for help researching the old Poor Farm graveyard at the county museum; Harry's mother, Opal, wanted to learn how to use an iMac. The children were in high demand for playdates. Nora Susak, an internist who was still nursing her youngest child, said she wanted to learn how to bake; her husband, Vinnie, eloquent attorney, asked for help with a letter to the editor. Ariel Delgado, the girl now lost in the river, asked for tutoring on the GRE and claimed she needed help writing a graduate school admissions letter six months in advance.

Over the last decade, half the town had brought Polly business letters, brochures, oral histories and obituaries, short stories, and even poems, the way you'd bring the sick to a shaman. Fix it, make the story come to life, make it true. Polly felt like a sham even before she smacked her head—she could only do so much. Now she couldn't move a paragraph. She would either wander away from a thought the way she wandered away from the stove, or she'd descend into a visual whirlpool, sometimes with an accompanying earworm melody. For an overdue mystery edit she confused character names, covered the printout with enraged comments, wrote *knight* for *night*, *toe* for *tow*, and—weirdest of all—*now* for *gnaw*. *Knew* instead of *new*, *passed* instead of *past*. *Right rite*, *bow bough beau*. When she picked up an old coworker's cookbook project, she shredded rather than edited and put the recipes back together in a novel order, with missing steps and fresh errors on quantities.

Polly's remaining independent source of income came from vetting scripts for Drake Aasgard, an actor she'd known since he was a teenager. Drake understood what had happened—Ned had been at his cabin when Polly went flying over the Bentley in March—and his agenda was so wayward that Polly could operate with little harm. He overpaid her to read and assess, to issue simple, graceful kiss-offs—this was sometimes a challenge now, given her damaged impulse control—to the scripts and novels his heartbroken agent still sent to Montana. Jane was snooty about the job, but trying to describe each script or novel plot was a good way for Polly to work toward making sense again. Drake, who hadn't filmed anything in four years, had no real intention of working soon, but he checked the notes before they went out.

The world became terribly fragile; the center, the imperfect brain Polly had been fond of, had fallen apart. The bleaks, short but sharp, swept over her after every error in judgment or memory, and when she sensed pity, she blew up in a nasty stew of confusion and panic. Polly felt sure she would need a minder forever, she would wear Ned out and he would leave, she would now be a horrible mother. What would Helen and Sam remember out of this mess?

You'll be fine, said Ned. We'll be fine. It wasn't as if he didn't understand her fear, and he knew having Jane around opened this question up like a wound. Polly had always known she was lucky to have Jane, but the bad mothers, cruel mothers, absent mothers, rang in Polly's head. She still loved the feel of Jane's fingers on the good side of her skull, fluffing her fresh-cropped hair, stroking her cheek.

Good mothers, good mothers were rarities, the center of everything.

On that Sunday morning, Polly had things to do, *errants*, most having to do with the looming arrival of Maude Swanberg, great-aunt, for whom they'd planned a large birthday party on July 5. These plans were now complicated by Ariel Delgado's accident—it was hard to throw a party for a hundred people when someone you loved was probably floating facedown in the river. It was almost equally hard not to have a birthday party for a woman turning ninety. "What if they find her right away?" asked Maude, her voice reedy on the phone.

"Fifty people, not a hundred," said Jane, who was depressed by the idea that Polly's younger brothers and sister couldn't come—they'd used their time off helping after the accident that spring. "The ones you truly care about. Do you want to come later, when we can do it right?"

Maude did not; she wanted to turn ninety in the town where she'd been born. Later was problematic. She thought she'd die soon, and she probably would, because she was eighty-nine. Consider the actuarial reality, she said.

Merle, designated asshole, called the guests who'd been cut. Ned canceled the tent and the cellist and planned pork specials at Peake's with one of the two pigs they'd planned to cook. And so the tasks for today, after Polly resisted the urge to loose the dogs on the rabbit, were simpler than they might have been. At the grocery store, Jane and Polly still looked like a ranch family on a monthly shopping spree, groceries as a sport and a pastime. They bought a cheap wading pool and squirt guns and new badminton and croquet sets to amuse the kids over the next few days, poster board for all the photos of Maude's life, socks and Velcro sneakers for Helen, who was still uninterested in clothing and liked to deposit items in corners of the garden. They picked up Sam's friend Ian, who was terrified about most things in life, and listened to the boys gibber about medieval warfare, Helen content in her own world. They dropped off containers of sauces at Peake's—the Berrigans' home kitchen was licensed, and despite her dented head, Polly still prepped some nitpicky things. She'd cooked the night before, drinking wine and only burning one batch of *carta di musica*. She hadn't ruined the lemon curd or meringues or duck confit, though she had eaten too much of the crunchy skin.

Polly found Ned in the restaurant kitchen, fresh from searching another stretch of the river with Harry. He was sunburnt, his brown hair bleaching out, and he shook his head—no news—before he kissed her and went back to prepping duck. He said the walk-in compressor was dying, but it was always something. Could she braise fennel and onions that afternoon? Would she remember to add the pistachios to the focaccia this time?

"I will," said Polly (though she wouldn't), floating off to the basement storage to determine how many tables would need to be carted to the house for the party.

Outside, the sky was dark blue, with just a breath of wind. Seventy-mile-an-hour gusts were routine on this part of the Rocky Mountain front, sixty miles north of Yellowstone Park, but at this moment the air was dulcet, and the town felt sweet-tempered, with only a few crushed plastic glasses in the gutter to warn a traveler of the place's roaring alcoholic heart. Livingston had only eight thousand people within a county that was twice the size of Long Island, and they were on the brink of peak tourist season. Polly and Jane and the kids stopped at a food truck in the hardware store parking lot and ordered coleslaw and fried clams, though Livingston was a mile high and a thousand miles short of an ocean. They drove to the river and walked toward a bench behind the baseball diamonds, where the dogs could run around. An osprey platform stood between the lights on the outfield fence, and the dogs sniffed for bones and scraps underneath. From the higher ground on the river path, Jane said she saw two small heads bobbing around an adult osprey in the nest, rather than the three Polly had counted the day before, and Jane wondered if the third chick had blown out during the wind the night before.

The third osprey chick was fine, said Polly. Maybe it was in the deep center of the nest. The dogs would find the body if it wasn't.

The kids and dogs zigzagged around the field. "Something else may have eaten it already," said Jane, who had an ancient view of life.

Polly pushed such thoughts away. The bench faced south toward the river, the still-green hills and white-tipped Absaroka Mountains, all the snow from the tops and the darker north-facing slopes still plummeting into the Yellowstone, where it joined the immense melt from the caldera of Yellowstone Park and plunged on to the Missouri, the Mississippi, the Gulf. The river swirled and thundered, but the level would drop quickly. This green world would burn up in August when the fires kicked in. If Ariel's friends had waited even one week to float, she might not be out there now, invisible.

Why, thought Polly, losing herself for a second, ripping herself back. They watched a disembodied kite flit above a lonely cow on the far side, above trees and rocks, below the osprey's circling mate. Jane's spaniel, a blur with millipede legs, hadn't seen much beyond her own Michigan backyard, and barked at a stroller, an alien. The couple pushing it showed no sense of humor. She barked at the oblivious day-trippers passing on the Yellowstone River, too. Jane and Polly avoided looking directly at the water until the county's search boats appeared.

"It seems like a tremendous waste of time," said Jane. "They can't see anything in that water."

"They're hoping she's alive on a bank," said Polly, who felt as though she should be looking, too.

"Not likely," said Jane. "After two days. When do they give up?"

"Not yet," said Polly. She waved to a man in one of the drift boats, her skinny cousin Harry Swanberg, grandson of the redoubtable Maude. It wasn't his first search.

Two days earlier, on Friday, June 28, when eleven people headed to the Yellowstone, putting in at about three in the afternoon just south of Livingston for their first float of the year, the river was too high to be safe, but the group wanted to stay ahead of the onslaught of summer tourists. An older crew had talked about going but bowed out—Vinnie was dealing with a client's suicide attempt in jail, Polly and Ned had an appointment in Bozeman, Josie and Harry were squabbling about their wedding. There would be nothing relaxing about a float when the river was flowing this fast, but many of this younger group were used to the Colorado and the Salmon. They'd floated a dozen times the year before and wanted to see which channels had deepened or filled with gravel during high water, where beaches had formed or banks collapsed. One drift boat held two people delusional enough to think they could fish in the cloudy, turbid water; a large raft carried seven others who only wanted to have fun; and a couple—Ariel Delgado and Graham Susak—chose a double kayak. The group packed beer, fried chicken, and coleslaw. They brought coats, though when they shuttled cars to their take-out, on the east end of town, it was ninety degrees. When they put in, ten miles south of town, it was slightly cooler, with a puff of clouds to the west.

They passed many downed trees, some hard to see in the milky water. The people in the raft and drift boat—bartenders, teachers, carpenters—watched the kayak, worried, but Ariel was careful, and Graham had spent his childhood on Puget Sound and the Columbia River and swum on a college team.

They saw two bald eagles, one golden eagle, many ducks, bank swallows, a fox, dozens of whitetails, hundreds of cows. Someone's goat ran along the riverbank, watching the flotilla. Graham said he saw a bear, but no one believed him. The river was too violent to hear much, and people shouted conversations. Hail loomed when they were an hour in, nearly to the canyon. You could feel a sudden sharp edge to the air even before an extreme darkness appeared to the northwest. The threat passed quickly, with just a little wind, and though the people in the raft and the drift boat decided to get home, Ariel and Graham pulled over on a pretty island. They waved, and Ariel disappeared from the world.

———

Something awful happened every year on the river. How could it not? Even during a spring when the flow wasn't record-breaking, whole trees shot down like Pooh sticks. A stiff dead baby bison had floated through town a few years earlier with its own golden eagle riding on top, watching the world between nibbles.

People loved the river Yellowstone for coolness, prettiness, peace, food, wildness, a dare, but touching it meant buying a lottery ticket. Using it was like driving on ice, flying a small plane, walking out of a bar with a stranger. It was easier if the unlucky person was a tourist, but usually it was someone the town knew, someone who loved the river, who understood what he or she might be getting into. This year it was Ariel, who'd been born here, played soccer and cello, tested high, been generally beloved.

When Polly and Ned moved to Livingston, Ariel, age seven, was one of the first people they met. Harry, Ariel's almost stepfather for three years before Ariel's mother found religion, stayed close with the girl and brought her to Polly and Ned's ramshackle house while they renovated, and Ariel swept sawdust or played with paint samples. When Ariel's mother married the next year, they saw less of her, though Harry kept up monthly lunches. Ariel's stepfather, who worked for UPS, was a conservative Christian and loved his stepdaughter but was jealous of his wife's history. Harry, who'd managed the impossible task of being a popular cop in a small town, was a difficult predecessor.

Ariel started helping with Sam when she was fifteen and he was two. She succeeded her joyless best friend Connie Tuttwilliger, whom Polly used for a few hours a week when Sam reached two months. Polly had been finishing a cookbook edit, and her notion of how things would proceed—she'd work at night and during the baby's naps, or perhaps while Sam was peacefully watching dust motes and attentive dogs—was shredded during the first weeks of colic and doubt and fatigue. Connie thought Polly and Ned were bizarre—so many books, wine bottles, the foreign and violently fla-vored condiments in the refrigerator, and the clean counter of cooks above an unclean floor of slobs—and was offended by the idea that Polly insisted on nursing rather than handing over the baby for a bottle. Connie generally lacked humor, or what Ned referred to as elasticity, but she was renowned for her first aid skills—when Bobby Lundquist had stuck his tongue in an outlet, she'd gotten his heart beating again, and this had made her services priceless to all the parents who signed up for her summer swimming lessons. She was in demand, and the Berrigans were relieved when Ariel, who was more their speed, was allowed to babysit despite their status as nonbelievers.

After high school, Ariel stuck close—college in Bozeman, an apartment with Connie. She was a good girl, a kind girl. She dated vaguely and rarely got in trouble. When Ariel did misbehave, Harry and Polly and Josie and Ned were the people she could call. Ned and Harry plucked Ariel out of a high school party during senior year and waited quietly while she threw up in an alley behind the Methodist church. Polly rescued her when Ariel, busted at an under-eighteen party in Bozeman, panicked and told the police Polly was her mother.

But Ariel was mostly a cautious girl, sometimes to her detriment. Prep-ping for a catering one night, drinking wine with Polly, she'd said she'd never gone out with anyone she'd been in love with. All the boys she'd dated had been assholes.

"All of them?" asked Polly.

"Maybe I didn't know them well enough to be sure," said Ariel. "All of them so far."

A little humor, a little bravado. She was still dabbling, thought Polly. But had she been in love?

Maybe, said Ariel. Maybe she was now, but Polly would laugh at the name.

Tell me, said Polly.

Nope, said Ariel. I'll be over it in no time.

The lack of bullshit, the frank doubt, impressed Polly, who'd always

seen life, love, the whole mess as a war of possibilities and had never wanted
to consider the bad odds. At Ariel's age in New York, Polly hadn't paused to
think. They were talking in late May; they'd run down to the Yellowstone
with the wagon to make the children happy after dinner, after wine, to see
if the river had risen during the day. Polly's curly dark hair was beginning
to hide her scar, and she was giddy, trotting along the muddy dike. In the
spring, even in years when there was little chance of flooding, it was hard
not to believe that all the water in the world wasn't rushing down toward
them. Freshly ripped trees, a broken pelican tumbling through the muddy
chocolate water. Or maybe a swan, but the flash of yellow-orange from a
beak or feet seemed too large. Ariel was sunburnt that day. It made her even
unhappier in her skin, but she was beautiful to all of them.

Over the hours Ariel worked for her, Polly edited a dozen mysteries and
cookbooks, on top of the scripts she vetted. Ariel did some work for Drake,
too, and he offered to help her get a real job in Los Angeles, but the futility
of the Hollywood process shocked her—all the back-and-forth, and Drake
never agreed to film anything; nothing was ever perfect enough to pry him
out of hiding. Ariel liked concrete things, and that summer, she'd begun
to help Harry with some archaeology jobs and think of a graduate degree,
even though Harry was clear that archaeology was as shitty a way to make a
living as writing or editing or cooking. He worried he would be responsible
for a life of poverty, while Drake promised riches.

It was an interesting tug-of-war, but Ariel had been happy and comfortable with herself, unlike Graham Susak, the boy who'd been behind her in
the two-man kayak. Graham had left Seattle to stay with his uncle Vinnie
that winter because of some hard time, some incident or depression. There
were so many possible ways trouble could manifest at twenty-four that no
one pried into it. Graham was two years older than Ariel, tall and handsome
and clearly lonely, but though he was articulate while bartending, he hadn't
been able to spit out a word in front of Ariel, and she had been noncom-

mittal. Graham was nice, but not for her—too jocky, too surly. Polly had no idea of how they'd ended up in a kayak together, and no one riding in the other boats seemed to know, either. Ariel's parents might, but it was unlikely.

Polly had talked to Ariel's stepfather only at graduations and when he delivered UPS packages; since the end of the relationship with Harry, she'd talked to Ariel's mother only when she called to track down her daughter. Now she felt queasy at the idea of seeing the family, and she'd given a little puff of relief when Harry said to wait to go by with food. Food meant death, and the Delgados still held out hope. They were bitter that people didn't share it. How long could you make yourself believe that your child was alive and lying on a riverbank, waiting for rescue, but what was the alternative? All the hard thoughts: Had there been pain? Had Ariel known she was drowning, or had there not been enough time to think? And how on earth had someone with as much experience on rivers as Graham let it happen?

The sheriff's department description for the searchers, as if they'd bump into another dead girl on the river: Ariel was five feet six inches, 120 pounds, a little long-waisted, with thick orange-gold hair and gray-blue eyes. She was wearing blue shorts and orange water shoes and a white T-shirt when she went into the river. She wore a Peake's hat, too, but there was no way it would have stayed on. She had a goofy deep giggle. She loved Tolkien and Frank Herbert, and her Subaru was coated in good-natured left-wing bumper stickers. She was tough—she'd placed second in the St. Patrick's Day Run to the Pub ten-kilometer race that spring. She'd been a lovely girl, funny and smart and ready to give the world wonder for decades. Or not— who knew what she would have been? Dead was all the things that would never happen.

Accidents, thought Polly, came like arrows. A plane in a shrill pirouette, the flicker of an oncoming car in the corner of the eye, the branch that took you into a final cold, wet, violent kingdom.

———

Graham told Cy Merwin and his deputies that he and Ariel had let their friends go on ahead so they could make love, that they'd been seeing each other for a while but kept it secret because of her family. When they put the kayak back into the river after waiting out the storm, they'd almost made it through a fast, braided section when a branch from a submerged tree hit the kayak just right at a dip, sweeping both of them into the water. Graham said he'd seen Ariel's face underwater, but given the opacity of the river, this was delusion. He'd crawled up a bank with water in his lungs, bleeding from cuts, and a raft of stoned college students had found him there an hour later.

By then it was almost 7:00. After a deputy finally managed to translate what Graham—who was crying, though he would not cry again—was saying, Search and Rescue was on the river within a half hour. Ned was already in Harry's drift boat before they understood they'd be looking for someone they knew.

Near the solstice, at this latitude and longitude, it was light enough to try to see sky-blue shorts and white limbs until after 10:00. There'd been no time to mount a true search before dark, though flashlights glittered on the riverbank all night. When Ned came home at 11:00, Polly heard the rattle of ice, the creak of the pantry door opened for the bourbon bottle. He came up and washed his face as she watched him, telling her about how little you could see in that water and along the green willow and red dogwood shore in that light, at that speed, the boat hurtling along. They'd done two five-mile stretches downstream from the bend where Ariel disappeared, shoulders popping at the oars to slow the boat down, and at the landing Ariel's parents had been waiting in vain.

Ned rubbed his eyes, finished his drink, and vomited in the toilet.

2

Sunday, June 30, 2002

Police cars and boat trailers had begun passing the Berrigans' small house, just two blocks from the river, before the next morning. The helicopter started at 7:00, and a dozen boats were on the river by 8:00. At noon, volunteer Gallatin County deputies found the kayak pushed against a weir two miles from where Ariel had gone in. If she was dead—and she was almost certainly dead—her body might still be close to that point, pinned down in a pool, or it could be shooting toward the Missouri. The current was still too high and strong for divers, and grappling poles could wrench a man out of a boat. All the searchers could do was try to reach every channel, scan every bank as they hurtled past the fishing accesses: Pine Creek, Carter's Bridge, Mayor's Landing, the Highway 89 Bridge, and eventually farther afield—Pig Farm, Springdale, Gray Bear, Otter Creek, Pelican. Harry said most drowning victims were found before Springdale, just twenty miles east of town. He promised that they'd find Ariel, though he complained to Ned about the other searchers and about methods.

Ned wondered if Harry—who'd gone from being a social worker to an archaeologist to a cop and back to an archaeologist—had begun to wish he were still a cop, so that he had more say in the search. The whole family bounced around between professions, but Polly, in particular, had excelled at not making up her mind. In grade school and high school, she'd wanted to be a veterinarian and a historian, a horse trainer and a botanist and an architect. She'd waitressed and worked on a grounds crew, babysat and sold tourist trinkets. As an adult, she kept zigging—cook to script girl to editorial assistant. She'd always minded the idea that she should stick to one thing. She'd loved drawing floor plans but hadn't taken the physics that would have allowed her to become an architect; she'd toyed with the idea of graduate school but never applied. Though she'd loved science as a child, she failed Merle, a biology teacher, by taking English and history and art history because she thought of them as her family line. But Merle himself had wanted to be a poet.

Back when Polly had had two-year plans, instead of daily swivels, Jane had said, "You'll be a late starter like me. And like Papa. A late second start, anyway."

Or third. There were so many ways to count Polly's forays. Despite having emigrated from Sweden with little money or formal education, Papa, Polly's great-grandfather, managed a whole mysterious life before going to university in his late twenties, producing movies in his thirties, publishing books in his forties, and becoming a legend in mythology. He worked as an archaeologist throughout, chased by war after war, and taught at Columbia until his death at ninety. His life was all about telling echoing stories, whether he was digging them up or filming them or writing about them. He didn't cash in like Joseph Campbell, but he was first and everyone knew it. Polly feared she hadn't inherited enough of him.

And Jane was rare simply because she'd returned to school for a master's in mythology and religion from NYU after Polly was born. She taught history for twenty years before abruptly producing a manuscript on the eternal nature of stories (*The Inherited Dream*) and another on ethnic and religious conflict (*Ages of Rage*) that somehow managed to give coherence to varieties of hatred. Both sold well and made the *Times* end-of-the-year lists.

Because she came from a family of writers, friends and family assumed Polly would write. She never wanted that—she liked to fix problems, not create them. Polly *liked* doing what she did. Editing recipes gave her both the anal, geometric satisfaction of quantities and process and the zen of variables. She liked the puzzle of scripts and mysteries, the who knows what when and why; she liked dreaming up solutions. The writhing, errant world was filled with good ideas that needed only a little air and discipline. Once a book or script was rolling, she stuck with it like a meth-addled Jack Russell on a large, juicy rat. She was a technician, with no interest in creating her own stories; she didn't mind that an idea wasn't hers in the beginning. She came from a family of special and strange, but she wasn't special, not special at all.

Though privately, she believed that the ability to turn a turd of a manuscript into a diamond was nothing short of magic.

"I thought, Why Polly?" said her internist after her accident.

"Why not?" asked Polly. She guessed the doctor meant that they knew each other and liked each other. They were almost friends, and he would rather misfortunes happen to people he didn't know. Polly wanted to pat his arm, but he might take it the wrong way. Just an accident, just a shame. It would be easier to bear if the damage had a plot, if she knew the point to this part of the story, or whether she'd ever make a living from her brain again.

Everyone had different acts. Montana had begun for Polly and Ned in 1987, when she talked him into driving out with her. He'd never been west of the Mississippi. They arrived in November, grimmest of months, and moved into the rundown house Jane had inherited from her greataunts. Ned passed the Montana bar and got a job with Vinnie Susak. Polly edited freelance and tried to get catering work. They spent what they made and more fixing up the house: new plumbing, new wiring, a roof. It had four tiny bedrooms, one of which Polly used as an office. They put new countertops in the kitchen but kept the old white subway tile, so dated that it was new again, installed a commercial range and double oven, patched the plaster rather than putting in modern drywall. Ned rebuilt the battered sections of brick wall around the garden, and they pruned the surviving fruit trees and vines, fiddled with old terraced beds (peonies, rhubarb, roses) that looked out over Sacajawea Park, soccer nets and tennis courts and a playground in what had been, back when the house was first built—long before the Yellowstone had been rerouted during the Depression and the park had been created by the WPA—marshy cottonwood lowlands buffering the river.

They mail-ordered olive oil and fancy perennials. They bought a lot of midrange wine and novels they never read. These sorts of decisions and expenditures set a pattern, and they danced in and out of debt. Their friends all loved food and wine and the occasional joint, memories of hallucinogens, music. They shared books, teacher tips, pink-eye medication, Ariel as an employee. They trusted each other without confiding too much, and when Polly had her accident, all these people helped.

Mostly, though, Ned and Polly worked. When they bought the businesses on the ground floor of the Elite Hotel, they leased the larger bar, which faced the brunt of the town and its tourists, but kept the restaurant and its small entry bar. Until the accident, Ned cooked three days and two nights and worked two bartending shifts, a Monday to mop up from the weekend, a Friday to start it right. Polly had helped on heavy nights, handled most of the specials prep, and dealt with the accounting.

But no more. Polly's problem after the accident, really one of her largest problems, was an inability to prune what she saw and what she thought, to stop her brain. She was both too easily distracted and too attentive. When she'd gotten out of the hospital, she'd gone on a looking binge. Ned brought her photography and gardening books, stacks of Sotheby's catalogues he found at the local Goodwill store, piling them everywhere as a hedge against her glitches in language. Polly spent one unnerving afternoon flat on her back in the yard, watching trees encroach on clouds. There hadn't been much to do but observe.

But she had always looked too hard at things. When she was little, in a decade of assassination and riot and war, people couldn't always scuttle her away from the news, but everything—books and records and magazines and calendars—played into some grand theory in her brain about lost people. Her dead aunt Evie gradually looked more and more like the woman on the cover of Durrell's *Justine,* and her dead grandfather Frank became a doctor in *LIFE* magazine. Jane had framed an image of a phoenix, a Persian fresco, from a magazine, and hung it in the bathroom—a golden bird, rising in front of a black sun. It didn't look reborn, it looked as if it wanted to scorch the world, and it became another tile in her mind, so that later when a neighbor had a parrot, she suspected it was a phoenix in disguise. Bird books, art books—the world was filled with strangeness. Gorillas playing flutes on the cover of terrifying Stravinsky albums, Chinese horses and Ray Charles, soldiers dead in the Southeast Asian mud, corteges on television instead of parades or cartoons.

Now, though, pictures sometimes scrolled around her even when her eyes were shut—a ribbon of color and random objects, usually beautiful but sometimes terrifying—and if she concentrated on a painting or photograph, she sometimes went inside of it, the way she had as a child. She saw the leaves in a van Gogh orchard and the graying wounded hands and feet of Holbein's long strange Christ. When Vinnie, an amputee from a forest fire–fighting accident in college, tested a new, unclad prosthesis, Polly was as fascinated as the children by the titanium and the hinges. She felt as if her eyes could enter any surface: the ground, the river, closed curtains, flesh. Sam ripped a hole in his leg in late May, and Polly, remembering another little boy, could not stop seeing his interior after he was stitched closed again.

Ariel, lost, would have the run of Polly's mind.

Few people seemed to believe her when she described this issue, certainly not her mimsy neuropsychiatrist, and so Polly was pleased when she was weirdly good at finding morels that spring in the river bottomland, the cream-colored honeycombs glowing up when you were right above them. Polly was the only one who found dozens, and the only one who didn't trip over submerged branches. She wanted to stay for hours, getting sunburnt, getting lost. Josie and Harry, Vinnie and Nora, Ned and Ariel and Drake and the kids tagged after, everyone getting a little drunk. Only Graham hung back and sat by the river, resentful and embarrassed, stealing looks at Ariel, her red-gold hair flashing through the trees.

When Polly went in for her first full cognitive testing, six weeks after the accident, the woman who administered the test wore a tight black T-shirt with black jeans and black lace fingerless gloves. The Testgiver (capitalized and one word in the leaflet Polly was given) was young, but she had gray streaks in her hair and her arms were doughy and profoundly pale, the pale of no sun, ever. Polly watched her and tried to imagine the life behind all this—the gloves, no sunlight, the CBGB look coupled with a face that couldn't love music, or drugs, or anything wayward on the planet.

The experience was innately hostile. When Polly made stupid, self-disparaging jokes, the woman took notes. When Polly misunderstood instructions, the woman said, "No need to be defensive." Four hours of general knowledge, definitions, story problems, arranging blocks, repeating series of words and numbers, looking at an image for fifteen seconds before drawing it from memory. Polly's reaction time was measured, and she was given a hundred-question yes-or-no psychological test: Do your parents like your siblings better than you? Do you use dirty talk sometimes? Are you afraid of the dark? Do you believe in evil?

Everything was cold: the woman, the lighting, the furniture, the pervasive flavor of humiliation in Polly's dry mouth. The fucking gloves—what was that about? The Testgiver said, "Some people complain a lot. We're used to it."

We, the wall of authority. Keep the patient small. In a follow-up, Polly was told her tests showed that she was perfectly average. "Well," said Polly. "Then why do I feel so odd?"

The youngish neuropsychologist, who said Polly and Ned should call him Dr. P ("for simplicity"), leaned back with his hands up, as if to say, *What can you do?* Polly scanned the sheaf of papers he'd handed her, passing them on to Ned one by one. She'd done honorably in language skills, not well at all in spatial skills and math. Ned asked about the comparison group, and the doctor beamed. Polly was stellar against sixty-year-old high school graduates, and a solid average compared to older college graduates.

As Polly watched Ned read, she began to bridle. How could the doctor be sure that her scores wouldn't have been higher before the accident? For a fast vocabulary recall, Polly pretended that she was walking through a fancy New York grocery where she worked in her twenties—had he seen the words she'd written? Celeriac? Pancetta? Why on earth had a clock face been flipped backward, for a month? The thirtieth percentile for spatial and math—Polly laid no claims to anything beyond algebra II and geometry, but before the accident, she'd measured out every inch of the house when they'd renovated.

"You might be depressed," he said. "Only natural, given your constant questioning of your state of mind. Or it could be a matter of stress. You said you have trouble sleeping. The aging brain, menopause."

Polly had just turned forty-two. Dr. P was getting a jump, there. It could be a lot of things, but she thought the simplest explanation might be best: Her head had slammed down on pavement. The neuropsychologist—whose bill would be paid by the old man's insurance company—was not endearing himself to his patient, or adept at luring her toward his chosen point of view. He had a sharp, tiny nose and the tic of pulling on his small, white fingers while he talked, as if he were taking off a ring or giving a tentative hand job.

Ned tapped her on the knee; Ned almost always knew where her mind was headed. When Polly snapped back into the here and now, the doctor was saying that everyone thought they were more intelligent than they were.

Ned, normally too composed for his own good, grew pink. "She edited.

She cooked at high speed. She didn't have to pause and think through every step."

"It may be unfair of you to set such a high bar," said Dr. P. "We would like to avoid a victim complex, fear of failure bringing failure, bringing on an even greater depression. She's depressed and thinking she's damaged or that someone was at fault will make her even more tentative."

"She has changed," said Ned. "This is not about grubbing money from insurance. This is about helping her to understand and be realistic and continue enjoying life."

Polly was locking into *we* and *she* and succumbing to agitation. Ned obviously wanted to hit Dr. P, but Dr. P needed to be Polly's victim.

"If you're hoping for medication beyond an antidepressant, there's no magic bullet. Nothing can make Mrs. Berrigan more innately intelligent. We are what we are. But I do recommend antidepressants, and counseling." The doctor pulled a prescription pad out, signed his name with a curlicue, and handed it to Ned, rather than Polly.

They all allowed a moment of silence. Polly imagined one of the hardest things to learn, as a psychiatrist, was how not to patronize your patients. "I don't want medication."

"Are you sure you don't already use something?"

"What do you mean?"

"You've told me you enjoy wine."

"You're a righteous little prick," said Polly. "Go fuck yourself."

You could take the girl out of New York, said Ned on the way home. He didn't need to point out that she had been drinking too much.

Polly's secret, which translated to a dozen small secrets a day: She was sure she was losing what was left of her mind. After the cognitive test, she abruptly saw the stakes and understood that admitting weakness was unthinkable. None of them needed another doomed, disintegrating woman. Polly started saying that she was fine, just fucking fine, better every day. She feigned calmness and deliberation, and those who knew her well, after briefly worrying this stance was some new manifestation of damage, went along with the whole thing. There was nothing wrong with pretending, Polly thought. People made it through cancer and jobs and whole marriages that way. And how different was she, really? If you couldn't remember normal, how were you to tell?

Polly didn't lie, usually, but she became good at leaving things out, eliding everything iffy that no one had noticed. Melted spatulas disappeared, bounced checks were covered, her children didn't fink on her when she put her purse in the refrigerator or the trash in the pantry or her laptop in Helen's toy box (despite the hysterical search that ensued). Most people didn't notice if she called out for a dead pet, and when she stopped commenting on her weird painless migraines and started to think of her seconds of paralysis as minor spells, she stopped minding them; what a trick. When she lost herself in one of the moments, she told people that she'd been thinking about something, which was true enough, and people welcomed the chance to ignore the fact that she'd turned into an awkward statue. It would be a fine thing if she could go anywhere she wanted to with her moments, on demand, rather than, say, while driving or burning down her house.

And if she could actually pick what she saw, where would she go? Dee's kitchen, a moment in a Michigan orchard, a French street, her own body at thirty with Ned anywhere, the minutes after Sam and Helen's births. Instead she was treated to a slideshow of Ariel, images clacking like slides as they changed in her brain: a little girl throwing a ball for a dog, a taller girl with a cello looking annoyed during a concert, a grown girl with a shovel on a high hill.

3

Saturday, June 29, 2002

Polly's great-grandmother Dee told her once that there were three kinds of dreams—not the passing filaments, the sorted trash from the day, but the ones that came back, over and over—about three kinds of things: wishes or desires, loss or being lost, and fear. All her life, Polly thought these categories felt true, and lately, they came to her in combination.

Right after the accident, Polly wandered around most nights, not quite sleepwalking, always with some goal in mind. She woke up confused about what was real and what was a dream. Did she still smoke, sometimes, or had she quit cold turkey before she'd had Sam? Was she having an affair? Had Dee made face cards come alive? Polly would smash memories and images together, and on the mornings when she was still in this state, she was half-blind while she made the children breakfast and tried to sort out the truth—had she bought tickets for Sydney? Was she pregnant?

Ned called these moments déjà you, and tried to be light, but during the night, Polly would lose the line between memory and the here and now,

Jamie Harrison

what had been, what should be. She was editing her story, surprised over and over in the morning to find the work was erased, and she was haunted by the in-between, true and not, the story bending once it hit her brain. Her occasional inability to distinguish what was real and what she'd dreamed was a torment at first, but she began to accept it, even look forward to it. Most of her dreams were pleasant, and she cosseted them. She wanted, in the privacy of the dark, to think about the good things, to spend time with people who were gone, to let the world be strange. During the daytime, she forced her mind to make sense, but at night, she told Ned, it was like doing mushrooms again, in the gentlest possible way, and thinking this way, indulging her strangeness for those limited hours, made her relax. She worried less about shorting out. If things got weird, she told people she needed to rest, to lie there and drift. Dreams felt true again, and often she could push them into whole stories.

But on the first night of Ariel's disappearance, Polly saw only bits of things, none of them good. She was tangled in grass, she was in a restaurant kitchen but the stove was over her head, she was running down the hall of Dee and Papa's house in Stony Brook, a figure following her inside the ocean-blue painting on the wall. She tried to stay in the dream but couldn't, and when she woke up, Ariel was still gone, and Polly cried quietly, while Ned talked in his sleep about tides.

They had to remember that this wasn't their tragedy. On Saturday morning, before Ned left to search again, before Sam and Helen could hear people blither on about how there was a chance that Ariel would be found, Polly and Ned told the children that Ariel was gone, that there would be no miracles, that she had felt no pain. Sam sobbed and wouldn't talk. Helen watched him, not entirely grasping what had been said, and told Ned and Polly that Ariel was scared of the water, as if that made her drowning impossible.

And what had Polly said in response? A half hour later, walking along the river while Merle and Jane watched the kids, she hoped it hadn't been

34

the wrong thing. She sat down on a bench and watched the water pass and thought, If I sit here and wait, I'll find her.

Saturday morning, overwhelmed by the sound of the helicopter beating over the house, Polly and Jane and Merle took Sam and Helen to the museum in Bozeman. They went through every room, read every label about Plains tribes and dinosaurs, inland seas and megafauna. They winnowed around vanished things, trying to make the children concentrate on giant lizards and bison and insects in amber and quilled cradleboards.

Everything disappeared. Maybe it would help, knowing this. Maybe Polly's childhood trips to the museum had been meant to bring home the same point. Look at all the wonders that have vanished, and yet here you are.

Polly of the visions, of the X-ray eyes: When she walked a stretch of the river with a group from town Saturday afternoon, people gathering at the city park for a quickly organized search, she truly felt that she held a new special power, that she would find their sweet girl. But she was delusional, in all ways. She found a dead bird, a river-smoothed arrowhead, and a yellow Peake's ball cap, already half-buried in mud. Polly sat down and cried until Josie, having her own hard time, tears rolling down her face, pulled her up and made her keep walking. Josie and Harry had been due to marry the weekend after Polly's accident, and then again on this Saturday, July 6, while Maude was in town. Two days before Ariel disappeared, Josie bought her a maid of honor's dress.

Before the baseball cap breakdown, Polly, who liked silence for the sake of seeing, listened to people in the search group go one way or another: Graham was lucky; Graham was doomed to a life of guilt. Imagine, they'd say, being the one who lived—the poor fucking kid. People in town would be watching him, grading his grief.

Graham was pretty and baby-faced, an angel with an athlete's body.

Working in his uncle's law office hadn't gone well. "He needs to keep moving," said Vinnie. "Not a candidate for a desk job yet." And so Ned hired him. Graham moved well enough in the restaurant bar at Peake's. He was attentive but polite, bait for women, though not great when frustrated, not adept at communicating with coworkers. But imposing physically and charming with customers, right until the moment he tried to push Burt's nose into his brain.

Burt was a notorious asshole, but he was also an investor in the Elite. He'd asked Graham to lean over the bar and whispered something to him—Burt had been too drunk to recall, and was annoyed to be writing on a pad, given his wired jaw. It didn't matter. Burt might have started the fight, but Graham almost started a lawsuit, and Ned and Polly lost any leeway when they learned that Graham had done two tequila shots in the kitchen after Burt began to hector him, and just before he knocked Burt off his stool and kicked him in the face. Their perfect, charming bartender had a short fuse when drinking.

"What did he say to you?" asked Polly.

His cheeks burned—Polly the editor hated meaningless phrases, but Graham's truly burned maroon. "I can't say it."

"Tell Ned, then."

A stunned look, then a flash of humor. "I *really* can't tell Ned."

Polly wondered about Graham's inner life, mostly whether or not it existed. Girls, sports, resentments, better angels blunted by envy and insecurity, the sweet kid who'd visited Vinnie most summers beaten down by the world's itchy bits. The Wednesday after the fight, when they tried him in the restaurant for prep, he was unable to peel a carrot or a potato in less than a half an hour, and they loaned him out to Harry for the archaeological survey at the site of the old Poor Farm—the defunct county home for the indigent, with a potter's field—that had been scheduled before Polly was hurt, or Maude planned her birthday, or Ariel disappeared. Polly was tormented by the thought that if they'd kept him in the kitchen, Ariel and Graham would not have worked together and might not have ended up in the kayak together on Friday. But there was Graham, telling the police they'd been in love.

Polly, however iffy her driving, was the person nominated to take Graham home from the hospital at the end of the day. While they waited for the doctor to show up and sign the release, Polly looked at Graham sidelong, which was easy because he had a patch on one eye. She'd remembered him as a shy teenager who liked to draw, a soulful boy who'd somehow grown into one of those kids who shone, almost obnoxiously, with good health and power. Rude health, Polly thought, and his good cheer felt forced to her now, a depressive's response. He was beautiful, but she was immune—maybe it was her age but she'd never found perfection inspiring, and cleaning that much blood off the bar floor after the Burt incident wasn't her kind of flaw. Now Graham had new bruises overlaying an older one on his temple, where Ned had dropped him with a chair in an attempt to prevent Burt's death, and scrapes everywhere else, stitches in his knees and on his scalp. The scratches on his throat were angry gouges, and river water in his stomach and lungs meant that he'd need to watch for both pneumonia and giardia.

Polly patted Graham's hunched shoulder and he stiffened. She turned away and piled up medical handouts, hoping and failing to find a get-well card. She wanted to ask how long he'd been seeing Ariel, how and why they'd kept it a secret.

"Can I grab anything at the store for you? Help you in the apartment?"

He shook his head and stared out the window. She tried again. Did Graham want to talk to someone? Help with the search? Visit Ariel's family?

"I can't face people," said Graham. "And anyway, they won't want to see me."

"I think they might," said Polly.

Graham stared at the floor. Polly, shaky from the sheer effort of the conversation, grabbed the release papers and went looking for the doctor, who happened to be her own doctor. She knew he was appraising her as he signed off on Graham's release.

"Is he on something?" asked Polly.

"Not a thing," said her doctor. "How are you feeling?"

"Great!" she said. Sanity was tenuous and life was burning by.

They climbed into the car. Polly pulled out onto Geyser a little abruptly and Graham flinched. "Should you be driving?"

"Of course I should," said Polly. "Would you prefer to walk?"

He didn't reply or apologize or speak again until she pulled up by his apartment, across from Peake's on the third floor of the old Masonic temple.

"No one expects you at work again for a bit. Maybe help with prep during the parade?" said Polly. "But Harry says he could use you, when he gets back to the excavation."

"Okay," said Graham.

"Can I help with anything?" asked Polly.

"Nothing to be done," said Graham.

He looked so young—no beard, freckles between river scratches. "Do you want to go home to Seattle and wait there for your parents to return?" she asked. Vinnie's brother and sister-in-law were traveling in Italy, and not volunteering to fly home to deal with their son's trauma.

"No," said Graham, still not looking at her. "I left for a reason."

Polly drove off carefully, wondering what horrible thing had happened to Graham in Seattle, and thinking of how sad it was to have something happen here, too.

In the dark, on Saturday night, the world fell apart again when Helen had a nightmare. Sam had already come to Polly and Ned at midnight, and so Polly climbed into Helen's bed. Maybe, two by two, they'd get some sleep.

The earth cracked open, said Helen. There were things inside. She wanted to look for Ariel.

Polly said "Sssssshhh," and "I love you," and shut her own eyes, wondering what Helen had seen. The cruelest thing, now that Ariel was probably lost forever, was that she was already on her way to being forgotten. She would now mostly make people think of their own dead or of things they should have kept doing in life, because they'd been reminded again that they were lucky. They would bring food, write notes, try not to say the wrong thing, and not allow themselves to think their way down to the dark, where Ariel's family lived now.

Polly dropped away from everything and saw Ariel's body unfurl underwater, arms and hair spinning like a pale seaweed weather vane, like car lights around a wet curve at night when Polly was a child stretched out on the back seat of the station wagon, passing stores and streetlights out on Long Island as Jane and Merle headed home from a party.

4

Spring 1963

Polly, who had known many people killed by water, and who now had a problem sorting the past from the present, was born with the name Apollonia Asta. Merle Schuster had been in a poetic phase, and Asta was the name of Jane's dead mother. Those cursive *A*s and *L*s took Polly years to master.

Some history, and a love story: Merle had met Jane at a cocktail party in 1959, thrown by some English major using his absent parents' fancy house in Ann Arbor, with a full bar, silver toothpicks for the olives and cherries and pickled onions, mixed nuts in an Italian glass bowl. People were dressed up, smoking and talking pompously about Bergman, while Jane was joking about the movies—admiring them, but comfortable enough to make fun of the boatload of symbolism in every frame. Merle heard she was well traveled and knew French and Italian and some Spanish. She was only nineteen, an orphan, but she'd started college early, and her grandfather was a Big Deal in archaeology and mythology. She was tall, with light-blue eyes that jarred against her thick dark hair and gold skin, which looked as if she'd been sunning on an island instead of stumbling through a dank midwestern term. All this, and she was from Montana.

Jane told Merle that Bergman had consulted her grandfather for *The Seventh Seal* and *The Magician*, meeting at Le Pavillon for feasts while they talked about death and old dreams. This level of sophistication, as well as the way Jane smoked a cigarette and preferred whiskey to beer, made various parts of Merle's body and soul expand. He'd grown up smart but poor, and he wanted the world.

What Jane liked about Merle: He was good-looking but gawky, with a high forehead and curly hair, a lanky Roman statue with an astounding, aquiline nose. He didn't patronize her, he admitted ignorance rather than feigning seriousness, he truly listened, and he knew how to fix things like cars and clocks and doorknobs. He was honest, and ardent, and read books. She pitied his polio-withered left arm and marveled at the brown, muscled right.

Jane didn't know Merle was a sweet but melancholic alcoholic who would have trouble, all his life, finishing anything—fencing projects, novel writing, the dishes. Merle didn't know that every member of Jane's family had at least one substantial secret, and that all these secrets had pooled in her body and her brain.

Jane was beautiful, as beautiful as her lost mother, Asta, who'd existed only in photographs since a car accident in 1941, and as Asta's mother, Perdita, Papa's first wife, who'd died soon after giving birth in 1917. Jane was so lovely that Polly could remember being eight, living with Papa and Dee, watching visitors—poets and academics—spilling things while they tried to have a conversation with her. On the first day of school, Jane was always the mother everyone looked at, and Polly would feel a bolt of pride make its way through her dread of the new. Even at the time she'd known, without minding, that she would never come close. Jane could beat Polly in tennis while hitting with the handle, and on the iced-over pond near the farmhouse in Michigan, Jane would make graceful figure eights around her daughter, who fell again and again. Jane was elegant; Polly was not. Whatever genes

Papa and Perdita had brought to the table—beauty, the ability to glide, the ability to kill with a look—very few had been left for Polly, whose figure was closer to that of Merle's sweet dumpling mother, Cora.

Jane was still a junior at the University of Michigan when she became pregnant. She managed to receive her bachelor's degree two years late, but everyone gave up something. Instead of hitchhiking around Europe, or writing poetry, or whatever escape he'd half planned, Merle signed up for a graduate degree in microbiology in Ann Arbor. They moved into married housing but spent most weekends at Merle's family's house a half hour away, a small plain place with linoleum and thin-planked oak floors, a cross on the wall next to school portraits. Merle's parents, Cora and Frank, fed them; a swarm of teenagers cared for Polly when Merle and Jane needed to be young and alone.

Jane, child bride with no siblings, became silly and giddy with the noisy, chaotic Schusters. Merle's brothers and sister and the flood of cousins in the neighborhood dressed Polly up and took her to church and for walks. Everyone paid attention to her, first grandchild, novelty—they read books to her, taught her games, gave her their best marbles. They took her to a cabin and towed her around a lake in an inner tube; they pretended she was managing to whip the cream or smash the potatoes on her own power.

The world was happy, accelerating—Merle would ditch science to write novels, Jane would get a doctorate someday, in something, because she knew everything—until the morning Merle's father, Frank, and sister, Evie, were given a ride in a plane as a gift by Merle's uncle, who hired an air force veteran to fly them. The ride was a celebration of Evie's fourteenth birthday, but the plane dropped into Lake Michigan a mile from Elberta, a place of beautiful white sand dunes. The pilot had been intent on suicide, waiting for an opportunity, and they were simply unlucky. Polly was three. A family can be snapped to the ground, just like that, and almost forty years later, the wounds still bled red tears.

As a result of these absences, Polly came up with some specific ideas about death. She believed that when people died, they disappeared but began anew somewhere else, disguised and hidden from the people of their old life. This explained all the youthful angels in art books, and Peter Pan and the Lost Boys. Polly didn't know what had ended up in Frank's and Evie's coffins, or how to explain the mangled airplane, but she believed they were hidden away, warm and unripped and safe, not understanding how sad they'd left the world. But when she tried airing her ideas, she upset Merle, and Jane explained again that Frank and Evie were gone forever, either buried in the ground in Michigan or up in heaven.

When Merle and Jane announced they were moving to New York a few months later, Polly assumed that the point was to find the dead again. Why else would they leave her world behind? She was bereft, and theories and solutions filled her brain. She would find Frank and Evie on her own, because clearly no one else knew how to go about it.

And so Polly and Merle and Jane set off for the city, three against the world. Merle drove the cat with a baggie of veterinary downers, and Polly and Jane took a sleeper train from Detroit. Polly remembered thinking through her task—she *remembered* remembering, even though Jane now claimed she'd been too young—on the ride from Michigan to New York, watching the landscape blur by in a frenzy of supposition. There was no photograph of the train.

In New York, they found a third-floor apartment on Thompson Street. Papa and Dee's place was a few blocks away, but it wasn't big enough to take in refugees. They were often traveling, and they were a blank in Polly's mind until she was six or seven. She was a denning child, given to blanket forts and shipping boxes, the queen of small spaces, and she refined her plan while hiding in a thicket in the muddy courtyard behind the apartment building, a secret trampled place among elderberry bushes that she made her own. The lacy white umbels gave the thicket a dizzy feel when they moved in the wind, and later the berries, though bitter, looked like jewels. Back then, she thought the older children never saw her, but now she was sure they chose to ignore her. They at least allowed her to listen to their games: If you were an animal, what would you be? What country would you live in, and how big will the kingdom be? How many children will you have, what will your new name be, what will you see?

You could pick whatever you liked. It seemed reasonable.

The three of them on Thompson Street learning how to live. They made coffee at the same time every morning, stopped letting the laundry mildew on the floor or in the washer, began to have dinner at 6:00, with an eye on Walter Cronkite. Merle put on his badly ironed starch-rippled shirts every day to be an assistant for a biologist he despised, and Jane took summer classes at NYU, though she was always behind, always late. She'd grown up with Dee, a world-class cook, without ever paying attention, and now she floundered through *Joy of Cooking* and *Mastering the Art of French Cooking*. She was only twenty-two, hot and resentful in a housedress, starch water in a Coke bottle with a saltshaker top, ironing work shirts badly while they watched Julia Child on television. Polly remembered the mundane moments, not just the laugh reel, the construction of a stew, a cake, a sauce. "Soufflé on a Platter," for instance—Jane was a real mouth-breather for that episode, watching with a steno pad and a pen. Some experiments were repellent (salmon soufflé with canned salmon, bones and all), but the triumphs— duck *à l'orange*, béarnaise sauce, éclairs—burned their way into Polly's soul.

Giddiness when a meal worked, hungover mornings. At night, even when she was three years old, Polly never dreamt of breaching the wall of the bedroom door. It was Merle and Jane's world. They were different people on Thompson Street, always whispering to each other, always close, and Polly was always with them but forever in her own world watching. They were nothing like the people she knew now, another point for memory over imagination.

Whenever she was out in the city, Polly searched for her dead aunt and grandfather. She always looked at the eyes, because it might be the only way she'd know. Evie had huge chocolate eyes with soft brown eyebrows. Polly didn't know how old Frank and Evie would be now—time seemed infinite, since they'd left Michigan, and she believed they'd choose whatever age they liked. Frank might be a teenager, Evie a baby, but Polly hoped they'd both be her own age. She spied on people in museums, circled customers in the fish store to look up at their faces. Back at the apartment, she'd sort what she'd seen against photographs in the grubby brown photo album.

That spring, she finally found Frank and Evie at the dry cleaner's on Sullivan and Prince and studied them from behind her mother's legs. Evie, fourteen when her plane fell into Lake Michigan, now looked as if she were about ten but still had flat dark hair and a small mole on her cheek. Her eyes were right, clear rich brown, and her skin looked the same, and her voice sounded familiar when she asked Frank when they'd have lunch (another convincing detail). Frank's eyeglasses were different, and he was pale, but everyone was paler in a city. He was counting a stack of brown-wrapped dress shirts while the Chinese woman who ran the shop scanned the shelves for a last packet.

Polly was stealthy; she was careful. She couldn't bear the terror of them looking back, the answering flash of recognition or the disappointment of being wrong or being forgotten. When another customer entered, a large woman with curly hair and a shiny coat, Polly wedged herself between Jane's leg and the counter, splitting the difference between strangers to avoid and strangers to watch. Jane counted the money in her red change purse while they waited for the man and his daughter to finish, coins tapped out onto the Formica counter. The old Chinese woman reemerged in a cloud of hot fabric and blue chemicals, and the smell of the place was like its own ghost. As she handed Frank a raincoat and hung Merle's only suit and Jane's blouses from a hook, the young Evie met Polly's eyes and smiled.

Polly felt her face crack open. She gripped Jane's leg so hard her mother gave a little yip and looked down in confusion. "They're not dead," Polly said. "I told you."

The other people in the store heard her. Evie looked away and Frank took her hand. Jane led Polly outside, into the wet pavement smell of spring, but Polly knew she'd been right. Frank and Evie still existed, though changed.

They'd come here to hide and she'd found them. They'd forgotten who they'd been, but she knew better.

That afternoon Polly and Jane wrote letters. Polly knew most of the alphabet but didn't bother with it on such occasions. Jane gave her a mug of cocoa and three pens, red, blue, and black, and they sat down to pale-blue sheets of airmail paper. When you're three, you can write your own epic in your own hidden language, and even after you've faced the fact that some sort of shared code is necessary, the mystery of the original story might survive, if it was there to begin with. Polly drew careful slanted shapes with spaces and exclamation points to mark shifts in the story. She knew she should write the way she talked, rather than the way she thought, but after a few minutes the pattern strayed, and her private handwriting circled the page. She drew human figures, birds, clouds, a cave in a mountain, jagged waves and fish with sharp teeth.

"What's all this, honey?" asked Jane.

"The people are thinking about whether to fly or swim or live on land," said Polly. "Now that they're someone else." She drank some cocoa and went back to her pencils. That night she explained again, and Merle told her that dead was dead. Polly tried to talk about it again when she was eight, but then she put it away, with other childish things.

5

Sunday, June 30, 2002

On Sunday afternoon, as Jane sat at the dining room table drinking coffee, her face was bleak as she read one of Polly's lists, this one highly specific:

> *Party menu: Just one pig now or extra shoulders? Ten loaves, salad*
> *Nicoise or Caesar? Spuds. Shrimp, cheeses, bagna cauda, make sure*
> *oysters cancelled.*
> *Work: Write Dan (myst in August?), give up on Helga?*
> *Clean baseboards, toilets, windows, lights, sinks, OFFICE,*
> *sidewalks*
> *Find Helen's swimsuit*

Polly poured Helen and Sam orange juice in pretty ribbed glasses, diner-style glasses.

"Do you know where I got these?" she asked Jane.

"From Cora," said Jane, uneasily.

"Do you know what I remember her doing?"

Jane pushed away the list and waited.

"I remember her pouring juice into one of these glasses, and then throwing it against the wall, and going into her bedroom and crying."

"Cora didn't throw things," said Jane. "Ever. Not so much as a ball."

"You weren't there." Polly could see the glowing glass of orange juice, and she remembered it from the perspective of someone who was thirty inches tall, nose an inch from the rim of the Formica table, the orange ribbons as the thing took flight. Not the why of it all, but the act. She had watched Cora crying in her bed, at eye level. "I'm sure it was after Evie and Frank died."

"Well, it certainly wasn't before," said Jane, marching toward the dining room and the boxes of photographs. "And we have a snapshot of you and a glass, taken in Cora's kitchen. It's black and white, so if you want to say it's orange juice, great. But you're mixing up life with pictures again."

Polly thought of all the things she wished she could remember from photographs, all the photographs she wished existed. She'd like photographs of herself being hugged by any number of dead people: Frank and Evie, Papa and Dee, boys dead in the first AIDS rampage when she worked in New York. She'd like anything from the year 1968, when her world blew up. She'd like photos of the casual lovers of her youth, to see why she'd done such things; she'd like a photo of herself in a bikini in approximately 1986, to see why they'd done such things; she'd like the look on Ned's face the first time he'd entered her; she'd like a photo of Sam or Helen, nursing.

If Jane could have anything, Polly guessed it would be one true memory of her mother Asta's face. Young, in the moment, no sense of doom. Maybe this was what they were arguing about, the idea that Polly could remember the dead and her mother could not.

"I'm not lying."

"I never claimed it was a lie. I know you believe it."

Polly stomped upstairs with a pile of Drake files. Her small office was at the head of the stairs, looking over the yard. This was the room, walls currently covered with notes and postcard images, pinned like ugly butterflies, that she would need to clean for Maude. Now she looked out the window to see Merle studying the perimeter fence, tugging on boards and testing looseness, peering up into the fruit trees to see if they needed pruning. He seemed to be counting her tomato plants, and he poked at the bean trellis to see if it was solid.

Merle looked up and waved to Polly in the window, Mr. Happy. Every one was so fucking cheery with her.

Ned was with Harry and Drake on the river again that Sunday afternoon, and Jane and Polly left Merle with the kids while they joined Nora and Josie and dozens of others in searching assigned stretches of riverbank. They thrashed through willow thickets and mosquito bogs; they were nearly charged by a bull, nearly eaten by an unnaturally vicious retriever. Nora, a filmy blonde who ran marathons, cut her ankle on barbed wire and promised to give herself a tetanus shot. She was a pediatrician, back to working mornings after her third child—Connie was her sitter—and this wasn't her idea of a break. As they walked, she gave them a graphic description of just how one died from tetanus, something she'd seen as a resident.

"I've never seen a dead person," said Josie. "Outside of a coffin. I've avoided it."

Jane always looked ethereal, even when she politely dripped scorn. "No reason to rush," she said mildly.

"I saw four bodies before I turned nine," said Polly, despite the fact that she despised one-upmanship. It was a blurt, a confession, and they all stared at her. Polly surprised herself, and she surprised her mother, too. Jane the athlete slid on the slimy green river rocks but stayed upright.

Josie opened her mouth to ask for some sort of accounting for these bodies—*who what where why*—but she knew half of it, after years of Polly, and started walking again.

Polly tried to concentrate on the good stuff, the wild iris, blooms long over, the wild asparagus, stalks bushed out. Today, instead of mushrooms, Polly found a dozen different animal bones, some owl pellets made smaller, stranger bones, a hiking boot, shotgun shells, an empty wallet and a half-dissolved copy of a novel. Jane found an old teakettle. Nora found a broken wristwatch. Josie saw something blue and screamed. It was a motor oil jug; Josie had no sense of naturally occurring colors.

They were shiny with DEET in defense against trapped flood pools, little spas for miasmas of happy mosquitos, as they struggled over ankle-breaking cobble, slick from the dropping river. They saw evidence of beavers, two dead deer, a pile of fluffy feathers from a fox or hawk or owl kill. They saw two black snakes and many indiscriminate live birds. Polly could identify dozens of perennials, but she was largely bird-blind, despite being dragged through the wilds and thickets of America by her father, grandmother, Maude. The dogwood and willow stands were dense and mucky, broken up by abrupt rock banks. Everyone but Jane fell down, everyone got blisters from bad-fitting rubber boots.

On the ride back to town in Nora's back seat, Polly flipped open the soggy book she'd found, looking for some meaning, and read:

Just because you can't see something doesn't mean it isn't there.

It didn't take much to make Polly's addled brain expand. She knew Jane was watching her. On the seat between them, a folded newspaper with Ariel's face smiling out at the world; next to that, a frilled baby summer hat, a pacifier covered with dog hair, and an energy bar. Polly squinched her eyes shut. Her brain teemed.

They brought their finds to the sheriff's office, where they learned that another body had been found on the river, probably that of a Chinese American honors student from Claremont who'd been on the wrong trail in Yellowstone Park the previous June, slipped in the wrong place, been swept away. Cy bagged the boot, saying it was a match to the one found on the body. "Hell of a long ride on the river."

"Who found the boy?" asked Polly.

"Harry, of course, in a tree, near where the girl went in. It wasn't fully a body," Cy said. "Just a tibia and foot hanging in a tree, stick with a boot."

Though Harry was no longer a cop, he still helped with forensic work throughout the state—lonely femurs found on talus slopes, the bleak final campsite of a runaway, the predictable assumptions that any older grave was a crime scene and any dog's tooth was a dead child's incisor.

"What side of the river were you walking?" Cy asked.

He was writing on an already-crumpled map, many colors of ink, initials, notes about density of vegetation. The map moved on Polly, as if the drawing of the river was running off the page. She couldn't grasp direction, and her face heated up. "East and south," she said. "From Harvat's Flats upstream."

Cy nodded nervously, sympathetically. "How are you feeling, lately?"

"I'm fine," said Polly, watching the map's river flow. "How about you?"

"In over my head," said Cy, who wished Harry was still the sheriff.

That night, Polly made a lovely chili—a 4-H beef shoulder and Chimayo chili powder, good tortillas and the last radishes. She took her time and concentrated, which lessened her new tendency toward the grand fuckup. Through the open window, while she prodded a chunk for tenderness, she could hear the high notes as Merle and Jane argued over blinds. Every morning, to keep the alley cottage cool, Jane would close the windows and draw the shades, and every night she'd raise the blinds and open the windows, and at both times of the day Merle would follow her around the house, making slight adjustments, while never taking on the whole task himself.

This squabble was about whether it was too warm to open up before dinner. The alley house was tiny, with a nice porch facing a small yard with roses. Papa had built it in about 1920 for Jane's two great-aunts, spinster schoolteachers named Odile and Inge. Now it was fixed up enough to rent to a series of forlorn friends and family, or at least friends and family going through forlorn times.

But it was too cramped for Jane and Merle, who'd retired the year before. They wouldn't last another week without a major fight, and needed to see a realtor. They'd been kinder to each other for a year now, with Merle not so resentful about life, Jane no longer telling him to exercise, drink less, mute his self-pity. It didn't seem fair that you'd start life with polio and end with cancer, but, as Merle pointed out, he hadn't ended yet. He was in remission, and in Michigan, he would still swim every day, either in a pool or a lake. In Livingston, there was no pool within thirty miles, and the river wouldn't do for laps, ever. He was an obsessive man, prone, when nervous, to bouts of overeating followed by bouts of exercise. He was going to lose his mind over the course of the summer, and take them all down with him, especially Ned.

Polly tasted the glossy meat and tried to concentrate on how delicious it was, how fucking perfect, rather than the next batch of dialogue warbling across the yard, Merle talking Jane through the nitty-gritty of drowning: how long it took, what it probably felt like, why a body stayed down, how a body came up, how far Ariel might have traveled, how little was known about river morphology.

Polly slammed a door to make him stop.

They ate outside at a picnic table shaded by the willows that ran along the property line. From Polly and Ned's yard you could see mountains to the south; from the upstairs you could see the Crazy Mountains to the northeast, and the slow rise of the Bozeman Pass to the west. During this kindest time of year, the wind rarely got over forty miles an hour, though it tended to hit that mark often during the fire season in late July and August. Tonight it was still clear, and in the garden, the roses were still blooming, and the tomatoes were surging out of a chilly June, not yet battered by bugs or heat waves or hail.

After dinner, they dispersed. Helen dragged a hose around the yard, Sam read in the hammock. Polly started a card to Ariel's parents, then gave up and wandered in the garden. On a normal day, in a normal week, she'd crawl around for hours, ignoring her children, watching things branch and bud, killing flea beetles by hand, one by one. She hilled potatoes, weeded, pulled out a row of bolted lettuce. She no longer heard the helicopter, out for a last evening run, but she noticed when it passed in front of the low sun.

At 8:00, Ned slumped up the sidewalk with Vinnie Susak, Drake Aasgard, and Harry. They were sunburnt, with bloodshot eyes, exhausted and quiet and mostly fatalistic, sliding into beer, trying to keep their heads in the beauty and rhythm of the river. After they finished off the chili, Merle opened a bottle of tequila and they had shots, though there was nothing to toast. Ned showed Polly the muscle on his forearm that had been twitching for an hour; when the current was this strong, you had to sometimes stand at the oars. They hadn't seen the downed tree Graham had described, but then no one who went through this sort of experience would probably have a straight memory. They talked about what was different about the river this year, after high water, about deeper holes and stronger currents and what the pylons on a new bridge east of town might have done to the flow.

Throughout the conversation, Drake watched Jane, and as she slid out of the room, he pursued her toward the back door. He said he was reading Jane's most recent book, *Ages of Rage*, and loved her chapter on Irish mercenaries in the eighteenth and nineteenth centuries, more at home in Venezuela or Mexico than Dublin. Had she thought of how cinematic some of these stories were?

The sheer physical blast of Drake was often too much. He was just *more*, all the time, a loud, fast, golden thing of beauty. At some point Jane might come around, but for now, he frazzled and annoyed her, and she snubbed him consistently. Now, when she fled, he stared out the window, settling back into sadness. He left a stack of files for Polly by the door; lately he'd accepted that he wasn't the center of her world, and tonight, anyway, he looked almost as rough as Harry and Ned, though he was only thirty-two. Drake had spent hours every week with Ariel, and offered to pay for her graduate school, even though he thought she should go to Hollywood instead of becoming an archaeologist. Now he was offering to pay for extra days of the helicopter search.

Vinnie, who was drunk, made up for Drake's silence. Would people blame him for lending the kayak? Blame him for bringing Graham to town, or blame Graham?

No one answered.

"Why did he leave Seattle?" asked Polly. "What happened?"

But Vinnie shook his head, finally noticing Sam's presence. Vinnie was a good person, a defense attorney from a Butte union family, a quiet serial philanderer. Polly wasn't going to peel his layers of guilt. They were all of them, at the best of times, amusing depressives and alcoholics. High functioning, Harry might add, in a better mood, and Harry was pretending to be cheerful, as if he hadn't lost someone he thought of as a daughter. He was impressed that Polly had found the hiking boot. Maybe they should start using her on the river, put her in some sort of balloon and drag her overhead.

"I don't like heights," said Polly. She pushed the kids outside, out of earshot. It was still light, warm and beautiful; if the helicopter was flying, it was east of town, out of sight and therefore out of Sam's mind. After Polly gave them ice cream sandwiches, Sam took his book to the hammock, and Helen pushed him from underneath, sometimes poking Sam's butt through the mesh. Polly dragged an old metal lawn chair onto the grass, ignoring the notebook and script on her lap for the sake of watching the bats. She did this most nights in the summer. She loved imagining what the bats saw, what the ping of a mosquito in an open mouth meant to them. She wondered where they roosted, if they were long-eared myotis or big browns or maybe endangered little browns, how old their pups were, what they'd think during the rodeo fireworks and if they would feel relief when the Fourth of July was over. She wondered if they hated her shrieking children and barking dogs, if they knew she was cuckoo, daffy, buggy, haywire, one watt short of a light.

Behind Polly, inside the open kitchen window, Ned slammed dishes and Harry talked about where they'd look the next day. This was supposed to be his year for building business back up as an archaeologist—teaching part-time at Montana State University, some contract work in Butte, a survey up at the old Poor Farm on Harvat's Flats, where the county had granted an easement to put in a road to a proposed subdivision and hired Harry to ensure the bulldozers and graders hit nothing problematic. Ariel had worked with him the week before, finding old plats showing the footprint of the burned and razed twenty-room dormitory for the indigent, a graveyard for paupers, farm buildings. But that Thursday, as a grader operated thirty yards from the closest foundation and ten from what should have been the nearest grave in the pauper's field, it ripped into old pine boards and Harry and Ariel looked down at the many bones of a human hand. Ariel was thrilled—when she and Harry stopped by afterward she showed Polly her field sketches. Harry, carrying the bones in a canning jar, was less excited.

The bats looped around a late-flying magpie and crossed to make a figure eight. Polly wondered if they herded the mosquitoes like dolphins herded schools of fish. All the small, swarming things of the earth—she thought of her childhood toes in the quiet water of the Sound, all the fry winnowing around, nibbling on her shins. She saw herself wading to the drifting rowboat, wondering why it was in the wrong place.

Helen climbed into her lap and started scribbling in the notebook. Polly didn't startle; she knew she'd dropped into another place, one of those pauses. Mix in some wine and fatigue and it wasn't that different from going to sleep, even if her eyes were open. But from the far side of the window, Harry's voice was real life, a steady murmur aimed at the other men. Harry could be calming when he needed to. Vinnie was back to ifs and thens and the unfairness of anyone blaming Graham. If Ned had told Graham he had to work in the kitchen despite his ineptitude, or in the bar despite begging for a lawsuit, Ariel would have been in the raft, and lived. If Vinnie hadn't loaned the group the kayak, Ariel would have lived. If Ariel hadn't decided to fuck his good-looking nephew—

"Stop it," said Ned. "No one blames Graham, but don't you ever blame that girl." The open kitchen window was beginning to throw a greater amount of light than it was taking in, the moment of reversal, day for night, and Polly could see the jut of his jaw. She knew how badly he wanted his good friends to go home, and now chairs scraped, Drake insisting he'd drive Vinnie, Vinnie saying he was fine.

Harry left through the back door. His face had been blasted by tears and wind and sun, though he would always be good-looking in a battered, geeky sort of way. He and Josie had been together, more or less and off and on, for years, but in his twenties and early thirties, here and in New York, he'd been cheerfully, openheartedly randy. Harry could walk into any bar or funeral in town and a solid percentage of women within ten years of his age would give him a fond, knowing neck rub. He gave Polly one now and talked about finding the Claremont student's leg, and about the parents of the dead boy, whom he'd gotten to know the summer before when he was still a cop. They'd quit their jobs to search the river for their son's body. When Harry called them after he'd found the bones, he promised to keep searching for the rest of his body.

"Hey," said Polly.

"What?"

"Why wasn't Ariel wearing a preserver?"

"Graham said she was earlier. They were sitting on them in the kayak after the island. He doesn't remember why they hadn't put them back on."

Polly thought of being young, warm sand grinding into your tailbone or knees. You finish and you laugh and you climb back into a kayak without weighing your skin down.

Not Polly. She could have been out of her sexual pea brain, drunk to her nose, and she still would have put on a preserver in a kayak in that kind of water.

"People fuck up," said Harry. "It's so easy to fuck up. It only takes a moment when the water is this high. Don't overthink this."

Helen touched Polly's cheek and whispered. Had Polly read the secret message?

Polly looked down at the waves Helen had drawn in lieu of letters.

"Is it about a treasure?"

Helen shook her head, disappointed. Her brown eyes, the spiral of blond curls, a hint of the family attitude to her mouth.

"Magic?" asked Polly.

Helen smiled. Harry leaned over and studied the notebook. "Working again, Poll?"

"Always," she said. "Just Drake's slush pile."

Harry tapped the notebook. "Is that Dee?"

They looked at the open page next to Helen's secret alphabet, Polly's paltry paragraph of notes about a script next to a doodle of tree leaves and a profile of an old woman.

Huh, thought Polly. It did look like her.

Helen was sad, Helen was quiet. She wanted a glass of chocolate milk and Polly didn't bother with a lecture about dental health. When Polly tucked her in, Helen said again that she wanted to look for Ariel. They'd get in a boat and find her. Polly was so good at finding things.

Ah, said Polly, lying down next to her. We will find her, but you have swimming lessons. She knew where Helen was going with this. Finding meant fixing. Finding was a cure, and being lost was horror. A kid could hear a word clearly but entirely miss its context. She watched the tiny wrist flex to drink the milk, listening to the stagy gulp, waited for Helen to close her eyes, remembering what it was like to be small, holding a glass like that, wanting to make everything better in the world.

Back in her own bed, Polly thought of drawing Dee in the notebook and of dropping into the moment, seeing Papa's drifting rowboat for the first time in years, the minnows circling her toes in Long Island Sound. Now she turned her mind from what they'd found on the beach that day, and made her child's body walk up the beach path to the house, climb the stairs to her old bedroom. She pushed the memory to another day, so that she could hear Papa and Dee talk, hear him follow Dee down the hall, saying something Polly hadn't understood but now guessed was sweet and dirty—the sound of it, the edge, had a small tangy vibration. The old-fashioned cadences of Dee's voice, laughing, and the lag of her bad leg as she and Papa walked to their bedroom

Was Polly right? She'd known them so well. When the rowboat floated back into her head, she struggled awake, nudged Ned so that he moved onto his side and stopped snoring. Why these thoughts, now? The drowned man on the beach by the drifting boat—she hadn't forgotten, precisely, but tucked it under the rest of what happened that summer, when she was eight.

Polly let herself fall back asleep. Now she was in the boat as it spun and bobbled. Ned was rowing and Polly was looking through the blue glass bottom at Ariel, who passed underneath and rose to face the moon briefly before she rolled over, fingers and toes dragging against the gravel in a shallow stretch of the river.

Polly woke again and listened to the rain. It wasn't until the next day that a man camping on an island just south of town came into the station and said he'd seen a woman pass by the evening before, cresting the surface and waving a stiff arm. A shallow stretch, but before he could wade in she hit a faster, deeper current and vanished. He apologized for the delay but seeing her hadn't made him want to get back into his kayak, in the dark.

6

Winter and Spring 1968

Her good friend Edmund, didn't she recognize him?

Polly stood near her mother and her great-grandmother on a Long Island sidewalk, on a mild day in the middle of January 1968, listening to Edmund Ward's mother, Rita, rattle on about old friendships, and pretending this wasn't happening. She and Edmund snuck quick looks at each other while feigning interest in the cars going down Christian Avenue or the dog on the chain, yodeling at the sight of the visitors. Edmund had brown hair and a sad, tired face. They were both seven.

Rita rattled on. When they were five or six, Polly must remember the day on Lake Michigan? They played in a creek, and there had been a puppy, and a campfire. Edmund's father got the car stuck in the sand.

"We saw each other just last summer, Rita," said Jane. "They moved the creek last summer, before that horrible day at Tommy's parents' house. And we have the puppy."

They watched Rita's mouth open. Her skin was so smooth she lacked expression. It was hard to look at her directly, as if something were wrong with her features, maybe even her smell. Polly turned away and let in a jumble of time and light: They'd cut off an oxbow in a creek along Lake Michigan and run through shallows while their parents were drunk and laughing. She mostly remembered the idea of Edmund, not his physical being. Yet here he was, paler and a little larger, now breathing noisily in her doorway, not a tan child standing in waves. She herself was a washed-out, skinny girl, nearsighted and born frayed, with black tangled hair.

No one had warned her that these people were coming to their house. Dee broke up the moment and pushed the children inside. She said things like, So, Edmund, this is the kitchen. We don't keep a lock on the fridge. Let's have a bit of something and we'll show you a room you might like. She had Polly lead him up to the little bedroom next to her own, usually reserved for their old friends from the city.

All afternoon, Rita talked about the earlier times, when she and her husband, Thomas, and Jane and Merle had been in college together, when Polly and Edmund shared a crib or butted heads on a lawn outside of married housing in Ann Arbor. She had an accent—she'd been born in Ireland—but her voice was too loud, too sharp and piping, and because her face was so blank the noise seemed to come out of nowhere, a trumpet from a wispy halo of red hair. Polly, squirming at one end of the living room couch, tried to imagine the sticky plastic of the crib floor she'd shared with Edmund, the nylon web blocking their sight. They were foisting Edmund upon her, and she was watchful, because she sensed an explanation that hadn't been offered, something wrong with either Edmund or his world beyond the clear issue of Rita.

When Papa came home, Polly saw disbelief and muffled anger. Dee explained the situation in a kind of a circle, moving right through any pause that might give Papa a chance to ask a question. Rita and Edmund Ward are living here for a bit. Let me get you a drink.

Papa followed Dee into the pantry with a set face. She could hear their voices through the wall, despite the fact that Rita grew louder and faster with every minute.

When Merle got home, Jane put him on the couch facing Rita's monologue and hid in the kitchen with Dee. Papa worked behind a closed door, and Polly and Edmund stuck to their rooms.

What does Polly really remember? Since the accident, the temperature of the air, the way a mosquito could balance on the peach fuzz on her small arm, a sticky line of dirt in the inner crease of the elbow. Childhood is a green knot, hiding places and suspended time. It is the speed she can run through grass, the heat of the air, the fear of pissing her pants on a school bus, the difficulty of returning someone's gaze, a bright object in the sand, the way a good moment can slide to bad.

Polly and Jane and Merle moved to Stony Brook from the city the year before. They were poor, with no money for both tuition and a young child. Papa and Dee were old—very old, in their late eighties—and Dee needed help. Jane stayed at NYU, but Merle transferred to SUNY, and Polly was enrolled in the Suffolk County school system. She had a new kingdom. Now, Rita and Edmund Ward were joining them because Edmund's father, Thomas, Merle's best friend and roommate in college, was overseas in the war, and because Rita could no longer stay with her inlaws, or they could no longer bear her. She said they were hateful, shriveled people. Leave Edmund with us, they'd told her, and they meant they wanted Rita to go away and die. This was most of what she talked about for the first few days. Jane gave up trying to herd Polly away, but Polly stopped listening on her own accord, and it seemed that Edmund did, too. They slid into companionship, silent at first. Later they were only quiet when an adult was around.

Edmund and Rita were given the rooms next to and across from Polly's. Merle and Jane had the big room at the top of the stairs, and Dee and Papa owned the end of the hall, a bedroom and study and a private bathroom. The house in Stony Brook had been a gatehouse of a larger, grander estate, most of it burned or sold off in the twenties and rebuilt in clusters of war-era starter boxes. Papa and Dee, needing a change after their daughter Asta's car slid off an icy road and into the Yellowstone River, left Montana during World War II and bought the house when Papa took a job at Columbia. The other remnants of the old estate were the greenhouse Dee now used for a pottery studio and a small stone house owned by a woman everyone called the witch, who had a mostly green parrot that Papa and Dee's cat May kept trying to kill. Before Edmund arrived, Polly never looked at the witch's house directly, despite passing it daily on the sanded-in path down to the Sound. Though the water was only a hundred yards from their house, it felt farther because of the trees, the curved path, the witch's vine-covered bungalow. On the beach the footprint of a boathouse was still visible, with a high-tide iron ring Papa used to tie up his rowboat.

Nobody mentioned how long Rita and Edmund would stay, though Edmund's father wouldn't be home on leave until at least August. Merle spent most of the next day dragging things to the attic: his still-boxed journals, a steamer trunk with Dee's old dresses, carton after carton of books. Polly was used to spreading her enthusiasms into the spare bedroom Rita now invaded, and spent hours cramming her dollhouse and her easel and a basket of her general mess back into her tiny room, which had been—like Edmund's new room—a dressing room when people still cared about dressing.

"Rita could have warned us," said Merle.

"She's clearly not well," said Dee, carefully.

Not well had so many possible meanings. After spending a week in the hospital with pneumonia, Polly connected illness with age, as in Dee, or with silence—Polly hadn't talked much when she'd been in a little tent the fall before, sleeping and dreaming. Rita did not stop.

Rita's mother-in-law phoned twice, and hung up on Dee both times when Rita wouldn't come to the phone.

Papa called her back. "You know you've treated her like something stuck to your shoe, madam. And no, we will not send the boy alone to you."

"Small-minded bitch," he said, when she hung up again. "Horrible bourgeois cow. They should never be allowed to see that child again."

"Do they want him or the idea of him?" asked Dee.

"Thomas will sort it out when he comes home," said Papa.

On the trip to Michigan the summer before, the Wards and the Schusters had spent a weekend at a cottage on the beach. Polly and Edmund hadn't felt compelled to talk to each other, but they slid into it, and they shoveled sand to redirect the creek while the adults sprawled, eating crackers and cheese and drinking from fancy-looking straw-wrapped bottles of wine. They didn't bother with the children, and the children didn't bother with them, and the night fell apart only when the six-month-old pointer Lemon jumped into the water and started swimming toward a freighter, Edmund and Polly running up and down the beach after their tipsy, weeping mothers while their fathers laughed.

The coast guard brought Lemon back. Merle slept in the tub that night and Tommy Ward fell asleep halfway up the stairs to the bedroom. When Polly woke up, she found Edmund in a chair with Lemon. Jane had Polly bring Merle water and ask how he was.

"I'm fine. Just fucking fine," said Merle, pulling himself out of the dry bathtub.

It was Polly's first crystalline recognition of bullshit. Merle and Tommy were giddy that day, in patches. They went out on a charter boat and both fathers vomited repeatedly over the side, which was funny at the time; Jane's serene expression would remain one of Polly's fondest memories. Then the beach again, people drinking again. Polly and Edmund, Jane slathering them with Coppertone, dug one more route for the creek, dozed with the waves tugging their feet, dangled from couches in the house, purple-lipped from sucking grape Popsicles.

The day, remembered as a whole (though Polly never was good at remembering the whole), was idyllic until they ended up at another beach in the town, near a break wall, to eat a picnic dinner of things from Edmund's fancy grandparents (Merle's description). Someone started screaming—the body of a girl had been found in the water near the break wall. Rita began to wail, and Jane and Merle and Tommy dealt with her while Edmund and Polly listened to the ambulance pass and watched the police and harbor men work with grappling hooks in the waves.

At dinner at a bar in the little town, they ordered fried perch, onion rings, a Roy Rogers and a Shirley Temple with flashy swords in the maraschino cherries. Merle and Tommy said they'd heard the girl's boyfriend had thrown her off the break wall, as a joke. When they were all in the car again, Rita, who had been uncharacteristically quiet—even then, Rita was not quiet—announced that the dead girl had been her; she'd seen the red of her hair. It was blood, said Thomas. It was me in the water, she whistled. Jane reached into the front to pull Edmund into the back, away from both of them, as Rita punched her husband and the car weaved on the curvy road. Merle, drunk but a mild-mannered man of science, offered that there couldn't have been much blood left, because there wasn't much skin left, and the water had washed the girl's system clean.

But Polly remembered red. How could she not? Rita crammed the memory deeper later when she showed Polly the tubes of color in her painting box, the smears on her palette. She said that if she painted Polly's portrait, she would use alizarin inky black for her hair. She told Polly that in the old days black paints had been made with wood soot and burned ivory and burned vines. When Polly said her hair was brown, Rita said, Well, of course. And I'd use a brown for your skin, too. Look at your wrist and my wrist. I'm pink. You're the color of wood. Very pretty, but you can't be pink like me.

That smile—Polly hated it, and later she would hate the memory of it, that beautiful silky red hair, the sandalwood haze on Rita's skin, the green stripes on her low-cut pants. At some point during the summer, Rita did a painting of Polly and Edmund. It was not, as Dee put it, a good likeness—Rita didn't make them pose for long—and they were each blurred, moving away from the center, or possibly away from the artist.

But before all this, at that Michigan beach, during the last week of July, in 1967: The next morning, while Jane scrambled eggs, they watched Rita walk straight into the water like the dog Lemon, moving forward until she was up to her neck and started to disappear. Thomas ran down and jumped in after her. Edmund went back to reading, and Polly, gathering that this was the way to handle such situations, did, too.

They packed and loaded the car, but when Tommy turned around in the driveway, he backed into a sandy dune, and for the next half hour they dug like dogs, having no shovel, while Tommy and Merle argued and Jane kept Rita from straying, sometimes spinning her in place so that she giggled and forgot where she might have wanted to go. They stopped for fish sandwiches and beer and drove on to Edmund's grandparents' huge house in East Lansing. Storm lighting, humid and still, ninety degrees. Rita said the color of the air was viridian and kept saying it until everyone agreed with her. She started on about the color of her hair again, Titian red. When Polly said that this was the color of Nancy Drew's hair, Rita went on about oxides.

When they piled out of the car onto the smooth black driveway in the midafternoon, the children were sunburnt, the parents drunk, and everyone was crumpled and filthy. Polly braced for hugs—all of her relatives hugged—and found with relief that none of the Wards were interested in touching anyone. There'd been tornado warnings, and Thomas's mother, angry from the minute she appeared at the front door, was hysterical about the idea they'd driven through death. She made the children go in the basement—the cleanest basement, still, of Polly's life—until Tommy convinced her that the warning was over, and the children should be outside.

Back upstairs, moving through the chilly immensity of the house, Detroit was burning in rare color on a large television. Everyone paused and watched. Tommy argued with his parents, and when he went outside with his father (who said, Let's get into it then, sonny) and Merle, who tried to make peace, the children and women fell into a horrible quiet as they watched police and crowds give way to footage of Vietnamese jungles on television.

"Merle is such a steady influence," said the elder Mrs. Ward, now calm. She had stiff frosted hair and huge diamonds on both hands, and she smoked Pall Malls. "Merle didn't volunteer for that silly mess. These boys have so many better things to do."

Merle probably would have served, like his brother, but for the polio arm. Nevertheless, he thought Tommy should have used his university exemption.

When the men came inside again, the children were released back into the yellow-green storm air, to a blanket of velvet grass. Polly had seen yards like this—lacking patches and dog piles—only from a distance. She and Edmund rolled on the lawn but there was nothing else to do, not a tool, toy, shrub, climbable tree. Through the fancy sliding screen doors they could hear an argument begin again—war now, and Tommy leaving for it. When they heard more voices raised, and a car engine, Jane came running toward them and scooped them up—Rita and Tommy had roared off without their child—while Merle stowed their bags and they followed in a fancy car borrowed from the Wards.

They ended up together at a Holiday Inn restaurant with umbrellas in the drinks and Hawaiian music. Later Polly and Edmund were left in a hotel room with peanut butter sandwiches and coins and a Magic Fingers bed, while all four parents drank.

Tommy's mother and father weren't dog people, and the Schusters promised to take care of the pointer Lemon when Tommy shipped out in October. Polly and Jane took the train back. The upper bunk, the sink that folded down, the ceremony of the dining car made Polly insanely happy. Merle drove, taking uppers while Lemon was on downers; at about 2 a.m., he said, they were moving at the same speed. Rita and Edmund lasted at the older Wards' house until Christmas, when she set their garage on fire.

Now, in January of 1968, no one made Edmund go to school immediately. Polly needed to go, of course, and when she came home on the second day, she found him on the couch, surrounded by her books. She guessed that he hadn't done this on his own, that her mother or Dee or Papa ransacked her room, but she minded, and she walked upstairs and slammed her door. When she couldn't bear it any longer—she was hungry, for one thing, because everyone was too distracted by Edmund and Rita to pack a lunch, and the cafeteria food revolted her—she nearly fell over the stack left outside of her door.

More stewing, some guilt, though what did you call it at seven or eight? Edmund's bedroom door was closed, but everyone seemed to be behind a door—Dee napping, Papa on the phone, a low grumble—but Merle and Jane, who were at class. Rita was singing in her room, and her voice was so unnerving that Polly dropped half the books back against Edmund's door and retreated to her room after grabbing a handful of cookies.

Neither Polly nor Edmund ever mentioned this later. By the weekend they went in and out of each other's rooms, and she had read his copies of *Bruce* and *Lad: A Dog.* The following week, he was put in a different third-grade classroom, but they saw each other at recess. He was quiet, and careful, and people grew used to him without any of the crap that often dropped on a new kid. When the prettiest girl in Polly's class teased Edmund, clearly liking him, it gave Polly a borrowed glow.

Edmund talked in his sleep, on the other side of the wall, and he picked his nose, though no more than a boy she liked in school. Rita talked to herself all night long.

Papa and Dee were very old, which Polly no longer noticed; they were from another century. When Edmund first arrived, Polly, who'd been living there for half a year, would catch him watching them—a little fear, some wonder, the same look that he gave to all the things in the house: statues and arrowheads and books everywhere. Within a week he no longer seemed to notice Papa or Dee's tissuey skin, pale as a photographic negative except for during summer, or hear a reedy sound in their voices.

Papa was the oldest person in the house, but he was also the tallest. He'd been an archaeologist before he taught mythology at Columbia, and had a way of moving through things, of looming without it feeling like a threat. He was a Presence, according to Merle, a Fucking Piece of Work, and he was known for writing about universal stories, the way they'd evolved through cultures, about shamanism and the archaeological evidence behind myth. Dee was tiny, with big arthritic arms below delicate collarbones, and a young woman's head of hair, still half-brown. She wasn't shaped like an old lady, and she dressed in slacks or straight skirts instead of what Papa called old ladies' bags. She was a year younger than Papa, who'd been born in Sweden by the ocean, both of them before cars or planes or plastic. She'd broken a leg in a fall as a child, and again when Jane was a child—one shin below her skirt hem was slender but dented—and she kept a grove of canes with different heads, of different shimmers and substances, like so many magic wands, in a pot at the front door and against a bedroom table that held her jewelry and perfume and medicine bottles. But she and Papa moved quickly, like young people, and their muscles were visible ropes, and they were sometimes drunk and silly and snappish. They did not fret over what the children ate, or whether they'd do something stupid near the road or in the water. They knew Polly and Edmund were terrified of both; why add to the humiliation?

Jane, who was getting a master's in history and mythology, planned to write her thesis about natural disasters and legends, though Papa thought she should focus on the universal nature of the flood story, and not get into variations. In the corner of her bedroom, above her typewriter, she'd hung a hand-drawn timeline of floods and volcanoes and earthquakes through-out the world, with bubbles of tiny handwriting for details. Sometimes she helped Papa with his research, tracking down versions of stories through the ages, trying to determine which were earliest, how they'd blended and changed across times and peoples, how they'd lasted.

Papa, surrounded by pens and books and bones at his desk, would let Edmund and Polly flop around on his old velvet sofa. He showed them crows dancing in the yard and pointed out that they seemed to perform for May, the one-eyed cat, who watched from a tree or climbed farther to the roof. He had maps on his walls, a poster of spinning souls, a photo of a tattooed Scythian mummy who'd been buried with her horses. He'd dug her up, and said he wished he'd let her be.

The bookshelves were topped by photos of Dee's children, Maude and David and James, taken in Montana and at all the archaeological digs they'd traveled to with Papa after their own father died. In most of the photos they were holding Papa's daughter Asta, the youngest. When Asta died young, Papa and Dee raised Jane, too, and Polly envied those photos: Jane at Polly's age on a French beach, in a Greek temple, riding a camel in a desert. And yet she'd had no mother. Polly knew even then she was lucky, that her parents might be half drunk and at odds half the time, but they were alive, and they did essentially love each other, and they certainly loved her, and they weren't like Rita.

Everyone told Polly she should help Edmund, but she was already doing so. They moved through their days with an almost British disregard for the chaos around them, barricaded together in one of their rooms or hidden in the arbor or down by the Sound, watching to see what was revealed when the tide moved out. Over the next few months, they were almost always within six feet of each other but never touched, except for two fights. But Polly was fascinated by Edmund's thick hair, the moles on his forearm, the way his skin would flame in bad moments.

Polly had friends at school, but she'd been so lonely. She took Edmund up to the attic to show him boxes of strangeness, the broken spinning wheel and treadle sewing machine and old clothes, or to Dee's greenhouse, with its kiln and wheel, nasturtiums and jasmine, a box of glass bottles that held powders for glazes. They'd watch Dee uncork the bottles, mix potions, spin the potting wheel, light the kiln. In the basement, where Merle kept salamander and frog specimens in an old refrigerator, they'd watch Dee add bleach and soap to the old open washing machine, the water gushing from a sheet when it went through the mangle, which looked like a deadly version of Dee's pasta-rolling machine. Dee said she'd once been distracted and put her fingers through, but nothing had broken except the tips of her fingers, which exploded and stained the sheets. She laughed, telling them this.

But mostly Edmund and Polly went down to the water. You could see a sliver of the Sound from the porch, even when the grapevines leafed out, and there was a ravine with skunk cabbage, which Polly liked to pretend was some sort of man-eating Venus flytrap. The house was on a rise off of the main road into town, Christian Avenue, and the lots were irregular and the streets were narrow and dirt, following the hill's contour, more paths than roads. The witch, whose house was wreathed in grapevines, burned wood (rather than children, as Papa joked) for heat and let out her parrot when the weather was nice. The only times she'd spoken to Dee and Papa over the last twenty-five years were to threaten to kill their cats if those cats killed the parrot.

The name on the old woman's mailbox, in stenciled letters, was Maw.

Edmund thought Polly was of a piece with the place, all of it so much better than life with Rita and his grandparents. The good part of his past was his father, but Tommy Ward had been around for only a few weeks since Edmund was five. By now, Edmund knew this place might save his life. The old magicians, Polly's beautiful mother, Merle's essential kindness, wild Lemon, given away by his parents but glued again to the end of his bed, the acrobatic cat arriving every night to lie on his chest—they all made for comfortable chaos, the people and even the walls buffers against his mother. Upstairs, when Rita muttered, the words echoed in the hall, but people were near, and his door locked.

He was sure his father would never come back.

In Edmund's and Polly's rooms ventilation grates, usually covered with rugs, opened on the kitchen below. In the morning, they could hear Papa walking down the hall humming, snapping his fingers softly. Next came the smell of coffee and some sort of pork, eventually toast. You could tug the rugs off the grates and see the top of his head, and sometimes he'd look up and smile. He taught at Columbia two days a week now, spending a night in the city at the apartment he and Dee still rented, on Bleecker near the corner of Sullivan.

Papa would bring coffee to Dee, who ached when she first woke and would not leave bed without it. Merle was first in the bathroom and rousted the children for school when he came out. Jane always got up quietly and was mysteriously and calmly ready at the table by the time they came down, whether or not she needed to go to the city. Merle dropped her off and picked her up at the train three days a week. She almost always came home for the night. Rita was never up before they left for school, and usually never came out of her room until noon on weekends. No one ever tried to wake her.

They did not have G.I. Joes, Easy-Bake Ovens, BB guns, spangled hairdressing dolls. Polly had two Barbies, both a little worn, origami and puzzles and books, glass figurines she kept on a high shelf after an experiment with roller skates as carriages. Edmund tried to trade a Batman figure for Polly's rock collection and a Lego set from an Irish uncle for her board games. They spent a stunning amount of time dangling upside down in a tire swing, spinning each other, occasionally using it as a weapon. Dee, with a fear of malaria that Merle considered irrational, made them rinse it out after every rain.

Edmund had arrived with a collection of wooden swords and shields and a crossbow-style rubber-band gun. Papa gave him a heavy German pellet gun, but after a flurry of wild pumping—Polly had been beside herself with the mechanical magic of it all—the first dead squirrel ended all but target practice. They both knew it was one of those moments that they'd despise being lectured about, but still Edmund stared down at the way the fur on the squirrel's chest gaped and closed around the wound for the last few breaths, and he pitched forward in a faint, giving himself a bloody nose. Polly never brought it up.

Arnold Galante, a poet who had been Papa's brother-in-law and was still his best friend, taught them card games—euchre and hearts and spades, games of solitaire that turned into feeding frenzies when three or four people played at once. Dee loved cards but didn't play well, and her insults were another game. Polly was a strumpet when she won a rare hand of hearts, Jane could learn to cook for herself, Arnold was an ass, Papa was an arrogant, horrible man. Merle was the best player in every game, especially poker, and card nights were the only nights when he was reliably not drunk. Jane tended to float away, and Arnold lost track while he told stories about the war in Spain, ocean liners, and the people he and Papa had known when they'd worked on movies together. He loved to goad Papa.

"Ask about what he did to the guy who called him a German in 1919." Or: "When you're older, ask him why so many people used to be afraid of him."

"We might not manage to be older at the same time," said Papa, who was almost ninety. "They don't need to know the bad stuff, Arnie."

Arnold was the only one who brought up the people who were missing. He said that Jane's mother, Asta, had loved to ride and fish and camp, and that Polly could be like her, someday. Asta's mother, Perdita, on a movie poster in Papa's office, was also dead and therefore beautiful and mysterious forever. She'd loved to sing and dance (even then, no one seemed to think Polly would ever sing or dance).

"Ask your great-grandfather how he acted when he first saw my pretty sister. I mopped him off a London sidewalk."

Perdita, frozen on the poster, looked nothing at all like Arnold, who was wizened and brown, with wild gray hair. Arnold had one blind eye, like May the cat, who loved him, and he drove out every other weekend or so—he taught poetry at Columbia, where Papa taught—and would spend the night in the last empty bedroom at the top of the stairs. Polly always put a rubber spider in the bed, and Arnold always screamed for her benefit.

People were always visiting—old professors and poetesses, ancient Californians from the movie years, Jane and Merle's friends. A convention of poets and historians, said Papa, was like a murder of crows, a conspiracy of ravens, a clamor of rooks, a scold of jays. He'd move through the crowd, people making way, and sit at the head of the table and have Polly open a window to let the smoke out while he showed off his superior cigarette-rolling skills. She did not understand the humor or notice what was being smoked.

It was a fine thing to be a rarity, a child. No one patronized Polly or Edmund. The view from the screen of the stair railing, after they'd been sent to bed, was sometimes bizarre, sometimes crushingly boring. It was hard for Jane and Merle's friends to compete with the strangeness of Papa and Dee, beyond the importation of an occasional bale of marijuana (this object, stashed in the basement, brought on a roaring argument between Papa and Merle; it was *going too far*). A friend of Jane's from NYU went to Peru and brought back ponchos, dried seedpods and tarantulas, quartz pipes and something he claimed was a shrunken head. Polly and Edmund knew it wasn't human and wondered what unfortunate species of dead monkey it might have been, but they loved the reaction when they brought it out at parties, letting the thing dangle from its hair. The head smelled acrid and funky at the same time, like a mix of cat piss and rotting tomato, and at some point it disappeared from the sill of an open window. Maybe the parrot or the cat was sick of smelling it.

Rita always seemed normal when other people were around—Jane said it was like Polly's fevers disappearing whenever they walked into a doctor's office—and her accent varied depending on whether or not she was trying to be charming. She said Edmund was no fun anymore, and she needed to have more children as soon as Tommy got back, so that the world would be silly again. She said Tommy's parents had a great deal of money and no taste, that she never thought she'd want to move back to the Old World (Papa curled his lip at this phrase) but if Papa and Dee would buy her an airplane ticket or drive her to a boat, she'd be gone.

Rita said "she," not "we," but Edmund finally went to Jane and asked her to please not let him be hauled away. Had Jane promised? Polly didn't know.

The point about Rita, at least in hindsight, was that she was a good painter, on her way to being a great one. Her artist father brought her over from Dublin when he taught for a year at Cranbrook, in Michigan, where Rita and Tommy met when she was seventeen and he was a senior. When Tommy received a Rhodes Scholarship after Ann Arbor, Rita started showing and selling her work in London. They stayed after Tommy got his degree, until Mr. Ward cut them off and summoned them home. After which—again, nothing Polly could know at the time—Tommy pulled off the ultimate fuck-you and enlisted in the army.

Rita without Tommy was unmoored, ineffectual. She'd lost her magic, said Dee. A Parisian gallery was interested in her work, and Rita's agent kept calling, but she only drew tiny shapes with Polly's pencils at the kitchen table, explaining that a pretty kitelike trail of triangles was actually a school of fish, a chain gang of slaves, the Virgin Mary's pixie dust. The galleries wanted large oils, Klimt-like abstracts with haunted mosaic faces.

Rita thought she'd lost her magic, too, and wandered around the house mourning it. By the third week, sometime in February, the push was on to give her whatever she wanted, do anything to shut her up. Merle phoned the elder Wards to ask that they send Rita's painting supplies. A huge box arrived, postage collect, but when Rita opened it, she complained about what was missing. Papa paid to have canvases and new paints delivered. She fiddled with them, and decided that the colors were wrong, and the canvases were too small. More paints, larger canvases. Dee volunteered the greenhouse. They'd only fired the kiln once since fall, anyway.

Your precious bolt-hole, said Jane. Our precious minds, said Dee.

All the conversations Polly couldn't understand at the time. In the moment—the slush of late winter on the Sound, the dreary, fraught hours at school, the jarring change of having someone out of key like Rita around—she and Edmund moved around the periphery, in their own new world.

At the end of February, Polly answered the door on a rainy day and looked out at two men in uniform. They had dirt on their foreheads, like Rita, who'd asked Dee to drive her to church that morning. On one man's face, a drop of rain made the ash bleed into a gray rivulet, which the man reached up and smeared as the other talked. Edmund was in the kitchen with Dee, discussing leap years, and Papa and Jane and Merle were in the city, and Rita was painting in the greenhouse.

The soldiers looked as if they'd rather no one was home. Dee told the children to go upstairs, and from the window they watched her lead the soldiers through the yard to Rita.

My father is dead, said Edmund.

But everyone told him no, not quite. Thomas was lost, a word that bounced in any child's head. It was everything you didn't want to be. People said missing, too, but lost meant something closer to a dog swept out with the tide or losing the keys to the world.

A crumbling, screaming shame, said Papa, in a letter to his stepdaughter Maude that Polly saw much later. Thomas Alden Ward, pride of his snooty family, who had cast aside a deferment and enlisted out of spite—toward his parents, his crazy wife, a needy little boy, himself—was in the process of disappearing, at that moment lying down to die near Hue.

The Tet Offensive played every night. Papa bought a larger television, ostensibly so that they could watch the Grenoble Olympics, really to distract everyone from Rita's constant babble. He realized quickly that the television was a mixed bag. The war and all the funerals and riots from the previous spring and summer, already Technicolor in magazines, were now larger, moving, echoing. Merle and Jane tried turning the news off, but Edmund kept turning it on and sat cross-legged in front of it, watching Walter Cronkite instead of cartoons. He studied every photo of the war in the *Times*, in *LIFE* magazine, every muddy white face in Southeast Asia that came his way. He dreamt of his father sleeping on a sandy path in a jungle, flowers and ferns blocking the hot sun, a line of ants walking around his head. It was possible Tommy was sleeping somewhere, even now. Polly would hear doors open when Edmund cried out in the night. Jane or Dee—never Rita—would go to him, and Polly would hear their whispers through her wall.

When they first moved into the house on Long Island, Polly felt a moment of hope, a blast of her old belief—maybe they'd find Evie and Frank. Now she told Edmund about her theory. It was stupid to think that way, she said.

I don't know, said Edmund. Maybe we should still keep an eye out for all of them.

After the officers visited, Rita was quiet for a day, and then she said she didn't know why people were acting this way—Tommy wasn't dead, he'd just gone off somewhere. Hiding out, like a smart person, she said to Tommy's mother on the phone. A week later, she announced at dinner that she was going to have a baby, and that she needed to lie down. It was exciting, but that night, when Jane tucked Edmund and Polly in, she told them it was hard to be certain about such things. Through the floor vent, Polly heard Jane say, Do the math, she saw Tom last in September, and her waist isn't much bigger than Polly's. Everyone said something like this but Rita, who stopped coming out of her room. She asked everyone who brought her food what she should name the baby.

Rita kept varying her information or imagination—Tommy was hiding out in Thailand, Tommy had been incinerated by some fiery bomb—but she never told them what the soldiers said. When Edmund tried talking about his dream, about Tommy sleeping on a sandy path, she exploded and slapped him, and after that, everyone kept him away from her room. Merle, maddened by the lack of information, and by the way Rita varied between candy optimism and horrific images, finally called his brother in the navy for help and learned that Tommy left on patrol in the middle of February with two other men to some warren of walled gardens—the Tombs? the Tiger Arena?—and never returned. Merle found a map in the *New York Times* and showed Edmund the area. Young faces, both of them, looking down in the light of the desk lamp. Papa talked to Edmund about dead heroes in myths and old wars, bad luck and the endlessness of love. They heard him say to Dee that because of Tommy they were all in limbo, and when Polly asked about the etching in his study—an illustration of *Purgatorio*, showing people whirling in a circle between a kind of ocean below and a sky above, and the title underneath said *Limbo*—Papa claimed he meant the limbo dance. He held out a cane and made them try, then whacked them gently with it when they fell backward.

Thomas Ward's family, back in Michigan, needed a funeral, but Rita said no, and the army refused to proceed without a body or a widow. The Wards tried for a memorial, and they insisted Rita and Edmund come. Rita refused.

Everything slowed down. During the long Easter break—true spring, tulips following snowdrops, all sorts of color popping upward in the messy yard—Rita worked on tiny painted shapes as if she were working on a baby's quilt and she talked about the baby's growth as if it were the plot of a movie. Dee made dye for eggs and the room smelled of the vinegar she added to help the colors set. Papa put the television on—Martin Luther King had been shot—and he watched riot and war footage sloped back in his chair, stretched out, hands behind his head. Every once in a while, Merle would get up and freshen their drinks. Between the sounds of the news, the spoons Polly and Edmund used to roll the eggs clinked. The tips of their fingers were maroon and yellow and bruised brown-green from the blend of colors.

Jane and Rita were trying for fancier eggs with Russian-style shells, and kept a book open to photos of jewel and folk-art eggs. They made tiny holes in each end, inserted a long, thin needle—one of Dee's trussing needles—to stir up the interior, and used a bulb syringe to blow the insides out. Rita held her colored fingers in the air and asked Polly to flip through the book until she found a design she liked. Jane, not as adept and unable to look away from the television, managed two and crumbled a last half-empty shell in her hand.

What, asked Dee, was wrong with simply boiling and dyeing and eating the things when we're done?

On the television, a Gerber baby food commercial broke into the news coverage. Rita watched and let her wet brush fall to the floor.

"I need to see the doctor," she said. "I worry something's gone wrong with the baby. It should be big like these babies."

No one said anything.

"Take me now," said Rita.

Edmund took his bowls to the sink and Polly started to clean up her things.

"Now," said Rita.

Dee dried the colored eggs and lowered them into the carton. "Jane, honey."

"No," said Jane. She'd joined Merle and Papa in front of the television. "Real people are dying here."

"Now," said Rita. "Call the damn ambulance." She picked up a paring knife and gouged the palm of her left hand, then brought it down again on the back, between the tendons below her first and second knuckles.

There was an immensity of blood. Merle and Jane took Rita in together. It was late when they all came back. Polly could hear Dee and Papa talking, Jane and Merle talking, Rita crying, Edmund talking to Lemon.

In the morning—no ringing alarms, because school was still out—Jane swept into Edmund's and Polly's rooms and told them to get dressed and pack up—they were going on a surprise trip to the city with Papa and Dee, maybe overnight, because it was their vacation, after all. They needed to hurry, but when Jane pushed them down to Dee and Papa's bathroom, past Merle, who was talking to Rita through the locked bathroom door, Dee was still lying with a pillow around her head, muttering about Irish lunatics. Through the wall they could hear Rita crying. Jane hustled Edmund and Polly through toothbrushing and peeing and shooed them back down the hall. They dressed and started to pack satchels in a lounging, scattered way until Rita started wailing in earnest, and Merle started to yell. Papa put Polly over the top of his shoulder and pulled Edmund along by an arm. In the car now, he said. He bellowed down the hall to Dee, to get a move on.

Polly and Edmund waited in the back of the Volvo. Papa reappeared and tossed some books and their bags and jackets through the window. He said they'd have to amuse themselves for a few minutes, and he headed back to the house, stooped and intent. Two of the books he'd thrown in were albums. One showed kurgans and mounds in Russia, where Papa had been on several digs. His strong, upright handwriting, different from Dee's because he wasn't American, surrounded the snapshots. The other album showed objects, gold birds and bright felt blankets, mummies and horse skeletons. The third book was *The Family of Man*. Polly and Edmund stared hardest at the section about war and birth, but eventually they each stuck a head out an open window, looking straight up at leaves and clouds, a strange whirlwind of birds that stayed within a pattern for long minutes.

The crunching sound of Papa approaching. He stopped at Polly's side. "It'll be a bit longer."

"Why are they doing that?"

Papa looked up at the birds. Polly brought her head back inside the car, and only saw his dangling hands, strong but old with a gold ring, dark trouser pants and a nice white shirt.

"They're starlings, and they're talking about a storm," he said. He circled the car and looked down at Edmund, who was also gaping at the birds. "Are you all right?"

"I'm fine."

"She'll be better after some sleep."

Edmund didn't answer, probably because he didn't think this was true.

Dee normally took her time with coffee, with dressing, with getting her body to move, but today she was fiddling with earrings when she hobbled to the car, and her hair was wet, in a ponytail like a girl's. Papa took off while her door was still open. From the back seat, Polly swatted the half-gray ponytail while Dee kept turning the radio louder to annoy Papa. She was fond of all the Detroit girl bands and she wanted Polly to dress in shorter skirts and bright colors, and fought with Jane about the necessity of leotards.

A weird, sunny mood in the car, as if they hadn't heard Rita howling for hours or seen blood dripping from her hand. The drive was new to Edmund, and Papa took the long way to point out the navy yard and the place where the British had packed Americans onto a ship and left them to starve in the Revolutionary War, skulls and bones crowding the shore of Wallabout Bay. People found vertebrae instead of seashells, crabs hiding in skulls. Then the swoop and darkness as they entered the city, the noise and blurring traffic when they emerged from the tunnel. They parked the car and carried their bags to the apartment on Bleecker, a bedroom and an office in the back overlooking scrabbly gardens, black-and-white tiled floor in the kitchen, clanking radiators. Polly and Edmund were put in Papa's office, Polly on the padded window seat overlooking the garden—she barely fit—and Edmund on the small sofa. There were piles of books everywhere and old movie posters with Papa's name as writer and producer: *The Tempest, The Amber Queen, The Window.*

They took the subway to the museum. The doctor's office was on Eightieth and Third, and Papa pointed west and said they'd all meet at noon in the south wing of the Met.

"Where?" asked Polly.

"Begone," he said. "We'll find you."

How, thought Polly. But they made their way west and Edmund ran up the massive steps. The guard at the door looked unhappy. "Our mother is inside," said Edmund. He put a quarter in the donation jar and looked levelly at the man, who waved them on. Polly was humbled by this ability to bullshit.

They saw Egyptian mummies and armor, naked women and angels and crosses, paintings about gods and violence. They were in the Asian section when Polly felt a hand mashing down on her head, twisting: Papa. Dee led them around the corner to a case with patterned cloth and jewels; she pointed to a gold belt buckle with a roaring lion and they read Papa's name—he'd found it on a frozen body buried in the mountains of Russia, in 1911.

Papa showed them all the stories hidden in amber and bone and marble as they moved through the galleries. Every civilization dealt with insanity and every story was an echo, an inherited memory. The oldest were about the father and the mother gone, a child starving, a beast waiting in the back of the cave. Or a false mother, or a trickster, or being lost—all these things happened over and over. This was why everyone wanted to hear fables and see horror movies: People like being reminded of their old fears, the idea that life had once been worse. The best stories—the birth of the sun and the moon, trickery and transformation, theories for the night and day and winter and summer—both explained and reassured: It won't always stay dark, it won't always stay cold, it's all happened before. Some cultures preferred these comforting stories.

"Not the Aztecs or the old gods," said Dee.

"No one loves the old gods," said Papa. "They ate their children. Mean fucks, every one."

They walked through a warren of offices in the basement and left the Scythian albums with a man who kissed Dee on both cheeks and touched her ponytail.

After they got off the subway at Astor Place, Edmund and Polly split a plain corned beef sandwich and Dee ordered a Reuben, saying that she'd never be able to finish it. Papa, who chose latkes and soup and a pastrami sandwich, ridiculed her when she did. Back at the apartment, Papa said he and Dee needed a nap in their dusty bedroom, just as they did at home. He gave Edmund and Polly the key to the front door and told them to walk around.

Downstairs, four Italian men were playing chess in front of the store next door. Papa called the place a social club. "Are you with the old lovers, then?" asked one man.

For whatever reason, they nodded.

"They're magic, you know. You the same types?"

They nodded again, like idiots, and the old men laughed.

That afternoon, while Papa watched the news—riots, more people being shot—Dee distracted them with treasures from the apartment's small safe. They played poker with animal teeth and gold and silver coins and old cards. When Dee phoned and heard Rita was still hysterical, and still in the house, she and Papa decided to stay a second night. Hiding out, said Papa. It would be their anniversary in a few days, said Dee, and they needed to celebrate anyway. She took the children up to Altman's for pajamas, new shoes, pants and shirt for Edmund, a new dress for Polly. At dinnertime, Papa hailed a cab. Dee wore a dress and a necklace and a fur coat, things she kept in the city, for fancy nights. At the restaurant, Polly and Edmund stared at the indoor trees and a pool and the people while Papa and Dee each ate a dozen oysters and gave them sips of Champagne. Scallops and crab, veal and potatoes shaped like roses, asparagus spears tied with orange peel, a baked Alaska. Dee said that the first time she'd met Papa it had been over a fancy meal on Fifth Avenue, but that when they'd married twenty years later, they'd done it in a courthouse, and eaten sausage and apples on a dusty sidewalk afterward. The world was filled with all kinds of good food.

After Rita stabbed her hand, she told the doctor that it was an accident. She lied well. But while Polly and Edmund were in the city, she slashed at her wrists with nail scissors, and the hospital didn't argue about keeping her. Jane and Merle took hours cleaning up the bathroom, trying to figure out what to do next.

Nevertheless, Rita was back in a week, sunny, calm, with bandaged arms, and the household stayed quiet through the spring. Rita set up her easel, but no one left her alone in the greenhouse. They all came up with things to do. Jane washed the glass panes and planted tomato seeds, Papa sorted his finds, Merle fixed the pavers, Dee ordered fresh clay and went back to making pots, keeping Rita company. Even if it kills me, she said.

In late May, Dee celebrated her eighty-eighth birthday, her *beiju*, which she said was a special year, especially if you were Japanese. Or a Cornish potter, said Papa, who made Merle grill steaks. Steaks were Merle's one culinary glory.

"What happened in Papa's special year?" asked Polly. Dee's birthday began every summer and his, at the end of August, ended it.

"You moved in, sweetheart."

Dee's daughter Maude visited for the birthday and dragged Polly and Edmund through marshes and along rainy beaches looking for birds. She gave advice to everyone, and she and Dee quarreled off and on for a week. Maude spent most nights in the city, visiting old friends, and Papa broke up the quarrels by teasing her about her days as a wild child. Variety, he said, was the spice of Maude's life.

For her birthday on May 29, Polly asked for lobster. Rita joked about it all one morning—"Have the lobster, little girl"—until even Merle asked her to stop. Rita talked about what she'd like for her birthday, in September, and though they probably all dreaded the idea of being together that long they nodded and smiled.

"When is your birthday, E?" asked Dee.

"March," said Edmund.

Polly had just taken a bite of ice cream, a beautiful Dee concoction with fresh strawberries, and she linked this moment with a kind of brain freeze. She watched, unable to swallow, as ice cream melted in her mouth and she

thought over the horror of no one celebrating your birthday, no one knowing. What had they done instead? Dee's lips opened in clear rage.

"You forgot your child's birthday?"

"Darling," said Papa. "Don't."

Rita was oblivious, scraping her bowl. Edmund didn't look sad, didn't
look anything. Dee pulled herself up, swaying, so old and so angry. "Edmund, come with me in the kitchen, and we'll plan your birthday. A little
late, but all the better."

Polly asked Jane once if Rita realized how much Dee hated her. Jane
thought Rita knew, but she wasn't sure the emotion was hate. Disgust, disdain. Dee loathed Rita for being a bad mother, for not controlling her mind
for other people's sakes.

A week later, for Edmund's belated celebration, they went up the Sound
to an old, beautiful house with a real sand beach, owned by a friend named
Mr. Porter. It was being restored—there were men on the roof, men on
ladders. Dee planned to have Papa's retirement party there at the end of the
summer, and for Edmund's birthday, she'd somehow managed to pick a day
that Rita planned to spend in the city, meeting her agent and a man from a
French gallery.

The house was built high above the Sound, with a flower garden below it, and below that a series of hedged rooms with fountains, a true in-
terlocking maze with tall yews. The hedges were neglected, but still dense
enough that the people who walked inside were mostly invisible from the
higher house, except for the center, next to the large dry fountain. There
were smaller fountains in different corners of the maze, vine-covered stone
animal heads—a horse, an elephant, a camel, a lion—that Dee had sculpted
for Mr. Porter back when she'd been strong enough, before she'd taken up
pottery. She'd seen fountains in Rome like this when she was young, and
she'd sketched the heads as lizards ran in and out of the statues' eyes and
mouths.

There were no lizards on Long Island, but the magic of all this green,
the way a person became invisible in the strange growing walls, did some-

thing to Polly's mind, led to decades of dead plant tags, a private mythology, and a false sense of what a garden could be.

Mr. Porter's grandchildren, who lived with their parents in a smaller place up on the hill, were a little older and slightly predatory. Edmund and Polly ran through the big house's stables, but eventually the fear of what would happen if they were caught was overwhelming. The Porters commanded that Edmund and Polly help collect tent caterpillars and put them in a marble trough on the side of the stable. The girl pried at Polly's legs while she was up in the tree, reaching for the caterpillars' tents. When the boy lit a match, and as the pyre of writhing worms shot up above the trough, Polly and Edmund raced down to the beach and hid in the maze, then parked themselves between Dee and Papa, who commented on the smoke and got the truth.

"The worms go in, the worms go out, the worms play pinochle on your snout," said Dee. "I hope they have nightmares."

"Those children have problematic eyes," said Papa. "Learn to recognize the look."

The Porters did not reappear, but Edmund and Polly sensed that someone was always watching them—from behind a corner, from the sea, from a hole in the hedge, from the eyes of Dee's animals. They ran around the gutted, echoing mansion and wallowed in the still, cold salt water with Lemon while Merle and Jane lolled on a blanket, sometimes kissing, and Papa and Dee read. Papa had brought his rowboat down that morning, and at dusk, at high tide, he rowed Edmund and Polly the two miles back to Stony Brook, as all the lights on the shore flickered on.

Papa and Dee talking, pulling them along through this dreamtime summer. Polly, seeing it in stanzas decades later, was sure, on every waking, that her memory was clear. She could hear the steady rhythm of the oars, Papa's voice with an accent, but not old, answering their random questions, both silly and earnest. His advice, moving over the water and under the moon, mixed with splashes in her mind: What to do if you're lost in the mountains? Find water and follow it down. What to do if you see a large bear, as Papa had in Mongolia and Montana? Play dead. What to do if you fall into deep fast water, a riptide or a river? Let it take you until you see a chance, try to stay on your back, feet in the current. What to do if you have an enemy and want to act in anger? Wait and do it right. What to do if someone is lost, but not dead? Find them. What to do when they had children, as they would? Love them. The glinting silvery head and eyes, old shoulders pulling them home.

7

Monday, July 1, 2002

On Monday morning, Ariel reached the big bend, as the Yellowstone, which ran north out of the park, turned east toward Livingston and the prairie. Bodies mostly float spine-up, legs dangling, but when she rolled in the current her limbs stretched out and she moved down a deep channel on her back, two feet under the surface, eyes open and facing the filtered sun, strands of hair or the occasional fish or boat or duck body blocking the light. The shadow of pelicans, a speckle of sculpins, her own water bottle keeping up a quarter mile back.

People still said disappeared. Polly was careful to stick to this etiquette, but she thought drowned, she thought dead. Lost. There was always a moment when a Search and Rescue operation became a recovery operation, though this point was usually a quiet reality days before it was announced. People could survive weeks when they went missing in the mountains, but although no one who'd gone into a river like the Yellowstone had ever been found alive after two days, telling a family to drop a fantasy of a wounded but breathing loved one on a riverbank was not the business of the searchers. Polly, for some doomed Drake project, had researched the mechanics of drowning, and she noticed that these were not the kind of facts that disappeared with the bicycle accident. Nor were they truly facts. If no one survived, who knew if the lungs burned as they filled or if the brain screamed in pain? The great mysteries of life, unanswered. Polly knew a body would rise only when the gases inside built up, and she knew a body would eventually turn into a kind of soap known as adipose. But before the body stage, at the end of the person stage, they were all stuck with the wonders of the imagination.

Ned was up and getting ready to go on the river again but Polly stayed in bed for another few minutes before morning sounds chased her downstairs: a flicker mistaking their metal furnace exhaust for an aspen with larvae, a neighbor whacking weeds at dawn, and the helicopter on one of its last scheduled tours. She was so tired she saw crackles of light in the corners of her eyes, and her brain felt grainy. She chugged coffee, rebuilding some sort of agenda as she shuffled around in an old nightgown, recoiling a little from the floor she hadn't swept, the dog hair, garden dirt, the stickiness of old spilled box juice. She found her previous day's list on her mounded desk and searched for something to cross out, then added:

> *swimming lessons*
> *go looking*
> *food for Delgados and Maude's picnic*
> *argue with Jane*

She added *sauces, etc.* to *restaurant* and an exclamation mark to her previous cleaning line, then scribbled:

> *get Maude*
> *deal with Graham*

In the yard, a flash of color caught her eye. At 7 a.m., Merle was drinking coffee in the chilly sunlight, reading while wrapped in a blanket, waiting for the house to wake. Having reached a plateau of boredom, he'd decided to fill their house with bookshelves. He was already measuring walls when they left him with the children to meet the search boats.

On day four, the machinery of drowning still included the helicopter and the county boat, a dozen rafts and drift boats and a dog team from Flathead County. A Yellowstone County crew arrived with a big motorized craft to give the Park County teams a break. Harry didn't much like them; bad blood from a case years ago, reawakened by a comment about Ariel becoming Yellowstone County's problem soon, anyway.

Polly, dropping Ned off at the Carter's Bridge take-out, happened to hear this. She was standing off to the side, studying the high, cave-dappled rock face on the east side of the river. If she watched for long enough, she would see something move, or something watching back. That much rock felt like the ocean, filled with invisibilities—something lived within every crack. The night before, a huge black Mordor-style cloud had opened up above the upper valley and Yellowstone Park. The river would rise and turn an opaque milky brown again, and Ariel's body might be lifted and dropped by this new surge. Some riverbanks would have to be searched again.

Ned swung a leg into Harry's boat, and she felt a blast of tenderness.

"What are you going to do before the shit hits the fan?" he asked.

The shit included cleaning and Maude's late-morning flight. The next day Polly would prep at the restaurant for the first time in months because everyone wanted parade day off, and then it would be Maude all the time for the rodeo, the picnic, the party.

The men pushed off and the river sucked the boat away, Ned looking uneasy as Polly took off her shoes and waded into the river to her ankles: melting snow, pure and simple. You didn't avoid the river, even though it was silver, loud, brutal. Of course it killed people, and of course she should bring her children back to play near it, and float on it. Polly watched the surface roar by and wondered if the deep pools beneath felt still and green. Once a diver found a body upright after two weeks in a fifteen-foot-deep pool—was Ariel standing under these boats, waiting?

Ned was worried Polly would go out for a walk and forget to come in, as it were. She'd wandered a few times that spring, and he always found her walking along the river. Didn't everyone walk toward the water? She hadn't felt lost. Polly took the dogs back down to the area near the baseball fields and saw three heads in the osprey nest, which made her feel smug. She'd have to tell Jane, who didn't need to know that Polly had also wondered whether one had been blown out, pecked to death by siblings, neglected by the mother, who preferred the others. Nature, tooth and claw.

No one needed to know every little thing that went through Polly's tattered mind, just as Ned didn't need to know about this walk. Polly was here to find Ariel, and she made it a half mile downstream, climbing rocks and going under fences, before she realized she was going to be late for Helen's swimming lessons. She jogged back across the golf course with the dogs to make up time. A man yelled at her, and she gave him the finger. This gave her the energy for a final burst of speed, even though she was wheezing when she remembered where she'd left the car.

It was still only fifty-five degrees at 9 a.m. when Polly unswaddled Helen's beautiful goose bump–covered body and walked her—fat tiny feet on Polly's sneakers to protect them from the cold crumbly concrete—to the edge of the pool, telling her that the water would be warmer than the air. Helen's skin turned gray in seconds, and Sam, who'd already survived this childhood challenge, catcalled from behind them, wearing a parka. But the teacher, humorless Connie Tuttwilliger, held out her arms, and Helen went to her.

Polly and Sam watched as Connie and her assistant seized small wandering bodies by their life preservers, held them gently for back floats, towed them back and forth, cooed over the roar of dozens of slapping hands and shrill cries. Polly watched Helen spin and splash, but when she put her face underwater Polly squinted her eyes shut against bad thoughts: child underwater, child changing shape. She stood, but suddenly both she and Helen were back in the daylight, the here and now of the bright pool. Helen lifted her head and laughed, and unloving Connie hugged her like she meant it. Really, the most dangerous thing that would happen to the child that day would be getting in a car with her mother.

The kids clambered out and Polly wrapped Helen in a towel. Sam was a rosy Irish American boy, but Helen was tawny, like much of Polly's family. When Connie swam to the side and waved, Polly plopped Helen down in the sun to warm up—the temperature was ten degrees higher than when they'd arrived, and Sam shed his parka—and walked over. Polly knelt when Connie gestured again to come closer.

"Mrs. Berrigan? Have they found anything?" Connie loved married names.

"One sighting, south of town, last night," said Polly.

"I meant," said Connie, "about how it happened. Have they found her preserver?"

"I don't know," said Polly. "It seems like that would be as hard to find as her body."

"She had it when we left them." Connie had been in the raft that day. "If it was with her in the kayak, she would have worn it."

"What do you mean?"

"I heard him tease her for wanting to wear it. He held it up over her head. I think he kept it away from her."

He. Connie, spiteful and jealous, wasn't going to utter Graham's name.

"He wouldn't. He's not some monster."

Connie studied Polly. "If he did, he wouldn't tell the truth now, would he? She wasn't a good swimmer. I never even saw her in the deep end without holding the side."

This didn't strike Polly, who was a side grabber, too, as revelatory. She liked swimming despite choking, terrifying misadventures. Water lurked, but it invited; Polly dabbled. Now she wondered if she'd ever seen Ariel swimming.

"And yet she climbed into a kayak." A little girl was actually waving to Sam, and Polly would have preferred to watch that show. "He says they were in love."

"She wasn't in love with him. She felt sorry for him. And why didn't he die, too?"

Connie rattled Polly. Pretty eyes in a flat, judgmental face, now filled with anguish. Helen was coming out of her hypothermic huddle, eyeing the alluring crew at the deep end. Sam, who couldn't remember Connie sitting for him when he was tiny but could remember disliking her, was watching the ducks on the far side of the fence, rather than keeping track of his sister or acknowledging the waving girl.

"I'm sure he feels horrible," said Polly. "He'll deal with this all his life."

"Good," said Connie.

Since her accident, Polly had survived many tasks that had never before been so difficult—bills, grade school registration, weighing whether to take medication, not killing someone during a psych test, not saying the wrong thing to the bereaved, not burning her kitchen down—but her cleaning efforts were so intermittent and spastic that she never made any real progress. Dust customarily lay heavy on the house of Schuster-Berrigan, the kingdom of dog hair, but Polly stripped beds, put away months' worth of clothing and handled the bathroom with broad, spray-heavy strokes, reached for cobwebs without falling off her shitty bent ladder. She'd brushed the furniture, scraped splattered condiments off refrigerator shelves, extracted bug bodies from lights. Now, she scrubbed one five-foot square of floor with Helen on her back, pretending Polly was a horse, before she sent her daughter outside to clean the sidewalks with the hose. She knocked spiders out of the garage shop vacuum and brought it inside, jerking open cabinets and drawers one by one. Sam and Helen would grow up thinking that vacuuming drawers was normal, but it couldn't hurt in later life.

Polly wasn't any better or worse at doing this than she'd ever been, and she lost herself only once, popping back into the here and now to wonder why she was on the floor, holding a soapy toothbrush.

In Polly's office, where Maude would sleep, Jane was waiting with boxes. It was hard to get her to admit defeat, but this room was taking her to her knees. They were trying a new filing system, and Polly, who guessed Jane's goal was to make some failed efforts disappear, handed over files docilely as they sorted a pile of the scripts submitted to Drake. Jane did the labeling. Polly loved Jane's handwriting, and she loved having her to herself.

Jane paused, pen in midair, eyes in a confused middle distance. "What do we call this thing? 'Untitled Stalking Killer'?"

"Psycho Fishing Guide," said Polly, not joking. Drake liked mysteries and always claimed he wanted to write his own, so Polly kept an ongoing list of variations on common fates—death by cars (cars hitting walls, hitting mountain voids, dropping into volcanoes), guns (shot in the ear, shot in the eyeball, etc.), and the local rarities that got him going (a backflipping horse crushing its rider, a rattlesnake in a boat as rapids approached).

Drake's absolute favorite way to kill someone off: falling.

Ways that Polly's relatives had killed or been killed: mostly water.

What it meant: She had no idea, but she'd keep looking for a pattern.

At any given time, half a dozen scripts were being written or revised or planned based on Drake's idly offered desires and curiosities. He was a holdover from the near end of Polly's time in New York, when she'd gotten a job with a producer. Only one script she worked on was made, but it featured Drake in a role that she'd suggested—in a ream of specific notes—be much larger and central. The film made a fortune, and Drake, a nice eighteen-year-old from trailer park Spokane, won awards and became someone else.

By then Polly had bolted back to cooking, and on to Montana. Drake, to his credit, thanked Polly publicly at two awards ceremonies, which brought in some extra freelance work. Polly wondered how different life might be financially if she'd stuck it out, but it was fine. She was out of there, and happy, and Drake handled success well. He was tough but not the boy next door, smart but not British. He was beautiful without being fey, funny without apparent bigotry, and he lacked the arrogance and childhood sexual wounds of some of his competitors. He could act, and he mostly behaved.

One March day ten years later, when Polly was pregnant with Helen, she answered the door and found Drake on her porch. He was almost thirty, and after a decade on top of the pile, niggled by thoughts of a deviated septum, a yellow fatty liver, he judged that things were likely to go downhill. He wanted to disappear, and he drove around the country and decided he liked Montana.

How to pull it off? Other famous people were tucked into pretty corners of the state. Drake was no fool, and he did everything right, simply dropped off the planet. Pick a town accepting of strangers and of the strange. Make friends, learn to row. Donate to the cops, hospital, food bank, local museum; volunteer for Search and Rescue.

Drake's sole professional issue these days was his reluctance to return to Los Angeles for work, his reluctance to go anywhere, for love, for money, for anything. He was energetic, locally. Ned fondly called him a remora after Drake spent time dreaming up a character much like Harry, an ex-cop and current archaeologist, river searcher, private eye, Romeo. He'd sucked up Polly and Ned's life, too, though he gave up playing a chef after two shifts at Peake's. The fall before, during elderly Maude Swanberg's extended 9/11 visit, Drake listened as Maude unspooled stories about Papa's years in Hollywood under the contrail-free sky of her childhood, both of them eating a tremendous quantity of Polly's tomatoes, and dabbled in the idea of a story set in Montana in the thirties. Now he was reading Jane's books.

Jane tossed another stack of scripts in the box. "He pays me, Mom," said Polly.

"He's an infant," said Jane.

They left for the airport.

When Maude Swanberg was a young woman, she'd been trouble, smart and wild. Her nickname was Maude Gone: she eloped with her first husband, a pretty boy from college, in 1931, but she bolted and they divorced in a friendly way the next year. These days, when no one remembered Maud Gonne, the joke fell flat.

Maude's next husband, a childhood friend, was shot down over France in 1944, and this broke her heart. "What would you have done if your husband died when you were thirty-two?" she asked Polly once. I'd have killed myself, thought Polly. But she smiled, and she wouldn't have, because she had children, just like Maude.

"That doesn't mean she didn't have a good life in other ways," said Jane gently, as Sam blinked over a photo of the deceased hero Swanberg. Maude never remarried, though she'd survived a series of subsequent lovers.

All Polly could see in Maude's face for the first few minutes of every visit was Dee, and now, with her new brain, Polly felt as if she could find bits of her great-grandmother, feature by feature. Everything that mattered was close to the surface these days. Maude, who had her mother's big, soft, hooded eyes, was regal without being tall. She did sit-ups, push-ups, and walked at least a mile daily, and ideally three, in place if necessary. She wore her dense but fine hair, once red-brown, now powder-white, in a Gibson Girl cloud.

When Maude walked into the house, she did the same thing with her hand that Papa did when Polly was little, smushing Helen and Sam from the head down, pushing them joyful and squirming into the ground. Papa raised Maude after her father, Dee's first husband, died in 1918. Both lovely men, said Maude. She believed her mother had understood her luck.

Luck, thought Polly, flashing there and back.

Usually Maude stayed with her widowed daughter-in-law Opal, Harry's mother, but this time she wanted to stay in the house she'd been born in, on July 5, 1912—before the millions of dead boys in World War I, before antibiotics, before her mother could vote—and she insisted on taking her old bedroom, now Polly's office. Maude, whose surviving children were in their sixties and seventies, said she loved the idea of hearing young children when she woke up. And she never minded a mess, because her mother was a horrible housekeeper. She thought it sweet that Jane and Polly kept up the tradition.

Polly followed Maude upstairs with the suitcase, taking in her spindly legs, the crumpled silk skirt, and tiny black heels. Polly could feel the fatigue in those shins, the effort of almost a century of movement.

"I worry all your good clothes will be covered with dog hair," she said.

"I brought some easy things, dear. And sneakers. I know how it is."

Maude needed a nap before dinner, but first she toured the garden, though she said she hated gardens, because they were the reason she'd been neglected as a child.

A joke? Polly found it close to home. Nevertheless, having Maude compliment her roses and clematis, her campanulas and the number of tiny plums on the oldest tree, the one Dee tree they'd been able to save, made Polly happy.

Maude wanted to nap outside, though she knew she'd never manage to get out of a hammock. The children dragged the most comfortable lawn chair under the old trees at the bottom of the garden and ran back up for a quilt, because Maude said she was thin-skinned.

"You can see right through it," whispered Helen, while Maude slept.

Polly, who had spent her childhood with old people, said Maude looked fine.

Maude, to be honest, was difficult. Before every visit, Polly constructed rosy scenarios—the things they would do for Maude, the way Maude would enjoy those efforts—but things inevitably went awry. Polly chose to forget this in another spastic push for happiness, a kind of *Groundhog Day* of hope over experience.

Nevertheless, the forecast was idyllic. Tonight they'd have the rodeo and fireworks, the next night a picnic on the river. Maude specified a place on the island a few blocks away, owned by old family friends, which made Polly nervous. Though she very much wanted to find Ariel, she did not want to find her during a picnic for Maude. On the Fourth, maybe some lazy cousin would volunteer to cook. On July 5, Maude's actual birthday, they'd have a party at the house for the same lazy, ancient cousins.

On the way back from the airport, Jane had fended off an attempt to once again enlarge the party and survived an inquisition. Was Jane happy, or at least content? How did she feel about her late career? Was she still in menopause? When things didn't go Maude's way, she retaliated with questions. Now, while she napped, Jane and Polly struggled with another request: Maude wanted to float.

They discussed this problem while Jane held Helen on her lap, drawing a floor plan of a castle named Chateau d'Helene. "Maude says it's the last time she'll be able to," said Jane. "She says everything is the last time."

Polly fretted about Maude in a boat, about everything having to do with boats, while she threw her body around for the last of the cleaning. Maude, on rising, noticed none of Polly's efforts. They gave her coffee and cookies after her nap, and watched as she made a pretty list with Sam's colored pens. Her handwriting was beautiful like Dee's, and still firm.

Things Maude intended to do during her visit:

> *See Harry's latest dig.*
> *Talk to him about his life. Give advice.*
> *Watch movies with the children.*
> *Sort photos and identify people who will then be forgotten again.*
> *Win at cards.*
> *See birds, float the river, picnic.*
> *Dabble in relatives. Give advice.*

Talk to Polly about her head. Give advice.
Eat well.
Receive accolades at parade and rodeo and party.

Polly filled a Maude request for chicken potpie ("With Mother's butter crust and all those lovely things you add? Morels, nice Italian salted pork?") and Harry and Josie joined them for dinner. Maude drank too many gimlets while showing the photographs she'd brought to put up at the party, and lectured Harry and Josie, who she thought should stick to the idea of marrying this weekend.

"I would like to be happy when we marry," said Harry.

"And when would that be?" asked Maude. "I'm here, now."

"Happier," said Harry. "Grandma, I'm a wreck. I loved that little girl."

Merle redirected them to the living room, where he'd set up Papa's movies. Drake had hired a researcher who'd found a few more snippets and put the pieces on DVD. Polly fled for her bats, and Harry and Josie and Ned followed. Through the open window they could hear the stagy music of Papa's films, hear Sam read the cards out loud—"'All lost! To prayers, to prayers!'" from *The Tempest*—between Maude's editorial comments: "Half these boys died in World War I," or "Horses were smarter, then," or "He was the first person to film almost everything outside," or "Wasn't your great-great-grandmother beautiful?"

Sam kept it up with the titles. "'O, I have suffered with those that I saw suffer.'"

Harry was crying, and Josie kissed him.

Ariel still tumbled along in the dark wet cold as Polly slept. The sense of looping was like having the spins as a drunken teenager. It was the way Polly felt for weeks after her accident, but now she knew that the middle of the night, the shaman time of true thought, was the time to give herself up to the girl, to see Ariel as she'd been at sixteen, in braces, or last week with a glass of wine in her hand. On a sled, with a backpack, in Polly's garden, holding Polly's baby. Polly fell through the river with her, thinking of all the lost beautiful girls who'd found themselves in water, in danger, in confusion, spinning. Asta, Evie, herself, now this.

8

Tuesday, July 2, 2002

When the alarm rang for a third time and she watched Ned's long arm arc up to silence it yet again, Polly thought, Marriage is difficult. She pulled herself upright, flexed her toes on the carpet, and flopped back into a last sleep, a dream of Rita, with bits of ribbon in her red hair and charcoal on her cheeks, tattooing birds into Polly's arm. There was no pain—the birds were jewel-colored, writhing in Polly's skin—until Rita pinched Polly and began to look like the Jabberwock.

Polly screamed, but no one heard her. Which was just as well, given that she was standing in front of the coffee machine.

Looking again: Polly had promised, and on parade day, she took Helen with her for the morning walk. The rabbit was waiting in the alley, but Polly ignored it, despite Fritz the dog's keening.

"I bet she's seen Ari," said Helen, waving to the impassive rabbit.

"How do you know it's a she?" asked Polly.

Helen was quiet after this shabby dodge. She perked up as they walked along the river and nattered about what flowers Ariel thought were prettiest, what she most loved to eat, how it was she could read so many books. By the time they reached the pool, Polly's eyes were hot and her throat was swollen, and she wanted to flop on the stained concrete and cry like a toddler.

But Helen the mermaid, Helen the fish, was in the water before Polly was through the locker room door. Connie crooked a finger. Ah god, thought Polly, trying for numbness.

"You should find out why Graham left Seattle."

"Do you know?"

"He won't tell me, but he might tell you."

"You talked to Graham?"

"We went out for coffee. I'm trying to be a good Christian."

"I don't believe you," said Polly.

"I want him to admit what he did," said Connie.

Because it was parade day, Polly was going to work at the restaurant for the first time since the accident. Tourist season, arriving with a bang and sirens, changed everything. Livingston's hotels were full, left turns impossible, and most people wearing cowboy hats were imports. If locals didn't own or tend a ranch, or run a realty company, they usually wore baseball hats, perhaps because of the wind. East Coast visitors who'd gotten up too early wandered around the brick downtown waiting for stores to open, peered suspiciously at art gallery windows and menus, while West Coast visitors got up late and shivered until noon. Every day, somewhere in Montana, a hundred people tried a chicken-fried steak for the first time in their lives and thought, depending on the gravy quality: Why?

The parade was always held July 2, and it signaled the beginning of the three-day rodeo and vast, ebullient public enthusiasm and drunkenness. Maude usually waved a snooty arm at this aspect of the town, but this year she was intent on going, and Ned put chairs out early in front of the restaurant door. Reliable highlights included the Shriners riding toy bikes, bagpipers, and the always-tipsy Statue of Liberty crew, celebrating a hundred years of drapery. In the old days, Clarence Darrow marched and Sally Rand showed up with her husband, rodeo champion Turk Greenough. These days, Livingston usually pulled in the governor, a senator, Montana's sole House rep, and too many people too proud of their antique cars. The rodeo queen and her court, the high school band, religious groups, Crow dancers, a defiant Planned Parenthood contingent. Josie was a Liberty this year and was surly when Polly didn't embrace the idea. Polly was a bad sport, but it was her nature. The only time she'd enjoyed dressing up on Halloween, she'd been a voodoo doll.

Peake's was at the epicenter of the mess. Ned was sending out food for an afternoon wedding, and at home, Polly made gnocchi and arancini and lamb meatballs studded with pine nuts. It was a day for round things, and she drove carefully, imagining an especially ludicrous accident scene. The clients had requested coleslaw on the side, not some sophisticated Italian version but picnic style. Hers was not to reason why. It was enough that people liked to eat.

Ned was blasting a wall of punk, confusing the twenty-year-old staff. Polly wanted to help serve the roast pig—the surplus Maude pig—in the alley parking lot, where they put out food and drinks for concerts and mud baths like the parade. Ned wanted her to work in the kitchen with Graham, who so far that morning had talked to Ned about his swimming career without once saying a word about Ariel. Hence the music.

Polly found Graham staring straight up with his unbandaged eye, watching a fly bash its head against a light fixture. Precision piles of folded napkins, his forte, surrounded him. Polly arranged a grater and three heads of cabbage, a knife and a board. When he gave her a blank look, she explained that he needed to wash the heads and trim them. This resulted only in a pool of water on the board and some tentative hack marks. Polly dried everything and trimmed everything and went off to pull Bolognese and tart dough from the freezer. She returned to see Graham leave his knuckles in the grater. They watched his blood drip onto the vegetables.

Polly was not squeamish. The squiggle in her mind was something about Graham, and his body, and the idea that he seemed to think this shit show was funny. The idea that he thought anything on the planet was funny right now. "Oh for fuck's sake. Wrap it up."

He shrugged, shoulders rolling, grin fixed, and she realized his own blood upset him. Polly found bandages. It was like dealing with Sam at four—she needed to explain everything. Rinse your hand off, use soap, dry it, hold still. She could feel Graham's breath on her neck while she wrapped his hand.

"I didn't realize your scar was so large."

Polly jerked back. "I'm fine." She finished and scrubbed off the feel of his skin, scraped up the bloody vegetables and threw the board in a sink full of bleach water. She gave him some parsley to chop for something, someday, and worked at another table with her back to him, happy for the wall of noise. Being around Graham made her feel both miserable and competent. When she checked, his mound of parsley was a combination of purée and stems, and she watched his slow, resentful fingers pull the stems out when she said they had to go. He repelled her, and this made her try to be nice.

"How are you sleeping? Do you wake up all night long?"

He looked up from his raggedy, slimy project, surprised and blank. "No, I've always slept well. I'm not sore any more. The stitches itch."

Ariel was nowhere in his mind. Polly stared at Graham's face and felt the room slow down again, the music moving into her brain. If your world is a monster, she thought.

"You look like you're going to throw up," said Graham.

Polly added two onions to his cutting board. He would reduce them to horse teeth and slimy mince. He wasn't a natural talent. "I'll be right back."

She pushed through the kitchen door. The restaurant proper was closed, and on the far side of the dark room, shining as if framed, she saw her family in the bright sunlight of the sidewalk. Maude, in a folding chair, was being greeted by a succession of people, Jane hunched on the curb with the children, drawing something again to keep them amused. The parade never started on time.

She ran back toward Graham, grabbed four glasses and a bottle of Champagne. "Take these to my mother and father."

He remembered Ariel now. "I can't. People hate me."

Man up, she thought, but how was Graham supposed to feel, when he was alive and Ariel was dead? Not feeling guilty would be hateful. She looked him over. He was a machine, an athlete with a tapered torso and a sulky mouth. He should have saved Ariel, and she knew, she knew, that Ariel would never have willingly kissed those lips.

"Just go."

His expression barely changed but she felt the hate blowing right through the freckles. She watched him navigate the crowd, pale and gouged. Graham wished he were invisible. Polly wished he were, too. He kept his head down, and no one but her family even looked. Of the ten thousand people watching this parade, a fraction knew a girl was floating in the river. Ariel updates were now tucked inside the paper, on page three.

A siren a block away, followed by the honk of bagpipes, signaled the beginning of the parade.

"Remember when Graham was little, and he seemed like a sensitive kid?" she said to Ned, in the alley. He was carving the pig, and he gave her a piece of perfect skin.

"I imagine he still thinks he is," said Ned.

Out on the street, Polly crouched by her children and blinked in the sunlight.

"You have blood on your apron," said Sam.

Polly took it off. Kids milled in the street, craning to see around the corner. The floats and marchers ginned up enthusiasm by hurling candy at the crowds.

Jane nodded to Helen, who'd scored two suckers and given the parade up to draw in a notebook. "She said she knew where to find Ariel. Have you been talking to her?"

"Feeding her lines? No." Polly asked Helen, "What do you have there?"

"A map of all the places Ari likes that she might be. I have to add the rabbit."

Polly reached for the notebook. Helen's drawing showed their street, with a cat and rectangle houses, several dogs, and a ribbon that Polly guessed was the river. The map portion looked like a macramé plant hanger, but Helen had also drawn clouds and the sun on top of the paper and the river on the bottom. The beginning of hell, thought Polly. Bring on the boat and the ferryman. Bring on the Jabberwock. The big *X* for Ariel was near the place where they planned to picnic, and Polly felt a little queasy. Helen was looking, and what if she found?

Polly told Helen her map was beautiful, waved her off to chase candy with Sam. She tapped the notebook. "I want to argue about memory," she said to Jane. "Evie drew pictures for me."

"That was Rita."

"I never once sat on Rita's lap. You drew horses and buildings. Evie drew birds and castles." Polly could see her teenaged aunt shuffling cards, cross-legged on a blanket outside. She shuffled like Merle, like a rural kid, a handy, competent, smart-ass kid. Polly would study Evie's big knees and her own small ones while the cards whirred, and she tried not to worry about bugs dropping from the mulberry tree that shaded them.

Polly might have the short-term memory of a hamster, but the deep past of her brain was just fucking fine. "Think of the things I don't claim to remember," she said. "The plane ride." Polly had been given a ride in the deadly plane with her grandmother Cora and Merle a few weeks before it fell into Lake Michigan with Evie and Frank.

Jane, watching the cheerleaders' float pass with a weird combination of glee and disgust, wasn't impressed. Subsets of people began to quarrel. Sam wanted Helen to be deferential to his greater age, Ned arrived with sandwiches and argued with Merle about whether the new bookshelves should be solid wood or veneer. Maude, surrounded by a clutch of old—very old— friends, disagreed with everyone about dates and names. Shriners on tiny bicycles rode in spirals and when one man, a retired teacher, tipped over and his friends ignored his plight, Merle pulled him upright, and the crowd cheered.

"I don't claim to remember the funeral."

"We didn't take you. We tried to keep you away from it all."

Tried and failed. "The garden," said Polly. This was the oldest argument, the thing that goaded Polly most: Jane refused to believe Polly remembered being with her grandfather Frank, tiny in a forest of tall, staked tomatoes. Frank blew his nose like a trumpet, and whistled, unlike Papa, who'd been a hummer. He led her down rows guarded by garter snakes and daddy long-legs. While Polly was the kind of child who'd throw up if someone forced her to eat a cooked carrot, she'd stand for hours picking raspberries, ignoring the fat buzz of bees, the potential touch of awful things.

A photo did exist of the big garden to the side of the house, and Polly and Jane both cared deeply about gardens, and Jane liked to joke that her daughter was poaching a memory from *The Godfather*. Did Frank put an orange in his mouth, give her a plant sprayer? But Polly could see her grandfather rip at a weed hiding on the far side of a green-painted tomato stake. He'd helped her pull at another, but she couldn't make it budge, and he sighed and swore when he saw a tomato worm, plucking it—writhing— from the half-stripped branch, crushing it with a boot. It hissed.

"No, it didn't," said Jane. "Worms don't hiss."

They do when your ears are three years old and two feet from the ground, thought Polly, watching Helen grub for a Tootsie Pop. Nearer my God than thee. Other things Polly remembered from a low vantage point: an ant crawling over a wild strawberry, spiders in lampshades, hair in grown-up noses, the daunting height of sweet corn. How was it any different than now, this bizarre tendency to look at something until it practically melted? The oddly identical scars on Ned's and Sam's legs; the brown flecks in Jane's right eye; the pale, vulnerable skull under the fluff on Helen's head.

Helen lost interest in the parade. "We have a worm that hisses in the garden," she said. "Near the raspberries. It guards the rabbit."

Polly and Jane fell silent on the curb. A second marching band passed, then the rodeo queen and her court. The women wore shiny western gear— turquoise, melon, lime—with jewels on their hats and in their horses' manes. Sam already looked sarcastic but Helen watched with awe, and Polly snatched her to her lap, just for a minute, just to remind her not to run in front of horses or clowns, just to hold Helen because she felt wonderful, and who knew what Helen would remember tomorrow, or in thirty-eight years.

The way time mixed: Whenever Maude visited, she looked at Jane or Merle or Polly or Ned and said, "Amazing that you all survived." She'd said it on her visit the fall before, during that extra week in September when all the flights in the country ceased, and she'd said it at Polly and Ned's wedding, repeatedly. But the first time Maude gave her survival line in front of an adult Polly, it was 1987, when Maude and Polly and Jane were all in Livingston for the joint memorial for the aunts Inge and Odile, sisters-in-law and lovers for seventy years who'd died within weeks of each other.

"How dare you," said Jane.

"Well, let's talk about it," said Maude, who was, after all, a psychiatrist.

This year, no one took the bait after Maude drank too much wine and tried the line. They'd lived through it, and Maude couldn't for much longer. Merle next politely declined to discuss the dimming of his hopes as a poet while they ate salmon with green sauce, a salad, and *socca* before the rodeo. Ned did not wish to examine his abandoned legal career.

"We are not in a reflective mood, I gather," said Maude.

Polly was; Polly was screaming with questions, but she knew the beginning of each trip was always about Maude. She wanted her childhood food, Dee's food, which was different than other people's childhood food. The list shifted with the decades—a few foreign entries from travels, posh restaurant items, favorites from previous visits—but it was an ambitious list, haute

WASP Continental: soufflés and consommés, the potpie of the night before, a bourride. A potpourri of Szechuan and Spanish and Italian dishes, *lapin à la moutarde*, lobster thermidor, boeuf bourguignon. Maude was less precise about desserts—a plum tart? "Something" with lemon curd and meringue?

"Can you manage this?" asked Maude.

"I've always managed," said Polly.

"I mean *now*. How is your head, anyway?" Maude leaned closer.

Ned left the room. Don't be angry, thought Polly. "Not bad," she said. "Helen can follow me around with a timer."

"I won't be asking you for this again," said Maude.

"Are you sick, Maude?" Jane asked. "Do you think you're dying?"

"I'm not sick, but of course I'm dying."

Despite Ned's resentment, despite Jane lines like "Stop and think before you say yes," Polly resolved to cook her brain into submission, vaporize thoughts of Ariel through movement. What, Polly wondered, was the fucking point in thinking? If Polly could avoid doubt and grief and Maude's clear sense of doom, why the hell not?

She would, however, no longer ask Maude what she wanted. Back when the large-tent, two-pig version of the party was on, Maude suggested they make "something simple, like fried chicken or some such." Fried chicken for one hundred would turn their house into a splatter of buttermilk and Tabasco, clods of flour, ribbons of grease. They were already dealing with the gift horse of two hundred oysters ordered by Maude's children. Everyone would wait for Polly or Ned or Merle or Jane to handle the problem of shucking, but at least they'd finally have a use for Graham, who'd put a good Seattle oyster house on his resume.

"She's not delusional," said Jane, speaking as if Maude were not at the table after she brought the fried chicken idea up again for the picnic. "She doesn't cook, and so she doesn't understand."

Maude smiled, snatched back her list, and added *confit de canard*.

Polly watched through the window as Ned casually threw an empty recycling bin half the length of the yard.

"Pasta for the picnic, then," said Maude. "One of my mother's recipes."

"You want me to bring a pot and boil pasta on the riverbank?" said Polly.

"Lasagna?" Maude asked. "Though I've heard it's bad luck for birthdays."

And so it was a plan. Not a hundred layers, or even ninety, but at least twenty. Polly would make a second tray for the Delgados, because they'd lost their daughter, and this was what one did, whether or not the family was ready to accept it yet. After four full days and nights in the river, they had to understand.

When Polly made the list, she added past days, for the sake of checking them off.

June 30, Sunday, home: chili

July 1, Monday, home: potpie

July 2, Tuesday, home: salmon & socca

July 3, Wednesday, picnic: lasagna, Caesar, molasses cookies

July 4, Thursday, home: leftovers? rabbit?

July 5, Friday, party, home: oysters, pork, etc.

July 6, Saturday, home: leftovers

July 7, Sunday, ??

"It might be nice to go to the restaurant toward the end of the week," said Jane.

"Oh, let's not," said Maude. "I do love Polly's cooking."

They went to the first night of the three-day rodeo, lest the world go downhill. Ned did not do the rodeo, though he helped with the fireworks. Horses gave him asthma, and the announcer's jokes about liberals enraged him and gave him an excuse to drink heavily, along with most other elements of the holiday. Polly packed blankets for the rest of them, an inhaler for Sam, an extra coat for Maude and for Merle, who never understood how cold it was at night at this altitude, wads of cash for glow sticks, cotton candy, bad drinks, popcorn. People paid homage to Maude, while Jane, who'd spent summers here as a child, worked the rest of the crowd.

Everyone stood for "The Star-Spangled Banner." During the opening ceremony two years earlier, a skydiver's parachute failed to deploy, and the man hit the arena dead center at a hundred miles an hour. Polly braced herself but tonight the men and women floated down like quieter fireworks. In other ways, the world frayed: A couple argued behind them and an old lady fell and split her face on the metal steps of the stands while nearby children stared with naked, exhausted fascination. Maude looked smug. A bull rider's rib-cage muscles ripped free from his spine as he was flung against a fence. When the rodeo queen and her court finished circling the arena, there was a minute of silence for Ariel, the riders' pastel hats held over their breasts, most of the out-of-town crowd not understanding because of the announcer's garbled voice.

When Helen fell asleep on Jane's lap, Polly took Sam behind the stock pens to the clearing at the golf course where the fireworks were launched by a ragtag, mostly sober group of pillars of the community, which included Harry and Ned. The fireworks started while they were passing the stock, steers and broncs milling in fear and dust in the light of every explosion. Polly could see lather on their mouths, the old stains of the saddles.

It was louder, colder, stranger right next to the launchpad. Polly clutched Sam with one hand and covered her eyes with the other, walloped by the way the fireworks seemed to run like water. Ned pulled her away, closer to the river, and she thought about how the water near the osprey nest would be changing color with every explosion. Maybe she could find Ariel this way, watch until the girl was revealed by colors, ashes and spent paper falling toward her face.

Polly and Jane lugged the sticky, exhausted children back to the car, while Merle half carried Maude. When Polly finally fell asleep, she saw Ariel rolling slowly, gently, onto her back, to face the falling lights. And it was true: Ariel was counting stars, upright and just below the surface, toes skimming the cobble. She twirled gracefully through a deep, gentle channel, with nothing to bounce against, nothing to cause more bruises, and that evening rose again until her face reached the cool air, startling a heron whose chicks were squabbling over the flayed corpse of a garter snake. Ariel moved down the center of the river like a swan, sometimes regal, sometimes spinning like a toy, but even though she passed the wedding party with Polly's round objects, nobody but the heron noticed her.

9

Wednesday, July 3, 2002

Maude talked of going birding in the morning, yet she was not an early riser. She would wake at 10:00 or so, drink coffee with a pastry (carried up by Sam or Helen, who came out of their post-rodeo funk to argue over who won the honor), bathe, and have lunch with distant relations. Sam and Helen would fetch the right pillows for the right chair, find her glasses, haul her huge purse between points A and B. Maude arrived with a stash of Bicentennial coins that she called silver dollars and doled out spottily. Sam thought they were insanely valuable, but Ned looked them up and found they were worth $1.38.

Lunches would be followed by a nap, more coffee, another outing.

Maude was therefore not awake when her grandson Harry arrived to pick up Ned for a day on the hill at the Poor Farm. The river was full of searchers from other counties, and Harry had possession of a rented portable ground-penetrating radar machine for only another three days. He needed to return to the dig.

Ned was still in the shower. Polly wanted to go with them. She wanted to dig far from the river, the kitchen, people she loved.

"Nothing is where it's supposed to be," said Harry, looking into the refrigerator for half-and-half. "So far, beyond that first grave site, a building foundation, an orchard."

"What else is there to worry about?"

"More dead people," said Harry. "Frankly."

The dogs and the children were at the front window, staring at something. Polly checked and saw Graham standing awkwardly on the sidewalk.

"Should I ask him in?"

"Not on my behalf," said Harry, blowing on his mug. "I asked if he wanted coffee and he said he had no addictions, which annoyed me, and so I left him out there."

Polly went out. "Hey," she said. "You got rid of your eye bandage."

"I had to walk to the clinic to get my eye checked," said Graham.

"Any lasting damage?" asked Polly.

"I think there is. It still hurts."

She wanted to say, Don't you feel lucky? Aren't you stunned that you're alive? Aren't you underwater in a different way, drowning in grief? Aren't you at least a little guilty to still be breathing? Both eyes were clear, the whites without a hint of bloodshot, Graham's face without a hint of expression. His scratches were scabbing over. "Why don't you have a car, anyway?"

"I was in an accident," he said. "I don't want to talk about it." He didn't say it as a plea for kindness. It was a shutdown, a Fuck you, Mom line.

"Harry won't be long," said Polly, deciding not to offer him anything. She walked back toward her house. Her children, who hadn't budged from the porch, were staring at Graham like ghost children planning his death. Even the dogs hadn't greeted him.

"What's the deal with Graham not having a car?" she asked Harry.

"I don't know."

"Is this about the bad thing that had happened in Seattle?"

"What bad thing?" asked Harry.

Polly and Helen were leaving for the pool when Drake walked through the gate an hour later, carrying a bouquet for Maude—they had planned to go for lunch—and another tote bag of Hollywood blather. Polly, forgetting about the lesson, had told him she could work, but Drake claimed to find the whole outing interesting, though his face dipped when Helen explained why they were taking a walk first: to look for Ari, of course. The three of them took the path along the river with the dogs. Drake had never noticed the osprey nest, despite floating by it a dozen times in the last four days. It was a little like the time he said he'd never seen the grapevine on Polly's porch, after two summers walking underneath it.

At the pool, Helen plopped right into the water now, a happy otter. At the far end, the city's athletic director was training the season's lifeguards, all teenaged and female and buzzing with Drake's presence. He made it worse by waving to them.

"Did you ever play a lifeguard?" asked Polly.

"Never."

"You won't lead Maude on at lunch?"

"I'm being led," said Drake. "I'm being used, but pleasantly. She wants me to know her stories. She thinks someone, someday, should do justice to all the shit she and her cousins got up to. Or the earlier stuff, all these strange stories about her mother and her father and her stepfather."

"Jane won't want anyone knowing most of it."

"I'm invited to your picnic, and I know your beautiful mother will give me the stink eye the whole time. I won't tell her secrets." He waved to Connie, who pretended not to see him.

Polly went to the edge to tell Connie about Helen's nightmare—boiling pool water—and Connie hissed that it was humiliating to be seen in a bathing suit.

She'd spent every summer morning in a suit for years. "Connie, you look great."

"I know how I look." The girl's face was dusty pink, a flush over queasiness.

Drake and Polly buzzed through script turndowns, as usual without acknowledging that there were only ever turndowns: Irishmen in Mexico in 1848, a romantic comedy about ecologists, a murder drama about cooks (though Drake found the number of available murder weapons compelling). He still liked a story about a predatory bartender; he was at this point attracted to anything that could be filmed in Montana and incensed that no one wanted a second fly-fishing movie.

The lesson was over, and Helen trotted up, dripping. While Polly dressed her—the drill involved sheltering a toddler's body with a towel while you pulled up pants, avoiding the funky locker room—Drake went to the pool edge and gestured to Connie, who was pretending that she was having a deep thought on the far side. She crossed with as much of her body submerged as possible. Polly watched them talk. Drake touched the side of Connie's face and kissed the top of her head.

All this while the teenagers gaped. Back in the car—a wet child, slavering dogs; it didn't matter to Drake, who'd grown up poor in a shitty part of Spokane—Drake said, "I wanted to tell her I was sorry. She lost her best friend."

Polly only then realized she had not thought to do something that simple.

That afternoon, while Maude and Drake drank mimosas and toured the county in the Porsche he usually kept hidden in his Mission Creek barn, Polly tossed chunks of butter around like playing cards. She steamed the chard, warmed the Bolognese, bickered with Jane about the proportion of butter and flour in the béchamel. She started batches of gingery molasses cookies, the easiest dessert option. She checked the clock, doomed to forget what she'd seen with each tray, but Helen followed her with an old alarm clock, one with a beating paddle that Ned had helped her take apart and put back together. When Maude was delivered back to them, Polly asked her to grate some cheese, just out of curiosity, but Maude wandered away to play cards with Sam. She would cheat, and then she would sneak upstairs.

They made the pasta dough and wrapped it to rest, put water on to boil, and cleared the counter again to set up the Atlas machine. They let Helen crank until it bored her, and the house was soon draped with handkerchiefs of pasta, Tibetan flags, drying white stockings. An hour later they were done. Merle took the pans to the restaurant to bake off.

"Easy peasy," said Jane. She'd been on a rant about the idea that Merle wanted to look at property outside of town, the better to have chickens and goats and other character-building animals for their grandchildren. "Maybe the problem will melt away."

They were sitting outside, and they could hear Maude snore through the upstairs window. Jane kicked into the inadvisability of drinking when elderly while Polly doled out the small harmless fireworks, coiled snakes and pooping chickens, cheap-ass tiny tanks and expanding pagodas. She wanted to purchase bottle rockets, smoke grenades, sixteen-chamber cakes that would vibrate the town.

Melt away, troubles as lemon drops—Jane, raised by old people, said things like this often, usually ironically, bits of the Jazz Age or Depression or even Edwardian slang, Dee words and musical phrases: lovey-dovey, criminy, rabbiting on, tempest in a teapot. People had druthers, things were done right off the bat. Why are you piddling around? When Helen had drawn a perfect circle the day before, Jane said, "Aren't you the bee's knees."

Helen was listening to them from her own little corner, an abandoned area in the garden where Polly was trying to kill off horseradish, and where there had once been a greenhouse. Helen liked finding old tin plant tags and forming the clay into castles, and she knew to watch out for glass and nails. Now she sat on her dirt heap and watched her bowl of ice cream flatten and pool, something close to fear in her face. Polly thought of the classic childhood question—could people melt to death?—good for lava situations and dissolving witches. Would Helen think Ariel melted into the river? If Ariel wasn't found, that might be the best thing. She could become clean bones, like river stones.

"Let's sweeten up," Jane said. "Let's enjoy the day, go down early and set up. We don't want to rush Maude's nap."

In the hammock Sam was visible as one leg and one arm, a fluttering comic visible, held up high. Everyone had a way of solving the problem. Helen's theory was that Ariel is melting. Sam would read her away. Shazam! Bop!

Every fucking moment since Ariel vanished was framed around what Polly worried the children would remember. The colored stink of the last of the smoke bombs wafted past the staked tomatoes and the things they'd collected for the picnic—blankets and card tables, camp chairs and tin plates, cups, coolers with half a case of Champagne and the Caesar salad, a crate with half a case of Nebbiolo, cheeses, and bread. Ned would bring the lasagna from the restaurant in a hotbox, which would give him a chance to arrive last.

"Let's go," Polly said. "Sam, put your comics in the house or they'll blow away."

"I'm perfectly comfortable," said Sam.

That was a Merle line. Polly flipped him out of the hammock.

They left a note, loaded one wagon with Helen and her pirate ship and blankets and glasses, the other with supplies, and headed off. A certain giddiness took hold, and when they reached the street Polly started to run, towing the wagon. Helen clutched her ship and shrieked with some wiggling combination of joy and fear. Jane and Sam, struggling to hold three dogs, sprinted, too, but as soon as they were out of sight of the house, they all slowed down.

The streets were quiet. Half of the town was eating dinner before the second night of the rodeo and the other half was at a concert at the park's crumbling pastel band shell. The sound of a swing band fluttered up the river with the smell of grilling meat. They kept the dogs on leashes until the far side of the bridge, and when Jane released them, they all ran onto the island and ducked under the chain blocking an overgrown two-track. The Sutton Ranch ran all the way from this wedge up to the area of the Flats where Harry was surveying. Back when this was the narrower channel of the Yellowstone, the Suttons had built their own bridge, gone in a flood in the fifties, to connect to the rest of their land and an old road that now dead-ended at the river and ran along the edge until it turned south to the Poor Farm and Swingley Road.

Everything that was frayed in life evaporated in the face of beauty. Polly and Jane and the children followed the two-track through green grass, the vault of tall cottonwoods opening to a view of the river, a sandy area, a stone foundation of the old ranch house, gone decades earlier in a fire. The beach was wide and shallow; upstream, the kids climbed on the five-foot dynamite-carved boulders of the ruined bridge's base. Downstream, they could see the metal of an old diversion dam, long useless, and Polly, who'd seen car bodies in that stretch—old cars were sunk for decades to reinforce ranch banks—told Sam and Helen to steer clear.

The shrinking channel was perfect, barely a part of the river but not yet funky with algae. Sam worried about how the minnows within it would be trapped and started digging a deeper outlet to the river, herding fish through this temporary gate. Jane and Polly set up Helen's pirate ship so that she could tow it with a length of surveyor's string in six-inch water, and she pulled it back and forth to flush the remaining minnows while making suggestions. Sam should make her a new island; someone should blow on the sails, or splash and provide some waves.

The light was almost the yellow of the Midwest during tornado season, with a big black cloudbank to the northwest, and Polly tried to guess how quickly they'd have to leave if there was a storm. No wind, not even warning puffs, nothing to disturb the spiral of fighting crows and magpies a hundred yards downstream. She fretted about the dogs, but they were staying close. Polly plopped down on the warm sand, exhausted.

"Let's go somewhere," said Jane, sitting next to her.

"I'd love to," said Polly.

"Seattle. Or even Butte."

Polly had already shot ahead to Spain, but she said okay. She lay back and saw some raptors, unidentified. It was a busy afternoon. "What kind of hawks are those?"

"I don't think they're hawks," said Jane. "Vultures? Buzzards?"

Helen was crawling in front of them, pushing at Polly's feet. They watched her pry up one rock, choose another and roll that.

"What are you doing?" asked Polly.

"Ari could be small now."

Jane lay back on the sand and covered her face.

When the cars arrived, they set up the tables, smeared on sunblock, opened wine. Harry was beginning to relax, Merle was looking at insect husks in the shallows and listing all the smaller creatures Helen and Sam could find in or near the river over the course of the summer: stoneflies, freshwater crayfish, tiny worms. Josie and Drake were skipping around, telling Sam and Helen where and how they should divert the trickle of the upstream channel. Maude hadn't been ready to leave the house, and Ned would win the errand of fetching her when he brought the lasagna from the restaurant.

But when the Civic bumped up, and Polly and Jane ran to it—somewhat animated after tequila, willing to forget most of the frantic, sad week—Ned climbed out, looking rattled. When Merle helped Maude out she put a hand over her face, still leaning against the dusty car, and looked straight up at the canopy of cottonwoods. Polly stared at her ancient throat, a strangler fig with a mysterious life at the center, a marvel of survival.

"Isn't it beautiful here?" said Polly, with a hesitant edge.

"It is," said Maude. "I'd forgotten that part. My sister loved it here. I suppose it's possible that's why they were on the bridge. But I think she wanted to get home, and this was the shortcut. She wanted to get out of that car, away from that person."

"What are you talking about?" asked Polly.

"My mother died here," said Jane. "Going off the old bridge. I wanted to see it, and Maude wanted to come here again."

"I will admit that it's all harder than I thought it would be," said Maude.

Almost nothing in life pissed Polly off more than not being part of a perceived secret, but everyone else rolled with it and ignored her until she came around. Jane sat quietly with Maude while the others opened wine, worked on stream diversion, took turns with Maude's binoculars. By the time Polly pulled the tinfoil off the lasagna, thirty layers in the end, the whole thing a miracle of salt and fat and flavor, Maude was talking about her cousins and gambling, about the trip to New York for Papa's tribute in the fall, about everything but death. They ate their delicious unpicnic-like meal, Maude picking all the anchovies out of the salad, Ned and Harry scavenging them. They sat with the tables perpendicular to the river so that they could all see both water and trees, swallows from the facing cliff diving for insects. Jane kept looking downstream at the bridge and the narrow road, and Merle switched their plates so that she would face west, instead of in the direction of Asta's death.

After they ate, Maude showed them the stone foundation of the ranch house. There were parties here, in a bunkhouse farther downstream, whenever the elder Suttons were away. If the police came, there was the city-county divide to cite at the first bridge, and the family bridge, gone soon after the house burned in the fifties, had been easily blocked. Before World War II, there'd been a warren of roads over on this now-abandoned south side of the river, more ranches, lost towns, Prohibition liquor drops and stills, the operating Poor Farm. They played cards and Maude's stories grew more baroque. Drake encouraged her, but everyone else did, too, and Jane kept her temper.

Helen pulled on Polly's hand. "When are we going to look?" whispered Helen.

So Polly filled her glass and they took off with Ned, doing their best to find happier things. A den for an otter or a mink, owl pellets with whole skeletons, quartz pebbles, petrified wood. They showed Helen a car body, an Oldsmobile from 1930 or so, and then Polly put her to work drawing another map, this one on a patch of fine, flat sand.

"What did Maude say in the car?" she asked Ned.

"She said that everything she looks at here, every hill or road, is a dead person."

Everyone had a core of hell and doubt and sorrow. Polly wanted to drink more, or much, much less. Helen drew and the wet dogs lay next to them, panting. A couple floated by and Polly could hear giggling before they came into sight, unfurling and possibly *en déshabillé*. It would have been lovely and funny if she didn't think of Ariel.

She flopped back onto the sand one more time and stared up. Tree crowns, beautiful clouds, the gyre of birds downstream near the old diversion station; in the corner of her eye a fast first quiver of bats, probably her bats. The cliff across the river changed color as the light left, and she wondered if it had been daylight or dark when Asta had driven down the road across the river, with someone. In early December, it always seemed dark.

"Are you all right?" asked Ned.

"I'm fine. A little woozy," she said. Woozy, muzzy. She should get T-shirts that labeled the condition of her day.

Down the beach, Merle called to Ned to play cards, and Helen skittered off with him. Maude was going on about her half-finished list. She hadn't seen an interesting bird or Harry's dig, and advice—she'd barely started with the advice. Why was Sam so slow at shuffling and dealing? Had no one trained him?

Another shadow across the sun, Jane passing with her binoculars up, an expert at work. Quite an act; Polly hadn't seen such a thing for ten years. Hopefully Maude noticed.

"What's so interesting?"

"Maude claims she saw a black vulture, so I thought I'd check."

Polly turned to an astounding sight, no rooks but a murder of crows, a whirl of magpies. What was the word for ravens? An unkindness. "Do you know what a black vulture looks like?"

"No."

"It'll be a dead deer, and the dogs will follow you and roll in it," said Polly.

"We'll be using your bathtub to wash them," said Jane.

"Jesus, Mom."

"Jesus, Polly." Jane was fiddling with the focus on the binoculars, and then she was gone. Polly could already imagine the stink of what the birds were eating, and then, with a shift in the wind, she realized she could already smell it.

She lurched upright. "Mom, stop!" Polly started to run, not easy on round river rocks and sucking mud, wondering if she was imagining the smell, wondering why she'd thought of a deer and not something far worse. "For fuck's sake, stop!"

She could hear Helen's happiest fuck fuck fuck singsong, Maude's raucous laughter, Ned calling her name. Polly called back, telling him to hold on to the children. Jane heard nothing and marched, oblivious, toward the spiral of birds, and Polly ran drunk in a carousel of images, her childhood of bodies on beaches. She was within a yard of Jane, both of them zigzagging through willow saplings, when they came into a clearing and saw the white outstretched arms, a back mottled with tentative pecks, thick reddish-gold hair spread over the drying sand.

Jane screamed.

Part Two

10

Summer 1968

One morning in late June—a steamy, midwestern kind of morning, not normal for a town on Long Island Sound—Dee took Edmund and Polly on errands to Brooklyn in the old car, a big blue 1944 Ford, because Papa had the Volvo. At the Italian market, where they'd stopped for veal cutlet and fontina, the three of them stared down into a full bucket of live squid. The owner had brought them from the Fulton Market; it was the feast day of John the Baptist, and the squid would be stuffed for one dish and sautéed for another. Dee listened to the Italians squabble over recipes, while Polly and Edmund backed away from the bucket.

"You can't possibly use all of them," Dee said, touching the moving water with a finger. "I'll take three pounds."

Everyone always did what Dee wanted. Her hands shook when she took out her money, but you wouldn't pity her. The shop owner scooped the creatures out, some listless, some wriggling.

Dee needed a pillow to see over the dash of the Ford. She was not much bigger than the children, an eighty-year age difference but none of them over one hundred pounds.

"I used to be taller and curvy," said Dee. "But you can't keep everything."

The children were alone in the house with Papa and Dee for the week: Merle and Jane were off visiting Rita at a hospital upstate and would stay for a few nights in the city. To be silly, said Dee. To be young. She wiggled her hand in the air as if she were a conductor, as if the knotted fingers were dancers, and talked about John the Baptist, beheaded by a beautiful woman, as saints were, back in the day. There'd always been a festival at this time of the year in most of Europe, because of the solstice, but these days you needed to go all the way up to East Harlem to find a parade. They were better off at home, anyway, getting the house cleaned up in Rita's absence.

Salomé, squid, saints. At stop signs, they could hear the lidded container slosh behind their heads. Edmund acted as though he hadn't heard Dee say his mother's name.

"She won't be out of the hospital for a few weeks," said Dee, who noticed everything. She stared at the windshield with huge eyes, and her papery eyelids seemed to take up most of her face. "She needs her rest."

But they knew Dee was happy—they were all happy—to have Rita gone.

The main point of the day was to hang canvases on the walls of the long upstairs hall, over the mess Rita made before she was taken to the hospital. When Dee drove into the yard, Papa was overseeing two students who'd arrived with a truck. The canvases, which reached the ceiling, would cover most of the splashes Rita left behind and fill the gaps between the bedroom doors. Normally—the wrong word when discussing Rita—Rita painted shapes that looked like origami or sand seen through a microscope, and both the shapes and the canvases were small and precise and lush in a way that reminded Polly of Dee's Russian or Turkish carpets. But after a quiet week, they heard her wander up and down the hall. No one came out, all of them holding their breath, and when it was finally light they saw wet red hills that looked like a roller coaster and awkward blue trees lurching across the walls like Matisse dancers. Jagged teeth at the top and the bottom might have been mountains or hell. Rita said that random circles, like blobby polka dots, were the planets, listening to the water.

"Jesus, Rita," said Merle.

"I can't see real things anymore," said Rita. She threw one pot of acrylic paint the length of the hall, hit Merle in the head with another, and locked herself in her room. Jane pried Rita out at lunch, but when Rita saw what she'd done she lay on the ruined Persian runner and cried. When she did not stop crying, Merle called her art dealer to see what she might have taken. Jane sat with Rita, and Papa called a doctor, and Dee loaded Edmund and Polly into the car and took them to a matinee—*Doctor Zhivago*, not childish crap, said Dee. She requested extra butter on the popcorn, whispered explanations of Russian history, and said it was good to leave the others to wait for the little men in white coats. On the way home, Dee thought to explain that this meant doctors, not miniature men.

Dee and Papa didn't see the point of repainting the hall or replacing the runner if Rita would be coming back. The only thing Rita liked to do, and usually did well, was paint. Thus the tall, white canvases, touching the spattered ceiling. If she was going to throw paint around, said Papa, they might as well catch it. The students carrying the canvases were nervous, but Papa probably made them that way at the best of times, even when he wasn't warning them to mind every fragile thing they maneuvered past in the cramped house. He loomed, and evidence of the bizarre was all around them in the other paintings and sculptures in the house, spears and bear skulls, the amused old lady, the green parrot on the grapevine at the entrance, telling them to go home.

"What will she draw?" asked Polly.

"I've no idea," said Papa. "Maybe the real things she was upset about. What would you draw?"

"A map of the world," said Edmund, who only ever drew maps.

"Go practice on the sidewalk," said Papa. "Make sure you add some live things."

They used the stubs of Rita's pastels, but it was hot, and inchworms dropped from the dogwood. Polly made her continents too large, Edmund too small. He used a squirt gun to clean away their mistakes, which meant a wait—not long at all, because of the heat—while the sidewalk dried. Their minds wandered and they whined their way into the kitchen, where Dee worked on a tomato sauce, rolling back and forth between the table and the stove with the rolling stool she'd begun to use. Polly sensed her lack of patience, but it was so, so hot outside, and Papa finally found a scroll, an actual stretch of uncut soft paper—he had every sort of object in his office—and stretched it out on the bumpy table on the front porch. He showed them drawings in an old bestiary and a children's atlas with bright trains flying over mountains.

Polly and Edmund ridiculed the atlas, but they were doing the same childish thing. How could they show the north and south poles, the sky and the water and the stuff boiling under the rocks, all on the same page? The bestiary showed creatures that had never existed, leopard women and sea monsters and single-eyed men. Papa said to try their best and disappeared with Dee for their daily nap in the bedroom at the end of the hall. When Merle and Jane were away, and Polly ran down to Dee and Papa's room after a nightmare, she would watch them for a moment before she woke them, and wonder why they looked so young in the dark, until they opened their eyes and let her climb in. We'll give you a good dream, they'd say. Don't worry anymore.

Most days in the summer were like this, as long as Rita was away or quiet: Jane and Merle would go to classes and work, and the very young and the very old, left in the house together, would swim around each other. For Dee, Polly and Edmund would pull weeds from the brick path, soften her clay with their small, hot hands, drift down the path toward the Sound during the daily nap. They took turns holding Lemon, who was strong enough to drag them. After Edmund first moved in, he spent weeks bringing creatures and plants up for identification: sea lettuce, knotted wrack, stone hair, periwinkles, surf clams, bloodworms. He did not try to catch willets and yellowlegs. He would ask questions—why was crab blood blue, how did clams mate—and return the animals to their exact place. Merle gave intricate explanations and would sometimes try to keep a sample for his classes, which bothered Edmund. Papa, who had grown up near a northern ocean, gave more convincing answers. Dee said he made most of it up, but Polly couldn't imagine that face lying.

Today was windy, and it was cooler down by the water, almost low tide. They popped jellyfish and seaweed pods, smacked mussels open for pearls. They waded for a while before losing the point again. They poked skunk cabbage until they caught the smell and saved a broken mussel with a shell bluer than most. But back up at the house, when they tried painting, the colors weren't right—the olive brown they used for kelp didn't shine, and the great curling water, green and blue and white, defeated their best attempt at translucence. They resorted to the bestiary, but their blue whale looked like a deflated balloon, ribbed with stretch marks, and the other sea creatures they tried to draw were all a flat gray, blobs that looked deader than rocks. In frustration, Polly veered toward the blues of the sky, and tried to draw the witch's green parrot, the one that May the cat wanted to kill. But this parrot's existence meant that somewhere there should be a tree to land on, tigers and snakes and elephants that would need grass and rivers and mountains to cross.

The whole wayward notion of time, usually pleasant or invisible, became oppressive.

"My mother will know how to do it," said Edmund, for the first time in his life.

They wandered away from the scroll, ate the sandwiches Dee left for them, and headed toward different corners of the house. It didn't do to spend too much time together.

By late afternoon, the squid stopped moving. Their bodies were about six inches long, the two tentacles almost the same length, and the eight arms were much shorter. Dee let Edmund and Polly stand on chairs at the sink while she showed them how to pull on the head so that the gloppy mess inside emerged. Dee wanted them to save the ink, and they found the sacs—silver beans in the head—and put them in a half-pint jar. They pried out the soft backbones, which were clear and iridescent: Polly held one up in front of her eyes and looked toward a lamp with a stained-glass shade. It was like looking through a soap bubble.

When Merle came home two days later he would draw a squid's body precisely, explain the why and how of shooting ink, propulsion, the three hearts, the invisible gills, each with its own heart. He would label each body part: mouth and beak; the third, central, systemic heart; the penis or the ovaries; the siphon the animal used for everything from shit to eggs. No one knew yet that squid saw light with their skin, or that they hunted in packs and their arms had a mind of their own, or that their beaks could punch through bone.

Dee saved the arms and tentacles, but she trimmed away the eyes, and the round cross sections with pupils on the sides shone up from a pillow of guts at the bottom of the sink, making Polly's skin shimmy. Dee scooped the mess into a bowl and let Edmund hurl it into the yard, and within a few minutes a crow and May were fighting over the bits, while Lemon, chained just out of reach, watched in despair. A flash of green, the parrot—male? female?—jeering from the fence, saying *poor doggy stupid doggy.*

Edmund and Polly didn't know how to cook yet. They didn't know how to do anything. Dee made dough, and showed them how to roll pici noodles, no different than rolling little clay worms while she threw pots in the greenhouse. She fried a few of the tentacles in a batter and they ate them with salt and a lemon from her window tree. Dee chopped garlic and some of the tentacles and mixed in parsley and an egg and bread crumbs she'd buttered and toasted in a skillet. Edmund and Polly helped her stuff the mess in the squid bodies but did not try to sew the slippery flesh closed. Dee's fingers were huge and crooked—she slammed around a pan Polly could barely lift—but the real problem was her eyes: She needed to bring the bodies up to nose level to insert the needle, over and over, as she stood on one foot and rested her other knee—the one attached to the bumpy shin that had broken so badly in a fall—on the stool.

The where and how of the fall had become a game. Polly loved to track versions: Dee had tumbled down a hill in Granada, she'd fallen out of a barn loft in Montana, she'd been looking at a man on a street and rear-ended another car in Los Angeles. Everything, always, was about having Polly and Edmund look at a map, having them know where the world was. The children would touch a shark tooth on Papa's sill, and he'd say Crete, or Cape May, and they'd add a pin to the map in Papa's study. A bone whistle: Persia. A piece of pottery: Lesbos. All your life long, said Dee, you must love your home but see the world. Papa claimed that the accident happened when Dee lifted a rock and fell into a tomb, that a slab cracked as she stood on it, and she'd fallen into time and onto bones. Don't look under rocks, he said, as they pried pill bugs from hiding places. A whole world might open up underneath you.

But the truth was probably the story Jane told them: In a cave in Morocco, during one of Papa's digs, Dee stepped into the wrong direction of darkness and fell a long way. As she dropped, she held tight to a small ivory moon she'd just discovered. Merle snorted at this detail in the story, but Polly and Edmund didn't have a problem believing it—if they imagined falling in the dark into some unknown place, they squinted their eyes and clenched their hands, so why wouldn't a person do it if they were truly falling?

"I'll tell you a secret," said Papa. "She'd gone off to pee and stepped into thin air. When I reached her she was proud she hadn't pissed her pants."

In both versions, Dee never made a peep until they got her into the truck and bounced into town.

Now she rolled the stuffed squid around in a hot pan until the bundles browned and shrank and bulged, then let them bubble with wine and tomato before she sliced them into rounds, dressed the pasta, and arranged them on top. Edmund and Polly ate everything; they were not fussy. Disdain had cured them—Papa wouldn't punish them for not eating, but he would ridicule their cowardice. Tonight he was in a good mood. He and Dee always drank wine, and Polly and Edmund were each given a shot glass while they heard about the color Dee would glaze a new bowl, the chapter Papa was writing on bird gods, the general stupidity of the world at large. During dinner, through the open window, they all watched the crows continue to taunt poor chained Lemon (Merle, in lieu of rent, was supposed to build a fence). Papa told the children that crows held funerals, but no weddings: They should put that in their hopper. He said they should use the squid ink to sketch out their map on the canvas upstairs. If Rita wanted to paint over the ink later, she could.

"Using what?" asked Dee, on her way to saying no. Dee did this often; she was the person who said no to him, and their arguments were rich and quiet and dense.

"Goose quills," said Papa. He laughed at her face. "I suppose brushes and inkwells, though their fingertips would work best. The carpet's already ruined, right?"

Dee planned it out—the door to her quarters at the far end would split the Pacific Ocean, so that Edmund would not have to face Southeast Asia every time he came out of his bedroom. Rita could paint over the lines later, or she could use them. It would be like a toast, good luck.

The children quickly gave up on the ink, and Dee used it to draw a perfect giant squid near the bathroom door. They sketched coastlines with charcoal pencils: it was night over their heads, a hot day in Asia, and the moon looked like the one Dee clutched in her hand while she fell. Edmund tried the Nile and did a good job: It looked like a snake or a lock of hair, but the mountains on either side looked like tents until Dee suggested he turn them into volcanoes.

"Add some beasts," said Papa. "What's a world without a monster?"

"It's a world where children can make it down the hall without being terrified," said Dee.

"They're already having nightmares," said Papa. "Drawing the teeth might help."

Polly and Edmund managed the outline of a sailfish, a single bird over the ocean, and a horse in what was supposed to be the American West. Then they scrubbed the different kinds of black off their fingers and went to bed, all of them sliding easily away into the dark.

Borderlands: the banister, the fringe of grapes on the porch, the tide's limit on the Sound, the edge of the woods, bedroom doors. When Jane and Merle came back from visiting Rita, the children could hear most of their story through the grates: Rita was mad, mad, mad as a hatter. She wouldn't draw, for the first time in her life, and she sat on an iron-barred balcony and yelled at anything that passed below—squirrels, nurses, other loonies. When her mood shifted, she went to bed with her eyes screwed shut. The hospital could keep her for another two weeks, at most. She certainly couldn't go back to her in-laws' house.

"She's burned her bridges," said Merle.

"Really only the garage," snarked Jane. She sat at the dining room table and wrote many drafts of a note to Rita's estranged family. Estranged, thought Polly, while Jane struggled with her wording. They watched her address the envelope, seal it, stamp it.

No one mentioned what the letter meant for Edmund, and he went to his room. Papa had given him an old record player, and now he played his two albums, over and over, right through lunch: *Camelot* and *Sgt. Pepper*. Polly's open bedroom window was next to his, above the crab apple, and she became dizzy with *fixing a hole where the rain gets in, and stops my mind from wandering.* Or was it wondering? She got things wrong, often. She'd looked for isles at the movie theater before she saw the word aisles one day. You couldn't ask about everything. Now she made her way outside to the grape-covered porch and watched Papa teach Lemon to sit, stay, lie down. He finally walked into the house, and a few minutes later new music floated down from Edmund's bedroom window: Vivaldi.

When Papa brought Edmund downstairs for a sandwich, they all walked out to help Dee in the greenhouse. Papa moved Rita's paintings to one side and Polly and Edmund arranged Dee's bowls and water and supplies before they lost track and started poking around. They found a wood wine box that held pieces of broken stained-glass windows Papa brought back from Europe after the war, the first war. Most of the ancient lead solder was gone, and the crate was filled with ragged jewels, a red wedge that might have been a lip or puddle of blood; a gold sliver born as a dagger or an angel's halo or the tail of Saint George's dragon.

Dee lifted a piece and showed them an air bubble. Polly put her face close and saw small cities, dark woods, and wild animals.

"If you break it, you'll let the old air out," said Papa. "Maybe there's a plague germ in there. Maybe there's a last breath from someone shot by a longbow."

"You're so full of garbage," said Jane, who was sweeping.

"I am, I am replete. And I am splitting my shrinking seams with things they need to know." Maybe he was a little drunk; maybe the world was already sliding toward ruin.

"You're daring us," said Dee. She smacked the glass with a knife handle, and they all leaned in. It smelled of candles.

Breakfasts over the summer were almost always the same: a soft-boiled egg, pork belly cured in salt and sugar by Dee, rye or linseed bread and jam or some peaches in syrup, or applesauce, or berries. On weekends, Dee served what Merle called a real Swede spread—sliced meats and soft cheese and herring and sometimes smoked salmon, more jams, special honey—on her fancy china.

On weekends, no one left for an office or classroom, but Jane would work on her thesis or Papa's research. She was trying to identify markers that could help determine the evolution of a story, whether the bean or the vine or the lost cow came before a similar story of a starving boy selling his baby brother and coming home with a baby sister or perhaps a frog. She followed them around the house testing out versions of stories. What story sounded right? Which one scared them more?

The scariest was always the simplest and shortest, and Edmund and Polly usually agreed with each other. Had they gotten the answer right? Jane didn't always know. That was the point.

But today, Papa and Dee needed to drive to the city for a doctor appointment, and Merle, having argued with Jane about who most deserved to drop a class, was the one to stay home with Polly and Edmund. He was in a fine mood, unshaven and humming Beach Boys songs with a stuffed-nose midwestern twang. He brought out stale cornflakes and did not suggest they dress. He turned on the television, and they watched one movie about Hawaii and another with Tarzan dodging dinosaurs, headhunters, lava, and pretty girls. Merle claimed to be terrified of everything, equally, and Polly and Edmund agreed this was a scream.

The villains sank into quicksand.

"Put that on your map," said Merle.

Which was worse, lava or quicksand? Was lava always red, and was quicksand the slime green they guessed? The movie was black and white. A few weeks earlier, they'd seen *Ben-Hur*, and Edmund wondered about leprosy. What else fell off, besides noses and fingers? Merle said quicksand looked like vomit, and penises fell off, too, and lava darkened to black as it hardened. He made them sit still while he read aloud a long story about freezing to death in Alaska. Was it better to burn or freeze, Merle asked at the end.

Polly and Edmund picked freezing, but Merle said he'd rather burn. He made hot dogs and canned beans for lunch. He used his left elbow to hold things against his body, to make up for the weaker arm. He told Edmund and Polly to find something to do, so that he could get some work done: He tried to write every day at a desk in the corner of the living room. He was teaching biology, but he wanted to be a poet; back then, he still thought he would be both. They heard him pour liquid in a glass as they left the room. He kept a bottle in one of the desk drawers, like a detective.

It was raining hard enough to make the stiff green clusters of Concord grapes swing. After the movies, though Tarzan triumphed and not everyone on the island died, it was hard not to see treacherous sucking mud and grasping killer vines lurking everywhere, beaks and tentacles and poison darts, whirlpools and hairy tarantula legs. Polly and Edmund stood on the back porch watching a little river run down the sandy dirt path toward the Sound, listening to the sound of the typewriter behind them, and when the rain stopped, they walked down to the water, forgetting to close the door though they did bring the dog and didn't quite lose her. Lemon pranced in the waves and ate the mussels they smashed open, Merle having forgotten to feed her.

When Jane got home in the late afternoon, she saw Edmund and Polly and Lemon walking up the lane without shoes and without a leash. Merle was asleep on the couch. Jane was upset, and they waited under the grapes. At some point, without really hearing the words of the argument inside, a phone ringing and ignored, they crawled under the porch, wary of spiders but distracted by the coins that had fallen through the floorboards. Lemon was down there with them. All this cool freshly dug dirt was her doing, and they lay together and watched the street through a screen of grass. A couple passed on Christian Avenue, and kissed, and Polly and Edmund didn't comment but they didn't look away. Sometimes during these plangent moments they almost understood it all, almost felt awkward with each other.

Jane and Merle stopped screaming at each other, and when the phone rang again, Polly and Edmund heard Jane's normal voice. A few minutes later she hurried them into the turquoise Ford and took them out for fried scallops and corn and told them that Dee and Papa were spending the night in the city so that they could see a doctor a second time in the morning. Jane started crying, and Polly crawled onto her lap and pushed her face into the tears on her mother's neck, while Edmund stacked sugar envelopes on the restaurant table.

They went to parties on the Fourth of July, and then it was down to doldrums, dog days, malaise, parlous times. Dee said she spent too much time reading news magazines in doctors' offices, and that while the entire world was a tragedy, all of life was a pain in the ass. The mood of the house was fretful. It was hot and the kitchen sink was plugged. Merle, overworked and almost always hungover, spent hours apologizing after he sniped at Dee from under the sink.

One night, after a week of rain, they watched Papa's movies. Arnold, as an early birthday gift for Papa, tracked down better prints of three of the movies they'd made when they were both young men, and the large reels lay on the dining room table while they tried to get the projector working again and argued about which friends were dead or still alive. Merle managed to fix the projector and hang a sheet. By then all the men were a little drunk. They watched a few minutes of *The Tempest*, the oldest. Papa said it was a snore and no one would possibly believe that was a real donkey's head. He left the room for *Tales of Arabia*, because his first wife, Perdita, had died soon after filming, and even Polly and Edmund, amused by the silly magic and the bad makeup of the djinns, were uneasy at the idea of her face disappearing. Dee wouldn't stay in the room for *The Window*, about an evil man with a bad conscience, but Arnold and Merle giggled to the point of tears when the villain first appeared—a mustache, eye paint, flaring nostrils.

"What was his name?" asked Arnold. "The inspiration? I can't recall."

"Hush," said Dee, from the kitchen. "It doesn't matter anymore."

The Amber Queen began and everyone quieted down, because Perdita played the queen, too, and the story had given Jane her love of flood stories.

Papa had learned the fable as a boy: It was an explanation for the amber trees that formed when a Baltic forest drowned and washed up for millennia, the amber traded as far away as Rome and China. It was an Ice Age story, told when the sea level was lower and people might still have found long chunks that still looked like trees, when the shapes might have been visible in the moment before tsunamis, from a boat on a clear still day. It was a perfect example of man constructing stories to explain mysteries, like creating dragons from the *Protoceratops* skulls on the Gobi. The queen chose the king of the sun over the king of the ocean, and the ocean sent a flood in revenge. She managed to save her people but gave up her own life to see the sun again.

Polly, already scared of still, deep water, imagined riding on Papa's rowboat and looking down at a ghost forest. She liked the part where Perdita's knights, one played by Papa's youngest brother, knelt in front of her—Polly could talk Edmund into playing a knight. At the end, when the queen was about to sacrifice herself, Perdita's face became huge and her teary eyes looked out at them. Her lips moved. *Dream me*, said the titles.

"Jesus," said Merle, who hadn't seen the movie before.

Papa left the room. Dee had Edmund pull her out of the soft couch to follow him.

"Wasn't my sister something?" said Arnold. "You know, half those knights died in the war, but not your uncle Per. He's still playing cards in Montana. He'll be here for the party."

In the fall and winter and spring, Papa went out rowing on the Sound two or three times a week. Most mornings in the summer and early fall, he swam. Dee called him a real swimmer, a fish, and Merle's warnings of pollution annoyed him. Life had polluted him for a full eighty-nine years, and he wouldn't do without the pleasure of water. In a concession, he used a hose to rinse off in the yard, something that never failed to stun Polly and Edmund: Papa, unflinching, voluntarily covering himself with what felt like ice water. Once he screamed when the water hit to scare them, and they heard the witch's door slam. He swiveled and stared at her door and put his thumb over the hose, so that it jetted almost to her doorway, flushing the poor green parrot.

Once a week, Jane and Merle drove Edmund and Polly to the ocean beach across the island. They would pair off by age; Polly and Edmund checked back only for food and small traumas. They built sand kingdoms, not just castles, and Polly had a store of scenarios she wanted them to act out: princesses in towers, dragons, *Sleeping Beauty*. In return, she played war. Which she didn't mind—Merle found toy wooden bows with rubber-tipped arrows, and a sword for Polly that wasn't as nice as Edmund's but was easier to swing. Sometimes they simply lay half in the water, feeling the tug of the ocean, pretending to be dead soldiers in Normandy. They'd watch the sand form around their bodies and wash away underneath, until the sucking feeling unnerved them. They'd tug each other around in the water, curl up in fake foxholes, pretend to be medics and stitch each other up. They never mentioned Vietnam.

And then, abruptly, they'd become sick of each other. One day in mid-July, Polly wanted Edmund to stand at the base of the dogwood tree, hold his cavalier's hat against his chest, and say, "Rapunzel, Rapunzel, let down your hair."

"No," said Edmund. "I don't want to."

"Why not?"

"I just don't."

You can't get away with this, even when you're eight. Merle, passing by, said, "Rapunzel, Rapunzel, push down your hair."

Edmund giggled. "You *can't* let it down. It's too frizzy."

"Say it," said Polly.

"No."

A nasty little boy wanting things his way, his way, his way. Or was she the nasty little girl? Edmund, who had hay fever, wanted only to be left alone. He was sticky and tired, sick of doing what Polly wanted to do. Now she was eating the last of the SweeTarts.

"I'll play swords," he said. "Or kickball. Or I'll be the one to ask for television."

"Say it."

"No." He wiped his nose with the back of his hand. His eyes itched so badly he wanted to scratch them out.

"Say it and I won't eat the last two."

"You don't even have long hair."

"You don't even have a brain cell."

Edmund roared and jumped for the tree, swinging up onto the first branch as Polly scuttled higher. He grabbed her foot and she kicked at his face, lost her balance, and started to fall, clutching at branches, following the SweeTarts down to the grass.

Later, while she felt her bruises, Polly would think of Dee falling, not dropping the ivory moon, not peeing her pants. She hit hard and stared up. Edmund was still dangling from the branch. She would have cried, but he wasn't looking at her. His eyes were on the battlefield, the candy in the grass next to her. Polly lurched toward the pieces and stuffed them in her mouth as Edmund gave another shriek of rage and jumped down and tried to pull the candy out. She bit down but he found one, scratching her tongue as he pried it out, and shoved it into his own mouth.

Polly spat at him, blood and bits of sugar. Edmund smiled and chewed, lay down on the grass, and looked up at the sky through the branches.

"You're not a princess. No one would rescue you. No one would even lock you up."

They didn't talk for three hours. That evening, they lay in their bedrooms, with matching open windows looking out at the crab apple tree, while May moved back and forth between rooms. Polly, tired with her rage and bored, could hear Edmund murmur to the cat, and then she heard a different voice, like an old woman's: *O little boy O little girl.*

It was the green parrot, calling from the crab apple. They both got out of bed and stuck their heads out the windows.

O stupid cat.

Lemon, trapped at ground level on her chain, whimpered. She'd been skunked the night before and she wasn't allowed into the house until Jane washed her. May watched from Edmund's windowsill, tail flicking, and flung herself at the bird in the tree. She missed, reached for a branch with her outstretched front paws, and missed that, too. She fell on her feet and looked up at them, tail slashing, and walked away sedately.

The parrot jumped to a closer branch. *O little boy O little girl.*

"Does he want us to jump, too?" asked Edmund.

Clearly, said Papa when he heard the story later, the witch sent her familiar to put a spell on them.

"Stop it," said Dee.

When Polly woke the next morning and opened her eyes and stretched, May shifted on her stomach, purred, and fell back to sleep. The window was still open a few inches, and Polly heard rain. She dozed, and when she woke again the blanket felt wet against her legs and the cat was cleaning itself next to a blue feather.

"You're evil, May," Polly whispered.

Being a cat, May ignored her. Polly lifted her knees to boost her off and stared at a huge red bloodstain, a half dozen more feathers, tropical purple and orange and indigo. At the same time, through the open window, Polly heard Edmund begin to howl. May had given him the head.

Merle roared through the morning. "That fucking cat. That old hag is going to knock at the door, looking for some bird named Alfie or Sailor. Or she'll poison the dog."

At first, no one listened to Polly and Edmund explain that the neighbor's bird was green, with a little gold on his head. The dead bird with more than a parrot's worth of blood had been a rainbow. When the green bird reappeared on the grapevine later, alive and warning of storms, they finally heard the old lady calling a name: Dwight.

Dee collected the feathers and hung some from each of their windows, to warn the bird away from May, who spent most of her time now on their windowsills.

Rita returned the next night, as if she'd been summoned. Polly was sitting in the bathtub; Dee's hands, washing her hair, were the strongest things she'd ever felt. Edmund, first up, was now wrapped in a towel, sitting on the floor of the hall just outside of the bathroom door so that he could hear the rest of the story Dee told, about six brothers who were turned into swans (Dee did not want May to kill another parrot). Vivaldi was playing again, because Edmund liked it now, and Dee said it made a perfect soundtrack—storms, rack, and ruin.

In any event, there was no warning. A door slammed and Rita's voice floated upstairs. Dee, stricken, finished rinsing Polly's hair so quickly that she left bubbles in her ears. Polly and Edmund hurried into their clothes. They could hear Rita's agent, a big blond pile of a man, explaining that he couldn't bear Rita's imprisonment, he couldn't bear to see beauty smothered. He'd freed her, but she wouldn't do well in the city. And so here she was, clean in a miniskirt, pretty bangles on her wrists that mostly covered the scars.

"I'm so tired," said Rita. "But I'm fine."

Everyone said things about that being good. Merle started to offer wine and stopped, and the agent finally left. Rita didn't move toward Edmund, and he stayed next to Jane.

When they all walked upstairs, Rita turned her whole body to see the new canvases, the children's unfinished squiggles. The last bit of paint visible from her rampage was a droopy tree to the left of the window at the head of the stairs. Papa insisted on not scrubbing it off the wall.

"These are for you," said Papa, pointing to the canvases. They all knew he was angry. "If you'd like to stay, you must keep your mind busy. You can cover what the children started."

"At least I managed one tree," said Rita.

"The tree is shit," he said. "Take a moment or two to plan."

The tree was shit—the effort of having to watch Rita's face while Papa insulted her, very calmly, sprang their brains.

Lemon the pointer was largely uncontrollable, or at least uncontrolled. No one ever trained her to a leash, and the first time Polly tried to walk her, she was dragged down the sidewalk, shredding her leotard and the skin on her elbows and knees. Merle sometimes said she was Edmund's dog, though Edmund resented the way Lemon had gone so willingly to the Schusters the summer before. He'd wanted to be given away, too, so how could he fault Lemon for taking advantage of the offer?

Lemon was Jane and Merle's problem, and they didn't do enough. They took her to the beach on a lunge line, and once Papa rowed out to a long sandbar and let her range. Dee let Lemon free in the greenhouse, where she would race the cat in loops around the old potting benches, somehow not breaking anything. Lemon shouldn't have been in a town or chained in a yard.

Merle promised he'd get to a fence, but not during a head cold or in the middle of a heat wave or when there'd be a Tigers game on television. Lemon got loose several times—Rita was incapable of shutting a door or a mayonnaise lid—and one morning Lemon was picked up down by the docks, having nearly been killed by several cars. Two nights later, when Rita went out for her nightly session in the greenhouse, Lemon bolted into the darkness. Polly went to bed crying and could hear Edmund crying, too, and Jane and Merle arguing. Jane slept on the couch.

They got up early the next morning, but Jane and Merle and Papa had no luck finding Lemon before they left for classes. Dee made Edmund and Polly waffles and said she had a plan. They were going to make little Lemons. She dropped lumps of clay in front of them and formed a third into the shape of a dog. "Like this," she said, pinching until she came up with something that looked like a pointer. "Yours can look like a hippo, Edmund.

It doesn't matter. The point is to believe it's a dog, and to go out and call for her."

Rita came through the kitchen and made a piece of toast without saying a word. She was painting again in the greenhouse, stacks of small oils tilted against every bench, ignoring the new canvases upstairs. Dee did not give ground and kept working there, too, but she said that Rita was at least quiet and the paintings were good. This stage would last about ten days.

"Now go down to the Sound, and wish for her to run home, and throw them in," said Dee. "Mine, too. And start calling for her on your way back."

Dee didn't say, This is a spell, this is magic, but what were they to think, and why would they doubt? They set off, feeling jumpy, and Edmund broke into a run.

"I see the witch," he said. "She's standing in the upstairs window, watching us."

Polly wouldn't look.

"I think she's my mother as a ghost," said Edmund.

Polly gave a shuddering skip and they ran through the skunk cabbage ravine. When they reached the sand, the tide was almost out. They hopped past marooned jellyfish, trying to land on bare sand rather than a mussel or a tiny crab. All this time they held the clay Lemons, and when they reached the water they were left with their errand.

"Does she know how to do things like this?"

"I don't know," said Polly.

They made wishes, threw in the clay dogs, and watched them sink and bump in the shallow, calm waves. No Lemon galloped out of the Sound. They made their way back through the ravine and were just short of the witch's house when a door or a window or some piece of wood on the property slammed. They stopped and waited. Polly felt as if her heart were lifting through her ribs, splitting into slices. A keening sound, a rustle. Edmund put his hand on Polly's back and pushed her forward, up the hill, and they were almost past the house when they heard the wail again and turned to see Lemon on the witch's porch. She was sitting there, not running, not looking at them.

Edmund called and Lemon didn't move until he walked onto the porch and took her by the collar. For a minute Polly worried they had the wrong dog. They trotted toward their yard, through the gate by Dee's greenhouse, and there was Dee, gaping at them.

"Where?" she asked.

"She was on the witch's porch," said Polly. "She acts like she doesn't know us."

But Lemon was waking up. She'd flopped over on the hard, dry mud of the ruined lawn, showing her stomach. Dee walked toward her slowly.

"Who is Mrs. Maw?" asked Edmund, finally.

"We've never asked," said Dee. "If people don't want to be seen, we don't force them." She bent down shakily and ran her hand down the dog's stomach. Dee left the hand there and they all looked: Lemon's long tail was now a stub, stitches dark against her blond and white fur.

When Papa came home and saw the dog's stump and looked at his wife and granddaughter drinking wine early in the day, he walked down the hill, and they all waited on the porch, listening, until he returned.

They spoke through a crack in the door. Mrs. Maw told Papa she'd found Lemon on the beach, tied to a log below the tidemark, as if someone was trying to drown her. Mrs. Maw hadn't recognized the dog, or at least known she belonged to Papa's house. She'd given Lemon a drug for pain, to make her sleep, and finished taking the tail off, and sewed it up.

"The woman's name is Mag," Papa said. A small smile: "Mag Maw, a witch name." Did he believe her? He wasn't sure.

It's true, it's true, said the parrot.

The next day, Merle started a fence around the property, despite a cherry-colored nose from his head cold. He would do it right; he'd grown up in Michigan, knowing how to do things. Knobbed posts, a pretty old-fashioned wire. He praised the chained dog as he worked unless she put her paws up on a post or the wire, and then he beat her.

Mostly, Lemon watched the witch's place, and Jane hid upstairs, typing her thesis.

One Wednesday, a new dog, a male Weimaraner, appeared in their unfinished yard and played with Lemon for hours. Merle worried that Lemon was in heat, and Jane said she would make an appointment with a veterinarian. Later, after some drinks, Merle argued that it might be wonderful to have a litter of game dog puppies. They could sell them. Papa asked him if he was out of his fucking mind and stomped off to his rowboat.

In heat; ah, the mysteries of the language. They were given a brief, non-dramatic explanation from Dee, of all people.

"Every mammal has a penis or a vagina, and mating is the way a species survives. So they're compelled, you see. They can't resist. When Lemon is ready to breed, she'll put out a special smell, and if a male dog notices it, he's going to do everything possible to have her. And we don't need puppies this summer. She's only a baby and she should have a childhood."

The visiting dog's tag read *Ham Armstrong*. The family must have lost him on vacation, said Jane, dialing the phone. She left a message with a maid. But when the Armstrongs called back, the conversation was confused. They lived in Connecticut, on the far shore of the Sound. It was twenty miles as the crow flew but eighty or so by land, through the city. Edmund measured out the miles, and while they looked at the map, Polly thought for the first time of the shape and enormity of the city.

Clearly, Ham had hitched a ride. The Armstrongs—eyeing the run-down house, intimidated by Papa—fetched Ham, and Lemon went back to watching Dwight and May and squirrels. Two sections of the fence were unfinished, but Merle planned to deal with them that weekend. He was short on wood and facing the semester's midterm week.

On Saturday morning, Merle tied Lemon up when he headed out for lumber. Polly and Edmund went down to the beach a little later, and on their way they passed Ham, dripping wet, all joy. When they returned, the dogs were next to each other, really on top of each other. Merle, parking the Ford, was close to tears.

"They're fucking locked up."

Locked up—the words of love didn't always fit. A hazy horror filtered in. "You can't get them apart?" asked Polly.

"It takes a while," said Jane, doing laundry. "I'll need to take her to the vet now."

Ham was retrieved that evening. There was no other explanation: He'd swum across the Sound. His owner wouldn't pay the bill for Lemon's spaying, but they would build a stockade.

"The dog swam for love," said Dee at dinner.

"I did that," said Papa. "The first time we were alone near water."

Dee put down her fork. She started to laugh—tears. "Oh, the vision," she said.

"We don't need to tell them everything, dear," he said. "The phrase will do."

The next afternoon, while Polly played solitaire on the dining room table and Dee and Jane cut Edmund's hair in the greenhouse and Merle, still short of wood to finish the fence, wrestled with the television, trying to get a boxing match to tune in, Papa lifted a book on Merle's desk and found a framed photo of Rita. "Why is this here?"

Merle said, "I didn't think it would help Eddie to see it."

Rita was the only other person who said Eddie, and Edmund hated her for this, too.

"And yet you needed to?" Papa watched Merle. "A boy should see his mother, even if the distance must be safe. And a man shouldn't keep his best friend's wife on his desk."

"I have my best friend on the desk, too," said Merle, pointing. Merle was in the photo next to Tommy, both of them wearing tuxedos at one of their weddings.

Papa ignored him and propped Rita's photo up on the mantel, next to the silver-framed photo of Asta. What was similar beyond the image of two women, one a redhead, one much darker? As an adult, Polly would have said a cloud of hair, soft eyes, full lips, and a big dose of doom, the frozen straying expression in the dead girl's photograph and Rita's eyes. Mad, mad, mad as a hatter, mad as some of the people who'd smelled the air inside the splinters of stained glass before it was contained.

Merle left the house, slamming the door, slamming the car door. Hours later Polly heard the car return, but instead of coming in, Merle lay down on the grass just inside the half-finished fence. When she went to bed she looked from Dee's window, and in the light from the porch she saw him still under the honeysuckle bush, petals falling on his face. But in the morning, when Polly went out with coffee, Merle said he was fine, just fucking fine, like he'd claimed the summer before with Tommy. Polly and Edmund giggled off and on for hours, and eventually both moments became funny in Polly's memory.

Rita moved between the greenhouse and her room. She didn't have dinner with them, a standing joke with the rest of the house, given the quality of Dee's cooking. Rita barely talked to Edmund, but it wasn't so much that she rejected her child as that she rejected everyone. She would sit on the couch at the end of the night, eating leftovers while they tried to talk, weighing all of them down.

Another trip with Dee, to Arnold's cottage in Port Jefferson, to climb his apricot tree with baskets, because Dee's greengages wouldn't be ready until September. They took the highway back to the Italian market and on to a Syrian market in Brooklyn. It was Jane's birthday, and Jane wanted a meal from North Africa, where they'd spent a winter when she was young.

"When you fell," said Edmund, who paid attention to all stories involving travel.

"Yes," said Dee. "It was a nice place to get over a broken leg." She bought shrimp and clams and tiny fish, a hard salami that Edmund swung like a baton, strange objects: pomegranates, long mulberry strands, dough as thin as silk. Back at the quiet house, Dee cut open the small fish and showed them the roe. When she found a magnifying glass Polly saw tiny fish inside the eggs, a skeleton seed inside the wet kernels of the split pomegranate, a tiny hair on each jewel of a mulberry. Years later, when she tried to sort her current life from the blooming past, Polly guessed Dee had found fresh anchovies, and was sure that one of the pomegranates was pale, like the ones Polly would see twenty years later in Seville on her honeymoon. Dee used a razor to slice a seed in half, but when she wanted to do the same things with the roe, Edmund screamed at her to stop.

They were breaking the pomegranates apart in a bowl of water when Rita came down and announced that she needed food. Dee told her to look in the refrigerator and the pantry, and eventually Rita retreated upstairs, where they could hear her voice from Papa's study. When he came downstairs, he said Rita wanted bread and cheese. Dee, goosing the children through what felt like hours of pitting apricots, ignored him, and he marched off, annoyed.

They all knew Rita's habit of picking a favorite for the day, the person forced to help her, but she'd never before picked Papa. As Dee basted the thin strips of dough with butter, she told them stories about times Papa had been truly angry, though not whole stories, not even full reasons. But he came down in the middle of it.

"Why would you not be generous to her?" he said. "No one is ever always at their best."

"Because she'll be happier when she starts doing things for herself," said Dee.

"If I said please?"

Dee finally put a bowl of leftover shepherd's pie in the oven to heat, and Papa climbed the stairs again, slower each time up. An hour later, Merle found the bowl untouched in the hall outside of Rita's door and put it on the kitchen counter. Dee hurled Rita's full, uneaten portion at Lemon, who was for once too scared to eat. May swept in while the crows gabbled insults, a conversation Polly almost understood.

That night, Rita emerged for the birthday party, because Jane, her oldest friend, knocked on the bedroom door and asked. She stared at her plate, pretty red hair dangling into her water glass, and finally ate the vinegary fried fish, the salad of mulberries and pomegranates and cucumber, the rice and shrimp and sausage. She handed Jane a drawing just as the caramelized apricots wrapped in pastry were being served with birthday candles. It was a pastel sketch of Asta, with swirls around her head, stars like a crown.

Jane and Papa left the room.

"Some people know how to clear a party," said Dee. "Merle, please make me a martini. And Rita?"

"Yes?"

"The drawing is beautiful, but what are you going to do with your life?"

A flash of venom in the pretty gray eyes. Rita pulled back her red hair, poured a glass of wine, smiled at the people who hadn't left. "I'm going to be a very, very good painter. You'll see. And then I'm going to walk into the water and be a ghost."

11

Thursday, July 4, 2002

Sam and Helen: What things did they see that were as strange as whatever Polly and Edmund had seen? Instead of Long Island Sound or the city, they had rattlesnakes, boiling water pouring up from the ground, rivers that could mangle, cold that could kill. Sharp edges, falling rocks; lions, wolves, bears. Daily, the dozen brown recluse spiders they trapped on sticky paper in the basement and the pit bull at the end of the block. Avalanches, earthquakes. In the mining town of Butte, an adit—a horizontal shaft—opened in a crumbling street, and Polly (tipsy on Ned's birthday) told Sam that five thousand men had died down there, and a thousand bodies were underground still. She knew, better than most people, that children didn't forget that kind of thing.

Polly, in bed but not sleeping, let herself see Sam and Helen's world, Polly style. No tides, no jellyfish, but the bank of a river where garter snakes sunned and stoneflies molted. The puff of fur at the edge of the willows that meant some small mammal's death, the varied pellets from grass eaters:

rabbit and moose, deer and geese. In the house, the way the cat played with mice while the dogs watched politely; the insect corners Polly never managed to clean. Silver spoons with devil's heads, a whale tooth, masks. The photographs that meant something half-remembered, the strange and holy significance of objects on the windowsill, which were people to Jane and Polly, ghost stories to Sam and Helen. The way Jane would read a book out loud and wipe her hand down their faces to make them sleep and the way Polly would type fast, roll dough, flick a bandage onto a bloodying hole in the skin so quickly it never quite existed. The way Ned was simply there, swiftly and always, gathering them up and smothering every problem, and the way Merle could name every part of any creature, whether or not it was the truth, and draw it with his good hand while the withered one twirled pencils. The way they felt sympathy and love like a blanket.

More than anything else, they would have the memory of their mother and grandmother trying to block their view of their dead babysitter near the river.

Harry, who'd spent his professional life digging up versions of the past, had seen more bad things as a cop than anyone Polly knew. While the others packed people into the cars, he said Polly needed to stay, to give a clear account to Cy and Shari Swenson, the county coroner. They sat upstream and upwind of the body, and Harry told Polly about a way to make an image or memory retreat: Change what you've seen to black and white, move it further and further away. They were both being matter-of-fact, but Polly's whole body was shaking. She had been looking for Ariel, and when she found her, she looked away. After all this effort, Polly was now intent on forgetting. Maybe this was the end of seeing too much, going into the painting.

"Or," said Harry, "you can look harder and face it. That's what works for me now."

It. He didn't mean the word that way. Polly watched him crouch near Ariel, then move around to the other side of the girl's body and crouch again with his face close to one of Ariel's hands. He did not touch her or move her. Polly would have to tell Drake that in that way, the scene was like a movie. In every other, not: the loveliness around them, the quiet, the way that Harry hummed. When Cy and Shari Swenson arrived, the second night of fireworks had just begun, and Polly huddled by the river facing the explosions rather than Ariel's body.

Polly truly looked at Ariel only in that first minute, and never her face. The girl was on her side, arms mangled and dropping away unnaturally. Her belly was swollen, feet gray, T-shirt up under her armpits but the bottom half of her black bikini in place. Now, as they waited, Polly's eyes slid over Ariel's thick red-gold hair, stretched over sticks and pebbles, matted with leaves and riverweed but still bright. In Polly's childhood book of Arthurian legends, dead lovelorn Elaine's hair looked like that, spread out on a wooden boat, a floating bier. Which was ludicrous—Ariel had not died, willfully, of grief.

"Is it harder or easier if it isn't a murder?" she asked.

But Harry shook his sad, bony, handsome head. "I'm not sure it matters," he said. "Especially if someone's young."

In the bed, in the dark, Polly asked Ned why this would happen again. At least it wasn't strangers finding Ariel, he said. Out of all the bad, this was good.

She tried to erase what she'd seen, and then she gave up and tried to remember. But in the morning, she would forget to ask Harry why he was looking at Ariel's hands.

The dream of the night, with some competition, had Polly towing a rowboat down a flooded cathedral choir, past walls of indigo and green stained glass that showed faces and houses and animals and everything in the world. She tried to pick her favorite pane as the boat, paneled with more glass, bumped and gouged her leg and fish followed the blood.

The other dreams were shorter. Polly lost her keys, lost Jane's dog, lost herself on a forested path in a glowing city. Each time she jerked awake and remembered Ariel was dead.

"Honey," said Merle. It was 8:00 in the morning, and he'd watched Polly stand by a window for five minutes. "What did you see?" he asked.

The vanished, she thought. Putting the feeling into a word made it stagy, took away its lightness and the sense of an endless pattern.

Ned was already at Peake's, dealing with a failed compressor, a dishwasher and waitress calling in sick. The overwhelming nature of the everyday, grinding over death, despair, and holidays like a glacier. Merle gave Polly coffee and she knew he kept an eye on her while he flipped sausages, cracked eggs, served up a massive breakfast for people who had no obvious appetite. Jane was still in bed, the kids huddled and quiet by the television.

"Do you think we should check on Maude?" Polly asked. Maude, drunk and not sweet after Ariel was found, a bullhorn voice and fragile bones staggering around their kitchen until Ned and Merle helped her up the stairs.

"I heard her make it to the bathroom and back an hour ago," said Merle. "Don't worry about her and go easy on your mother today."

"Well, sure," said Polly. But Jane was no delicate flower. "Didn't she sleep?"

"It's hard. She can't help imagining her."

Polly's glitchy brain shot through images: Ariel's hair, the woman near the break wall in Michigan, the man on the sand in Stony Brook, Rita and her own private ocean.

"Her mother," said Merle. He almost snapped. "Asta." He was looking through the bread bag for slices without mold, a reminder that Polly couldn't manage the simplest things.

"Who died in a car accident. With someone. No one ever mentioned that part."

His voice softened. "Who was trapped in a car after an accident and drowned."

Polly's skin shimmied. "How did you expect me to know that, if you hadn't told me? If I've never been supposed to talk about it, because it upsets her?"

"Don't be angry," said Merle. "Janie's never said it upset her. She was fine last night, before the girl."

The girl. "Aaargh," said Polly, bursting into tears. "Jesus, Dad."

She went out to the garden and dug up a rosebush she didn't like, a sacrifice: The rose was hot pink with no scent. It attracted aphids and frosted to the ground each year. Polly's ratty brain sought and garbled *King Lear*— *Why should thou have life, and her, none*—and when she threw the bush in the trash she felt infantile only because she'd have preferred to spray it with gasoline and light it on fire.

Ariel crowded back around her head and Polly pushed her away. She ran back in the house to make a list:

Ariel's shorts? the man in the car? Ask cousins about Asta?

Merle by then was measuring for bookshelves and talking to the kids, who had seen a monarch butterfly the day before, about metamorphosis and the difference between a chrysalis and a cocoon, and how completely different any of it was than, say, molting a carapace. He said that butterflies remembered the aversions they'd learned as caterpillars, despite an intervening existence as undifferentiated goo. Polly was considering what this meant when Maude's cane rapped on the floor. It was possible that she'd been rapping for a while, but Polly ignored this call for help and ran back through the yard to the alley house. Jane was still in bed.

"Mom," said Polly. "Mother."

"I should never go near the water," said Jane. "I can't stop thinking of my poor mother drowning. Did you know she was almost as young as Ariel? I can't bear it."

Jane covered her face and wept, and Polly sat with her. What could she say? Live through this? Remind her of how much worse it was for the Delgados? Some things aren't survivable.

But Jane knew all this. Polly wanted to ask about the death Jane owned, about Asta: Was the other person in the car driving? Did they live? Did they leave her to die?

Instead Polly said, "I love you, and I'm sorry."

Jane pulled a pillow over her face.

Everything meant too much, again. Back in the main house, Polly heard water running in the tub upstairs, and the coffee machine was empty; Maude was ambulatory. Merle walked through the kitchen, dangling a measuring tape. "She's been on the phone. She invited the Duerrs and the Kings tomorrow night. Since Ariel has been found, she said."

"She's not easy, is she," said Polly.

"No."

Merle puttered off, willfully oblivious, his own carapace hardened. Polly felt as if she'd been glazed with some mild form of novocaine. If this were a normal day, if she were still thinking clearly, what would she be doing? It was the Fourth of July, and there were no swimming lessons, even if Connie could have handled giving them. People were supposed to be happy, and Sam and Helen might still want to try to be happy. Polly had to think up something normal.

Upstairs, Maude was singing. Polly finished the card she'd started twice, pulled the extra tray of lasagna, the one in the nicest pan, out of the refrigerator, picked a large bouquet of roses and delphinium, clematis and astrantia, stuffed it in a fancy tequila bottle, and set out for the Delgados' house.

When Harry talked to Ariel's mother, Inez wanted to see her daughter's body and wanted to know if Harry or Polly were able to recognize the girl. She wanted reassurance, but Polly wondered in what way. To know that Ariel hadn't been untouched, or maimed? After five days in the water, she'd been just barely human. Ultimately, Cy would take a careful photo in the hospital morgue to give to the family.

Harry told Polly to visit with the family when she dropped off food.

Josie said call first, leave the dish at the door, and run for it. Polly didn't know these people well enough to see them in their probable state.

Polly drove carefully, missing only one stop sign, to the Delgados' big new house in a subdivision in the hills. She parked in a driveway full of cars, but the house showed no sign of life. She knocked tentatively, looked around, and slid the dish and a card onto the stacked firewood. She was halfway down the sidewalk when the door was ripped open. Inez looked out at her, and down at the pan.

"Thank you," she said. "Funny how no one wants to linger."

Polly walked back up to the house. Inez Delgado, usually haughty and beautiful, was now gray skinned, bundled in sweaters, sinking into a big chair but calm. Polly had brought some photographs—Ariel in the garden, with the kids and dogs, with a glass of wine (Polly wasn't going to fret about the Delgados' religiosity). They talked about the memorial the next day, what food people should bring and which of them might speak. There would be a private funeral, once the state lab returned the body.

Connie sat in the corner of the room, picking at fading bouquets. Two of Ariel's sisters came and went. Everyone but Polly had sent lilies, and while she and Inez talked about Ariel—her sweetness, her silliness, her intelligence—Polly watched an ant climb out of her bouquet and hesitate at the bottom of the tequila bottle. Connie reached over and crushed it.

When Inez asked about Ariel's body, Polly, in a half-truth, said she'd looked away. By the time she left, she understood that Ariel hadn't gone out with "that boy." The notion that anyone thought Ariel had done so bothered the Delgados. Perhaps the boy would clear up the conflict? Their daughter wouldn't even touch wonderful Drake, who liked her so much. They'd tried telling Cy, but could Polly tell Harry?

Polly said she would. It was amazing, how people still wanted Harry to be a cop.

Connie followed Polly out in silence. When they reached Polly's car, she only asked one question. "Was she still wearing clothes?"

"Yes," said Polly. "Bathing suit, T-shirt."

Connie started to cry. "What about her shorts?"

"Maybe they came off in the water," said Polly.

"She wouldn't have taken them off, any more than the preserver," said Connie.

Polly slumped home, feeling like a softening balloon. Cousin Hans, who looked more and more like an albino crow, had taken Maude to lunch, a true community service, and Merle and Jane planned to hike.

"This wasn't easy on your mother," said Merle, redundantly.

Boy howdy, thought Polly. She went outside, because it was eighty degrees and clear, soft and lovely, and her family was alive. Who were they to know their allotted time or even, sadly (in Polly's case), what time, day, month it was at any given moment? If she lay on her back in the yard—which she did now, Sam and Helen and the other animals finding nothing odd about it—she saw mountains, swiveling tips of trees, clouds scudding by at a hundred miles an hour. Birds, a roofline with a loose shingle. If she turned her head to the right, she could see the old dog Pearl looking in the garden for the old dead cat. Cats weren't meant to predecease their dogs, just like women weren't meant to leave widowers, and children weren't supposed to die at all. If she turned to the left, she could see the new cat watching a chipmunk with the other dogs, all of them still immune to time.

Sam lay in the grass next to Polly, seeing how long he could bear the feeling of an ant on his skin. Helen wandered off with a bowl and a bucket and a hose to her corner of the garden. She liked to form the clayey soil into mud animals—mostly variations on dogs or rabbits—then say a spell to make them come alive. It involved throwing the finished sculptures into a bucket of water with great force, while saying voilà and some gibberish. Polly had given her the idea, because she remembered Dee doing something like this once.

Find something, save everyone. Helen lifted her arms, dropped them, started an argument among her creatures. She had so many theories and worlds and Polly worried about the way they'd quietly dissolve over the years, fall away after reckonings with real life. Forgetting her own over the years felt like giving up, even as it happened, and she didn't want Helen to lose the magic. Polly could just barely remember grasping the pattern to time, days and weeks and seasons. She could not recall her baroque rationale of how locks, toilets, cars operated, let alone sex and birth. She remembered death and her ideas about Frank and Evie, and the weird magic of the map, but nothing religious, no glimmer of that kind of a higher god, a soul beyond trees and sky. They hadn't been that kind of family.

Polly's overriding theory, since leaving Long Island, was that shit happened, and you molded the mess into the next best option. Even if nothing needed to be romanticized, everything was still a wonder. But what did you say to Ariel during the dark, harsh night, your mind on a pillow of needles, brain writhing like a panicked earthworm?

Helen's big, clear voice: "Mom, what's this?"

A flicker shot overhead, followed by two peevish magpies protecting a massive twig nest in the oldest apple tree. Polly waved to Helen, delaying, and by the time she got up, Helen was back to her mud trance.

"What did you want to show me?" asked Polly.

"What do you mean?" asked Helen.

Polly, feeling neglectful, watered her beans and lettuce, her fennel and cabbages and twenty tomato plants. She weeded, and she did not scream when Maude, who wasn't usually capable of a silent approach, spoke.

"A terrible thing," she said.

"Yes," Polly said, straightening. As if Maude hadn't been tottering drunk and raving about death the night before.

"Your father said you had a moment this morning."

"I'm tired," said Polly. "I drank too much."

Maude excelled in sidelong looks. She was, after all, a psychiatrist, though never the talking kind. She'd worked in hospitals back in the days of Thorazine and shock therapies and lobotomies, specializing in veterans with head injuries, and she'd authored one of the first papers suggesting that explosions damaged the brains of people with no obvious injuries.

But there had been no prize in the past for people skills. Maude had essentially been a single parent, and her children seemed sane, but her training had come in the neurological Stone Age between world wars. According to Jane, Maude thought Polly's damage was nonprogressive but akin to wet brain, a kind of benign fabulism with false memories. The only way to talk Polly out of them was for her to keep a notebook and check herself. Hence the ongoing battle: Polly felt as if Jane was testing out Polly's stories the way she'd tested fables when she was a student, trying to determine which version was scariest. A game of telephone, this time with Polly's head.

Polly tried an evasive maneuver. "Will you help Sam with the family tree? He needs a simple one for school, and it seems like the party would be the time to ask questions."

"A simple one," said Maude with a little smile. "How funny. Now tell me, do you still get those migraines?"

"They don't hurt," said Polly. "Now they only cause daydreams." A lovely, innocuous word.

"But they must be so hard on Ned."

One of Papa's better-known essays had been titled "The Emergent Past." Polly thought she should reread it. "No," said Polly. "I think he's fine." And a counterattack: "So who was the man in the car with Asta?"

Maude looked away. "Everything needs to come from your mother."

"Was he driving? Was he drinking?"

Maude arched a thin gray eyebrow, skin creasing above it, the big eye below suddenly smoother and younger and sarcastic. "Back to you, dear. Does Ned find your injury frustrating?"

Polly started laughing. "No, I'm the one who's angry. Everyone watching me, everyone asking questions and not believing my answers. No one believes me."

"Do you find that in grief your memory is even worse?"

"No," said Polly. "Maybe it concentrates the mind. It all feels much closer. I have so many questions."

Helen was watching them, and Fritz the mutt and the old poodle were watching, too. The new edge to Polly's voice was like a special radio frequency. Maude looked as if she wanted to retrench but Polly didn't give her a chance.

"Think of your own childhood," she said. "What would your parents have not believed that you'd remember?"

"Tricky girl," said Maude. "Probably them having sex in the pantry, when they didn't think we knew. My father's face, his voice, or being carried by my mother. And you?"

Polly started to speak but stopped herself.

Maude waited, leaning toward her. "What were you going to say?"

Polly thought of a lawyer's problem: If you're not sure you want to know the answer, don't ask. And what was Maude searching for, here? "Dee told me something, and I wondered if you agreed. She said there were three kinds of dreams."

"Ah!" said Maude. "She meant *lasting* dreams, the kind that return. I suppose it's as true as any theory. Do you have the same now that you did as a child? What are they?"

"Boats," said Polly. "Men in boats. And women in the water."

They were quiet for several minutes. Helen went back to her mud creatures. She was covering their heads with flower petals, tiny bits of bachelor button and calendula. Maude was watching closely, fascinated, and said her mother had done this with her when she was a child. Polly didn't admit that she knew this already. They watched Helen line up her figures, sing some gibberish, and blast them with a hose.

"Will you have a nap before dinner and visiting Harry?" asked Polly.

"I will," said Maude. "Hans and I each had a gimlet or two."

Polly went back to her garden, picking up dog toys and shovels and everything that took away from the new blast of color, this moment of perfection. Despair was a default setting in this climate, but this time of year was the best Polly could hope for. Nine-tenths of the year it was too hot, too dry, too high, too cold. Spring brought floods, high summer brought fire and smoke. Dee's ratty green taped-together garden notebook said the same thing: *flea beetles, HAIL, wind flattened corn*. Polly wrapped it in scrap silk they'd found in the attic, and she took it out once a year or so, usually in the dead of winter.

Polly wanted to hear certain voices. She wished, ferociously, that Dee could see this new world in her old yard, even Helen covered with mud from the neck down. Polly was tempted to use a hose but splashed her clean with a bowl of warm water. "Did you remember what you wanted to show me?"

Helen handed her two pieces of greenhouse glass and a rock, a gouged marble. "See how pretty it is?"

Polly rolled it around in her muddy fingers. She hadn't seen one of these since she was eight, and Dee allowed her to paw through her jewelry box. They carried the stone inside, and Polly scratched the side of a canning jar, then the side of the stainless sink. She explained the hardness scale—Merle would have been proud—and put it in a bowl in the window, trying to imagine Dee dropping rough diamonds around the property like so many bread crumbs.

Polly's drifty afternoon ended when Ned, marooned at the restaurant, called needing grocery items. Polly threw the kids in the car and shopped for Peake's, for the memorial, for what she remembered of Maude's party. The phrase "threw the kids in the car"—what percentage of most post–World War II childhoods was taken up by inexplicable errands? Polly was treating Helen like a sack, Sam like a dog. The actual dogs hid in the corners of the yard as she pushed her children toward the Civic.

At the liquor store, the owner couldn't look at her directly. At the grocery store, the clerk, who had gone to school with Ariel, burst into tears when she saw Polly. A moment of confusion when she got back in the car—where was the clutch and the gear shift?—and as she felt her children watching her, she broke into a sweat, and turned around to buy time, looked at her bags, and realized she'd forgotten to buy the brisket for the memorial, the primary reason for going to the fucking store to begin with.

She ran back in, dragging her whining, exhausted children. Another checker, seeing that Polly had been crying, patted her hand, and Polly started crying again, ran back to the old Civic, slammed it into reverse, and crunched the bumper against a concrete signpost.

Helen and Sam made no sound whatsoever. Polly hauled herself out of the car. The damage to the post was invisible, and any new dent on the Civic was indistinguishable from the last dozen years of abuse. Polly started to get back in.

"Hey, lady," said a man. "I saw all that. Hold up."

There was always some such fucker. He was snub-nosed, overly groomed with ironed jeans, her age, not a local. Polly could tell her appearance did not impress him, nor did her car.

"I haven't damaged a thing that doesn't belong to me," she said.

"Someone should make sure."

"Really?" asked Polly, warming up at the same time she started to shake. A sunburnt man trotted toward them with alarming speed.

"Can I help?" asked Drake, sweaty from working with Harry at the dig. He touched Polly on the shoulder—nice, not proprietary. "I came down for food and water."

The man, uneasy, looked at Drake's clothes, not his face. "She backed into that."

"I saw!" said Drake. "Awful! Clearly she's having a difficult time!"

Polly managed the trick of weeping while enraged. It probably saved the man, who finally focused on Drake's face. People were sometimes overwhelmed by a weird sense of familiarity. Did they know him? Maybe when he was twenty and saving a battalion or a city or fucking the girl, rather than being dressed like a guy who might dig up bodies in a field.

Maude would enjoy this, thought Polly. Were she to know.

"No harm done, I think," said Drake, wrapping an arm around Polly.

"No," said the man, retreating.

Drake got into the Civic and drove them home. By the time they turned into the alley, Polly was shuddering.

"I'm not rescuing you, I'm saving that asshole," Drake said. He parked, carried both Helen and Polly's groceries, gave the kids ice cream sandwiches, once again sifted through the photos on the table. "You're not getting anywhere with these."

"I know," said Polly. She wished she could go to bed.

"I'll get them enlarged. Will you give me the Delgados' address for a note?"

Polly fished through her purse. "They appreciated the fact that you were a gentleman," she said. "That you wanted to help with tuition, that you were sweet to her."

"Well," he said, "I liked her. Very much."

He was flushed and blinky. Drake was not a demonstrative man, at least about sad things. Sometimes this amused Polly, but Drake had grown up in a shitty, run-of-the-mill abusive family, and he kept things tight. He was good at looking impassive—he and Ned and Harry and Vinnie played poker all winter—and having a subtle listening face was not a bad thing for an actor.

Right now he looked almost as ruined as he might have if he hadn't retired. During two years of working for him, Ariel was often the only person he'd see in a day or even a week. Everyone in their own world of sadness.

"I'm sure she didn't like that little shit Graham," said Drake. "I'm sure she wouldn't willingly touch him."

No one can be sure, thought Polly.

"Harry didn't want the kid around today. He didn't want to look at him. He says she has rope burns, like she caught up with the kayak and wrapped the rope around her right hand and was holding on with her left. Like she tried to save herself."

Despite the risk of maiming the car again, Polly decided to take the groceries to Ned herself, because all she could see were Ariel's hands, outstretched, bloodless, mangled.

She found Ned in the office, working on the calendar. He'd already heard. It wasn't the sort of thing he would have told her over the phone. It was a horrible detail.

"How could Graham not have seen her reaching the rope?"

"Who knows what it's like when you're at water level, drowning." Ned slammed things around, trying to get out of Peake's to go help Harry on the hill.

"I hate him," said Polly. "I can't bear to think of this."

"We're done after the party. I'll talk to Vinnie."

In the kitchen, Graham was folding napkins again. She took her time looking in the walk-in for the stew Ned had made, but Graham folded on, placid and careful.

"How are you doing? Is it upsetting, or are you relieved?" asked Polly.

"About what?" he asked.

Polly went back into the walk-in and nibbled on some pecorino, thinking about narcissism, thinking about how a person who was truly nuts would likely fail to recognize this fact. When she could no longer feel her nose, she grabbed the containers she needed for dinner, cracked the door, and saw to her relief that Graham was gone.

Polly was sliding down the hall when she heard him laugh through the doorway of the closed bar. There he was, with a new waitress named Emily: laughing, pink-cheeked, human, holding a corkscrew just out of reach, teasing her.

Graham didn't have Ariel in his brain, anywhere. She was gone.

"Jump higher," he said, corkscrew in a cocked hand, at the end of a strong, long arm, just like Connie said he'd held a life preserver high above another head. He could have knocked Emily to the ground like a feather. Polly wondered how he dared to breathe. She shouldn't think he should have saved Ariel, but she did think it. He should have made sure she was wearing her preserver. He should have to see Ariel now.

Emily saw Polly and stopped hopping. Graham handed Emily the corkscrew and gave Polly as pure a look of hatred as she'd ever seen. Blink and miss it, but it happened. She wanted to kill him. She wouldn't, but it was a pure, honest desire.

Polly topped Ned's *lapin à la moutarde*, a bullet on Maude's list, with some fresh tarragon and served it with new potatoes and the first green beans. The children ate without irony or comment. Polly made a plum cake with last year's frozen Mount Royals, another Dee recipe. Everything was Dee, for Maude, at the beginning and end.

Maude and Jane were still arguing about the guest list, though it was silly to bother: They'd bought four extra pork shoulders, doubled the sides, chilled another case of Champagne.

"But I won't see these people again," said Maude. "Whether I like them is moot."

"How can you say that?" asked Jane. "Has there been some diagnosis?"

"I know," said Maude. "I just know."

"We'll see you in New York in October, for Papa's tribute." A big shindig on the seventy-fifth anniversary of *Myths and Variations*, his seminal book on myth and archaeology and how the two didn't always coexist comfortably. They were all going, and Polly intended to walk half the blocks of the city and try four restaurants a day.

"Yes," said Maude, but she didn't seem sure. "But I can't just sit around in the meantime, counting on it. We should go see Harry's project."

"When?" said Polly, opening one eye. She was in a lawn chair, daydreaming.

Now, apparently. Maude was intent on a trip to the Poor Farm on Harvat's Flats. For the view and to change the day's mood, and to support her poor grandchild, she said. Perhaps they'd see a bird.

It was only eight in the evening on one of the longest days of their lives. "We'll watch the fireworks," said Merle. "All good."

It was not all good. In the car, a Suburban they'd borrowed from Vinnie so that they could fit everyone at the same time, everyone was irritable. Helen drew on Sam's leg with a purple pen, and Polly climbed into the way back to divide them. They bumped on, Maude and Jane still squabbling about the party, Maude pointing out markers: the lane where a beau had lived, the house that served as a sick ward during the flu epidemic. They passed the ranch on Ferry Creek where Papa and Dee had hidden a still with some friends, as a hobby and a way of using Dee's grapes and plums and apples. Mostly, Maude said, people would make a run up to the Canadian border for whiskey; she showed them a ravine that had been a drop point.

As they neared the site, they could see Harry's skinny frame. Ned was fifty yards downhill, holding a survey line, while Drake dug farther up the slope near the flagged road, the flags vibrating in forty-mile-an-hour gusts. This was what people meant when they said "high plains," and Harry did seem to be starring in his own Sergio Leone movie.

"Well, this is lovely," said Maude, who was one of the few people who could remember the ruins of the first poorhouse, lost to a lightning fire in 1916, and the life of the second, abandoned in the fifties and gone to arson in the early sixties. "I distinctly recall Mother dropping a drunk off here in 1926 or so. And food, surplus apples and potatoes and beef for the inmates. Some of the wardens were criminal."

"Not very birdy," said Merle.

"It's about poor Harry and the tour, dear," said Maude, as Sam pointed to a bird, at least trying. "Only a crow," she said, the huge papery eyes turning to him. "You know they have funerals, don't you?"

Sam shook his head. Papa told us, thought Polly, head swimming. But of course it wasn't this "us." She slapped herself on the top of her head and Jane stared at her. "Bug," said Polly.

"You'd do well to be as smart as a crow," said Maude to Sam.

They spilled out toward Harry's field of stakes.

"I don't believe her," whispered Sam, struggling with Maude's tripod, her binoculars, her five-liter purse. Helen carried the cane.

"It's true," said Polly. "Or at least I heard the same thing when I was your age, and I did see some crows standing in a circle around a dead magpie, once."

From the Poor Farm, perched between the Absaroka Mountains and the river below, you would have had the best view possible of the town that didn't want you, the thousands of people who didn't care, the whole world you didn't own. The landscape bowed around them in three directions: the river and the Crazy Mountains to the north, Livingston to the west, the Beartooth Mountains and Big Timber to the east. The mountains behind them still had snow, but the lupine and forget-me-nots near the poorhouse's ruined foundation were giving way to silvery artemisia. From town, the domed flats looked as if they were covered in rich gold grass, but it was really orange lichen on gray rock, the soil blown away in the Depression. There was nothing lush about this place, and almost nothing standing of the buildings that had housed hundreds of unhappy people. Poor farms had been a gentle Victorian response to the extremes of the past, streets and debtors' prisons. If you had no money and no way of making it, if you were ill and had no relatives to care for you, you were given to the care of the county, which fed you, clothed you, gave you a bed, and did its best to tend to your medical and psychological needs. In practice, this meant a catchall of orphans and withered alcoholics and widows, tubercular miners and paralyzed cowboys, the simpleminded and the harmlessly insane. Once an orphanage opened in Gallatin County, and a mental hospital opened in Warm Springs, it increasingly meant the elderly.

Up close, Harry and Ned and Drake had a vague look, a kind of padding over grief and fatigue, and Polly guessed they'd been smoking. There were shot glasses on the hood of Harry's truck next to half a bottle of tequila, and Polly poured herself one.

"So," said Maude. "Show us the problem, darling."

"I have a surfeit of bodies, Grandma. Dead in the middle of the road."

He was definitely stoned. "Well, move the road," said Maude.

"That's not an option. By contract, I need to relocate them and identify them."

"Idiocy."

Harry's whole life was a fight for exactitude, for something beyond reasonable doubt. He showed them what should be where—the poorhouse proper, barns and an orchard, the potter's field. He waved an open notebook, and when he put it down, Polly flipped through.

The sight of Ariel's handwriting was a smack in the head, but as Polly paged, the girl's handwriting shifted back to Harry's and growing confusion, question marks and rectangles. Harry, meanwhile, was trying to explain ground-penetrating radar, its uses and its issues on boulder-laden heavy clay. The machine looked a little like a large-wheeled lawn mower. Sam and Merle were fascinated by it, but Maude's eyes filmed over. Helen had wandered away with some old binoculars and was using them on some ants.

Polly stuck with Maude as she stalked off toward the edge of the ridge. Livingston lay below them, on the north bank of the curl of the Yellowstone as it headed north and bent east. To Maude, the river was filled with dead people, and she pointed a knobby, beringed finger as she said their names. "Maggie Strand, only three I think, about 1924; Fred Byrne, in his teens in 1917 when the bridge went; Connor someone, a pretty Irish kid, in a car like our girl, sometime before the war."

The dogs chased curlews and the kids chased the dogs. Cruel little shits, all of them, and all of them ignoring Ned's warnings about snakes. Normally Polly would have been worried, but it was almost dark, burrow time, and she was now on her second shot. Merle tried to point out a golden eagle and Maude showed no interest. She was back on the dead, a local history of drowning, and her toll had reached the Korean War.

Harry fidgeted.

"You can go back to your gizmo, if I'm so boring," said Maude. "I won't bother with irrigation ditches. The Schmidt boy fell in down there near old Clark City, the Gallianos' drunk father just downstream. Mostly boys, of course, poor idiots. But there is the road our beautiful girl followed to the old bridge.'"

"Don't forget our beautiful Ariel," said Drake, walking back to his shovel.

It was as close to a criticism that Polly could imagine him doling out.

"Don't you want to see the bodies?" said Harry.

Of course they did. There were four tarps. Polly, looking at the outlines of the coffins, was horrified. "You have four bodies that shouldn't be here?"

"No," he said. "Four bodies in the wrong place, though the tags match the records. I think the gravediggers ran into some rock and went with the easy solution." He flipped tarps off to show them half-excavated, half-crushed pine boxes. "We have a Marjorie Pince, aged sixty-two, dead of apoplexy; S. Oditz, an alcoholic; Ferdinand Zapruder, bowel cancer."

Polly looked for the children, but they were still chasing the dogs or curlews, whichever came first.

"Here's the problem," Harry said, lifting the last tarp.

They saw a fully excavated skeleton, facedown on top of a crushed coffin, arms outstretched. The right hand had been the one taken by the grader. "I think someone put him in here when the ground was still soft," said Harry. "In the coffin underneath, we have Vincenzo Speri, dead of blood poisoning in August of 1940. The guy on top has a bullet in his head"—he knelt down and pointed to a hole centered above the eye sockets—"and it looks as if another is lodged in his pelvis. Tall guy, good dental work, some sort of fancy class ring on his finger—I haven't tried to clean it off yet, and maybe I shouldn't."

"My, my," said Maude. "I wonder what he did to earn this."

"Maligning a possibly innocent man," said Harry. "Did you know him?"

Polly wasn't sure he was joking.

"Of course not," snapped Maude. "Have you looked into people who've gone missing?"

"I will when I get him out of here. The coroner just left."

"I imagine it's been too long," Maude said. "I imagine plenty of people are never identified, or never found. I knew a girl who simply disappeared, one day in the late twenties. Knocked up and never seen again."

"She'll turn up someday," said Harry. "That messy human shell."

Disappeared, Polly thought, looking at a long femur. Almost no one truly managed it. And now it came to her, all those hints of family murders wavering up for air.

"Maude, is this the man from the car? The man who killed Asta?"

"Why on earth would you think that?" asked Maude.

"Several reasons," said Polly.

"I wish it was," said Maude. "But sadly, no."

Jane didn't hear this; she'd run off after the children because Helen was screaming at Sam, enraged about some injustice.

"What if I said I'd cancel the party unless you told me about Asta?"

Maude smiled without futzing with her hair or another tell. "I'd say you were a manipulative little girl. The story is horribly simple," she said. "Asta met a bad man and she died because of it."

"Did she know him well? Or was it only chance that they died together?"

"Oh, he didn't die for years," she said. "Despite our hopes and dreams, as it were."

Graham would probably live for decades, too, thought Polly bleakly. "So he was no better than the man who abandoned her? Please give me his name."

Maude seemed to think about it, then shut her eyes. "Ask your mother. I will tell you that he was drunk and driving. He'd beaten her earlier that day and he left her to die in the water. He could have saved her, and he didn't." She opened her eyes again. "Just a bad man," she said. "That's all it takes."

———

It was the Fourth of July, the night with the best fireworks. Ned and Drake put their shovels and brushes in the truck, and Harry stretched out his tarps while the rest of them bundled in blankets and watched the show in the river valley below. Merle held Sam, Helen was on Maude's lap, and Jane bounced up and down to stay warm. Polly's eyes went wonky with the first few explosions, and she backed up, as if ten feet would make a difference, until she was near Ned. A firework for every body in the river, she thought.

On the way back, more bits of Maude's past: the wooded lot where an arsonist had burned her favorite roadhouse bar, the lane to what had been the last whorehouse, the place where Asta had boarded her pretty Thoroughbred. Every familiar road or house was a lost world, like every photograph.

"I'm not sure why I wanted to come home," said Maude. She started to cry, but, being Maude, she stopped immediately, and began being shitty to Merle about the way he was driving.

The list of the day, at the end of the day: a last stab at pretending there was some sense of order to the universe.

> *memorial: brisket, flowers, basket for cards*
> *passage to have read?*
> *pick berries*
> *photo boards*
> *cook cook cook*
> *sleep*

Polly gave up, threw the notebook on the floor, and reached blindly for the stack of books on the bedside table. Jane was coaxing her back into reading, as if reading were medicine. When Polly pointed to her pile of manuscripts, Jane had said, "All shit," and went to the library for a stack: Dorothy Sayers, Oliver Sacks, Nabokov, Elaine Pagels.

Polly could tell that Jane was trying to disguise her theme. "I've read most of them," she said.

"Read them again," said Jane.

Tonight, Polly flipped open *Speak, Memory*, skimming along until she reached

> *Aunt Pasha's last words were: "That's interesting. Now I understand. Everything is water,* vsyo-voda.*"*

"For fuck's sake," said Polly, dropping the book on the floor.

"The idea was to read," said Ned.

"Please don't patronize me."

Ned stared at her for a minute. His face was tired and angry, and his pretty gray eyes were bloodshot. He was brown all over, and when he rolled over to face away, the scars on his back showed white. Harry said they'd been swimming on these hot days of searching, and this reminder that Ned gave her a reason to worry annoyed Polly even more. But when Ned got up to tell Sam to turn off his light, she picked the book up again, and read a few more pages, until she hit

> *The mirror brims with brightness; a bumblebee has entered the room and bumps against the ceiling. Everything is as it should be, nothing will ever change, nobody will ever die.*

12

Summer 1968

Despite the fact that no one was talking to her, Rita paced up and down the hallway, looking at what the children had drawn and the books they'd left on the carpet. She knocked on Papa's door and spent an hour inside, murmuring. Art books and copies of *National Geographic* pressed open to giraffes and orchids climbed up the margins of the hall. Rita used Polly's chalks to trace new mountains and islands, seabeds and clouds. She brought out her valise of oil paints, stowed under a bench in the greenhouse, covered with clay dust. She began to paint the ocean.

Merle left in the Ford to visit his brother in Boston, and the next morning Edmund and Polly both woke up with his cold. Jane was getting ready to defend her thesis and planned to go to the city apartment to try to keep her mind clear, to be away from Rita. Now Jane said she'd stay, because Dee was fragile and shouldn't be near sick children.

Dee was offended. Jane left, but any sense of getting away with something dissolved. Dee said they needed to spend the morning sleeping. She said if they took a long enough nap, they'd have three dreams, not necessarily happy but not terrifying, either. She gave them each a bowl of sherbet, put cold wet cloths on their foreheads, and shut their doors. When Polly tried opening hers five minutes later, Dee's voice whistled down the hall: "No."

So they fell asleep. Edmund's dreams were always about jungles, and he did have three. Everything in the first was gold and fragile, leaves breaking as he brushed by chasing a turtle. The second was cluttered with spots of color, as if he were trapped in a soft, moist Christmas tree, and it was talking to him. In the third the jungle was his bed, leaves crackling and whispering out of the wood frame, telling him a tiger was coming, but not to worry.

Polly's dreams? Jane being plucked from the roof of the apartment building by a giant eagle, Polly riding on a train in a snarled tunnel that became the maze from Edmund's birthday party. In the last, she looked into the sand at a jellyfish, then realized it was a watching whale's eye.

When Polly woke, she smelled toast. Rita was living on toast and cheese and Dee's underripe fruit—it drove Dee wild that Rita would touch her plums—and there she was in the open doorway, still in her nightgown, staring at Polly as she ate her toast.

Rita floated off.

Edmund's voice: "You should go away. You don't want to get sick."

"I'm immune," Rita said. "Silly duck. I need your feathers. I woke up needing them."

"Promise you'll give them back."

"Of course," said Rita.

Back in Polly's room she reached for the second bunch, not even looking down at the little girl in the bed.

"They're mine," said Polly. "Dee wanted us to have them."

Rita shrugged and took the feathers from the window. "You're all fucking crazy," she said.

She left, slamming her bedroom door, and a minute later they could hear Dee on the stairs.

"I see she was here," she said. "It doesn't matter. We'll make more." She led Edmund and Polly downstairs and plopped them on the couch and draped them with new cold washcloths.

When Arnold arrived, he said, "Hearts," and they all sat down. Dee dealt. She told them to study the faces and symbols, warlike and malicious and sidelong and seductive, and they spent an hour in shifty delight, cunning and joy, before their throats and lungs burned again, before they remembered they were sick. They had never truly looked at cards (just as they had never truly looked at dogs, feathers, berries), or considered what they meant. Clubs were originally clover leaves, spades were pikes. The jack of clubs was Lancelot, the jack of diamonds was Hector, the queen of hearts was Judith (not that Dee bothered telling them that story).

"Look at the blood on his sword," she said, running a finger over the face of the jack of hearts. "And look at her beauty. Her hair is blowing, and you can hear trumpets. You should be playing euchre instead of hearts, E, look at those jacks and aces. But Polly has the suicide king, and you will not shoot the moon."

Polly stared at the king of hearts. Charlemagne, according to Dee— why would he stick a sword in his head? Dee said that he was only brandishing it, that over the years, printers muddled the image until it looked as if he was plunging a sword into his brain.

Arnold was supposedly helping to plan Papa's retirement party. Really, he and Papa and Dee sat on the porch and talked for hours, drinking better wine than usual. One-eyed May loved one-eyed Arnold and ignored Polly and Edmund when he was around. Man and cat could look in and out at the same time, said Papa. When Arnold learned about Edmund's nightmares, he drew a tree on his hand. Polly wanted one, too, and he drew a vine.

Rita was moving too quickly again, singing to herself, darting around the house. To no good end, as Dee put it. Steer clear.

Rita tied the bloody feathers into a bouquet that dangled above her door. She'd begun to paint flying things near the tops of the canvases, above every continent: pterodactyls and hummingbirds, bats and a World War I–era airplane, all topped by stars, clouds, curls of wind like the wind on old maps. She added sharks and sailfish and jellyfish and eels, dangling in the southern Atlantic: Papa explained that eels traveled to the Sargasso Sea to mate and floated together in a huge mat, in the center of the Atlantic, a place where slaves and horses were dumped when ships were becalmed on their way from Africa to America.

Rita put heaven on top, above a layer of polar ice and white bears—no angels, but birds with halos—and hell below Antarctica, the bottom of which was blue ice, and made of skeletons. Her half-finished Jabberwock was reaching for a penguin chick. Lowest of all, a black-red skim of hell and lava, gray outlines of ghosts and more feathers on a devil.

Papa was amused. "Do you believe in hell?" he asked Rita.

"Of course I do," she said. "Don't you?"

"Myself am hell," he said. "Did you ever hear that phrase?"

That afternoon, Rita drew phases of the moon and sun, burnt landscapes of deserts, white-blue mountains. She left Dee's moon where the children had drawn it, but it now hung over an orchard, in what was becoming Central Asia. Rita added bright dots, red and orange and purple, to the trees. The Garden of Eden, she said, but she drew no snake and no people. She drew pyramids in Egypt, and mounds in Mongolia, but when she began a jungle, a greener Asia, she did not draw her husband, sleeping on the path of Edmund's dreams.

After Rita finished the jungle the next day, just after Arnold left, she ran away with Papa's Volvo. Edmund and Polly, sicker than ever, were propped up at the kitchen table eating coddled eggs when they heard the engine start. Papa looked up from his paper, and went back to reading.

"Will you call Bennett?" asked Dee. Bennett was the Suffolk County police chief.

"I'm too annoyed," said Papa.

"How will I take the children to the doctor without the car?"

"They'll be fine. We've all survived worse."

Fevers are different when you're young. For an adult, any second's physical status is a gray area, because nothing in your body is ever entirely right. When you're a child, the baseline feeling of wellness is so profound that any variation—a sunburn, an itch, gas—is intolerable, mind-boggling. Sometimes an adult gets a glimpse of this past paradise—swimming, a moment before orgasm, tasting food—but small damages coat mind and skin and muscle with a kind of indifferent hair shirt. To healthy, first-world children, the body is an absolute, and discomfort brings collapse.

Their fevers were hallucinatory, and Dee fretted and gave them ice cream and baby aspirin and honeyed whiskey water and propped them up for games of gin. Out of the corner of her eye Polly was sure, over and over, that the horse on one of Papa's Chinese paintings was running across the wall, that the flowered curtains on the glassed-in porch, meant to shade it from the sun, showed faces flowing out of the patterns as they moved in a breeze from the window, a closing door, someone passing. Ten years later, tripping in college, she would think of these days.

May and Lemon took turns on their beds. There were new feathers in their windows from Dee, orange and turquoise. Polly didn't know where they'd come from and Dee claimed she didn't, either. May went back and forth between their rooms, soaking up the heat of their fevers, window to window, and at dusk Dwight took up position in the crab apple tree. Polly and Edmund heard *teatime*, and *puddy*, and *evil, pretty girl* and *storm*. They had begun to like him, and think of him as theirs.

When it was dark, Dee rubbed Vicks on the children's chests and opened their windows wider, because they were hot, even if the night wasn't.

"Look at the stars," said Dee. "See the largest, just over the crab apple?"

Edmund did, but Polly said she only saw a blur. A spinning night world, a blind milky eye. The lights in her room were a blur, she explained, and the words on her posters were blurs. Dee panicked and called for Papa, who crouched in front of Polly in the hall, holding a hand close and moving it far away, while Dee went on about how they didn't have a car, because of damn Rita, and couldn't they get legal custody, and would they need to call an ambulance, and how awful it was that she hadn't simply taken the children to the doctor.

Papa smiled at Polly, who rocked on her small toes in the green of the hall. Gray-blue eyes, old brown skin. He lifted his glasses off the top of his head and slowly lowered them onto Polly's nose. Suddenly the world glittered, even from a distance: She could see Rita's waves, and swaying trees, clouds ghosting above and rain falling on low mountains. Dee pointed to Rita's jellyfish and eels and Polly saw them begin the long swim to the Sargasso Sea, to all the bones of horses and slaves. Her eyes filled with tears. This was too much, thrashing, drowning horses and black children and a continent of eels waiting to devour them.

After they'd comforted her, and said they'd buy her eyeglasses, Polly insisted that Dee was making the world wake up. But why, and to what end? What would happen? Papa said Dee only wanted them to be better, and that helping them imagine more meant helping them know more. "Dee is not magic," he said. "She is reality pie."

Dee laughed and said she wanted to be a myth.

It was all bushwah, Papa said in the morning, after Arnold arrived and they used his car to go to the doctor. Polly and Edmund each got a shot of antibiotic in their butts. Merle found Rita a few days later. She'd darted around Manhattan, bug in the light, selling paintings. Edmund pushed his trunk against his door the night she returned.

After the night of the blurred night sky, everyone understood that Polly was blind as a bat, so nearsighted that when they took her down to the harbor, she couldn't see the swans, or the large schooner moored to the dock—she thought it was a building, not a boat. Merle made an appointment with the eye doctor but they missed it and the next for one emergency or another. Polly didn't care, because people would only ridicule her at school. Rita, who never seemed to be listening to any of these conversations, took Polly to the greenhouse, arranged her canvases, and asked her to say what she could see from five feet, ten feet, twenty feet. She'd scribble down notes, let Polly wander off, and rework the paintings.

"Well, they're beautiful," said Dee, when she saw the canvases. She gave Rita $50 for a small oil that might have shown a bird. Dee finished her vases, which were about eighteen inches high, plum colored, with blue and green and gold vines that seemed to run from one to the other, linking the two. She asked Merle to cut some corks for the tops, in case someone wanted to use them for storage. Polly asked if Dee would make one for her, and Dee said Polly would have these someday.

It was still hot, and almost unbearable in the upstairs bedrooms. They spent a chunk of every day lounging outside on a frayed, brightly colored quilt with Lemon, who lay on her back panting, and sometimes with May, too. One afternoon, Polly, with her fuzzy vision, was slow to realize that Dwight the parrot was on the blanket next to them, and he and the dog were nose to beak, Lemon cross-eyed and seemingly paralyzed. A second later May floated through the air and dropped onto Dwight's back.

Edmund ripped the cat away while Polly grabbed the shrieking parrot. She ran him down to the witch's house, and Dwight talked to her the whole way. He said *watch the cards, dear, watch the crazy lady, be nice to the boy,* a lifetime of advice along with *dumb dog, pretty hair, turn on the news, tell them to go away.*

When she reached the witch's porch, Polly put Dwight down and felt his breast and back for blood, and asked him if he was okay. *Tell them to go away,* said Dwight again, this time to the closed door.

Polly knocked. "Thank you, dear," said a voice. "But go away."

"The cat jumped on Dwight," Polly called. "I think he's fine. Please don't kill my cat."

Mags Mags Mags, said Dwight.

The woman said nothing. Polly backed down the porch steps and watched from the lane. The door opened and Dwight hopped inside. Polly ran home and found Edmund on the stoop, May sitting next to him.

"Is he dead?" he asked.

"No." Polly sat next to him. "I didn't even see any blood."

"Did you see her?"

"No. She wouldn't come out."

They both thought about what that might mean. Polly flopped back and May crawled on her chest and purred. Polly turned her head to see past the ball of fur and watched blood ooze down Edmund's back, through his torn shirt. She made him go upstairs to Dee, who said that they needed to go in for stitches and antibiotics. She admired his bravery but cat wounds were beyond her. Papa drove. Everyone knew them at the hospital.

That afternoon, Papa picked some of Dee's roses and walked down to Mrs. Maw's house. Polly and Edmund skulked behind, assuming the door wouldn't open for him, either.

But it did. When Papa came out a few minutes later, he said he'd asked Mrs. Maw if she'd like him to have the cat put down. She said no and wanted Papa to give Polly something as a thank-you, a pretty embroidered handkerchief. When Papa explained the scenario, she opened a drawer and pulled out a small ivory pocketknife for Edmund.

Polly wanted the knife.

"She has no hair," said Papa. "She wears a turban. In her head, she's still young, and she wants to stay that way in other people's minds. She's not like us."

As penance for giving Edmund and Polly a cold, Merle said he'd stay home when Dee and Papa and Jane needed to go to a friend's birthday party in the city. No one suggested that Rita was up to the task.

Jane was apologetic and said she'd change her plans.

"No," said Merle. "Let me. Have some fun." He kissed Jane—not many things made Polly happier—and sent her off. He made them a real breakfast, frying bacon and eggs, hashing some potatoes on the side. He wiped the counters, and did the dishes, and even swept the kitchen floor. He would write for a while, he said, and they should go upstairs, since they were sick and it was raining. He didn't care that Edmund, who avoided whatever floor Rita was on whenever possible, didn't want to go. "Get your butt up there," said Merle. "You can shut the door to Papa's office. You can lock yourself in, for all I care." But he patted Polly, as if it was a joke.

Upstairs, Rita was cleaning her brushes, still in her bathrobe. "Is everyone gone?"

"Dad is here," said Polly.

"I know that, silly," said Rita, going down the stairs.

The hallway was wet and shiny, overwhelmingly green and blue, oceans and sky, just like the world. They could hear Rita below in the kitchen, laughing at Merle's jokes. When she laughed again, Edmund touched both hands to his head, to his earaches, and together they walked to the end of the hall, to Papa and Dee's door, and shut it behind them.

The bedroom was on the left, with open pocket doors, and a dressing table covered with Dee's things was in the center room, under a window looking out on the green cloud of the dogwood tree. Papa's study was to the right, behind another set of pocket doors. You could see a strip of the Sound but the real show was what lay on the sills, nothing glittery, but still strange: the bone whistle (be careful who you call, said Papa), tiny statues of round women, a sperm whale tooth, an aqua shot glass with red dots and the words *Two Dot*, a disintegrating piece of celluloid, and a curly lock of dark hair, dangling from his cantilevered desk lamp by a blue velvet ribbon.

Polly and Edmund were still woozy and weak. They flopped on the sofa and looked through Dee's jewelry box, all the different drawers with pearls and earrings, baby teeth and stones; one tiny silk bag was filled with lumpy rough diamonds. They heard footsteps on the stairs, whispers and giggles, sliding furniture. The study door rattled and a minute later

189

Rita's door clicked shut. Edmund tried to push the door to the hall open, but it was blocked—they could see the blue wood of the dresser that held the towels.

"We could climb out the window," said Polly, looking at the top of the dogwood.

Edmund shrugged. May, a glowing orange caution sign, looked back up at them from the grass and Dwight preened himself on a branch above her head.

"It doesn't matter," Edmund said. "Where would we go, anyway?"

The laughter from the hall ended, and the pins on the map in Papa's study jumped to the rhythmic slam of Rita's bed striking the other side of the wall. Polly and Edmund retreated with their books to the bedroom, where the bed was dented for two bodies, one heavier and longer. Edmund took Papa's side, Polly took Dee's, and they read and faded off into daydreams and other thoughts that weren't as good, not so much about people who made walls rattle but about people who went to see doctors for tests. There were pill bottles all over Dee's bedside table.

"I don't want her to die," said Edmund.

But they knew she would. They knew endings and other old truths Jane and Merle wouldn't speak about but Dee and Papa could: that the world needed monsters, even if it made it hard to walk through the dark; that the oldest horror story was the beast in the back of the cave, and that babies giggled when someone pretended to eat them because being eaten was the oldest fear. That vines could see nearby trees, that people had always drunk too much, and you couldn't blame yourself if they did; that people had always gone mad, and sometimes it wasn't malevolent. That you couldn't fault anyone for pretending there might be good news. That people sometimes died without pain. That you had to treat your memory like a violin and play the bits you liked so that you wouldn't forget. That your lizard brain made you jump at a snake or a spider, and that people inherited this fear and the special landscapes of their own dreams, some aching for forests, some loving hills or deserts, snow or rivers. That Polly and Edmund would always know the right thing, and they would always at least try to do it. That they weren't fools: They knew that people had to die, make room, and that when you died, you disappeared. The world didn't hurt anymore, and you didn't worry anymore.

It was dark when they heard someone move the dresser. Downstairs, Merle left out glasses of milk and grilled cheese sandwiches. They could hear him talking in Rita's room, but they didn't see him until the next morning, when Dee and Papa and Jane returned, and Rita moved on to another continent, singing as she drew long hills, seas of trees. She was so good when she was painting, so sane. She let them powder Dee's broken pieces of stained glass and add it to the paint for the ocean, so that the water glittered as if it were full of krill and silver fish. Sometimes she tucked Edmund in even when Jane returned, even on nights when Dee wasn't in the hospital.

13

Friday, July 5, 2002

At 4:00 in the morning before Maude's party, Polly found herself young again, standing in the hallway at Stony Brook in front of a section of Rita's map. Polly was worried that if she looked too hard at the wet paint, she'd find dead faces. Instead she saw a beautiful beach, a shack and scrub trees, a woman and a man coming out of the water and lying down together on the warm sand. In the dream, Polly was surprised: She couldn't remember Rita painting these figures. They were so unlike her.

When Polly started to wake, she clung to what she saw, because it was so much better than thinking of Ariel. Downstairs, she studied their two Rita paintings as if she might find the faces there, but the paintings showed what they'd always shown: origami-like birds and a portrait of two children. The couple had never been painted, and now they disappeared again. The dream was a dream.

A list for a difficult day:

> *lessons*
> *everything for memorial done by 2:00*
> *party: chairs, tables, forecast before tablecloths or bouquets*
> *photo boards—enlarge or give up? Sic Drake on Maude*
> *Sam family tree*

At the pool, the children practiced jumping from the edge.

"I've picked some passages for the memorial," said Connie. "I'm not sure if I'm going to be able to read them myself. I might have to ask someone else to do it."

"That's nothing I would be good at," said Polly, drying Helen off.

"No, I want you to read them now." Connie pointed to her backpack on the far side of the pool, a girly shade of purple. "Main pocket," she said.

Polly walked over and unzipped the pocket. She looked down at a switchblade, a can of mace, and a can of antiperspirant, and unfolded a sheet of white ruled paper. At the top, in irregular spiky handwriting:

> *Everyone who knew Ari trusted her. She made people feel safe and happy, and we all assumed we would have her around forever.*

Connie had scratched out *to take care of us* at the end of the last sentence.

> *I know it is harder for her family, but she was my friend from daycare on, and I don't know what to do with myself. I understand this takes time. I have in the meantime reminded myself to abide by His teachings.*
>
> *"Judge not, and ye shall not be judged: condemn not, and ye shall not be condemned: forgive, and ye shall be forgiven."*

"What do you think?" said Connie. "Will everyone freak out?"

Yes, thought Polly. She would try to gaze off into the clouds for this part of the memorial. "Forgive him for what?"

Connie stopped acting as if it were a game. "For whatever he did. It's his fault."

"What are you trying to accomplish? Do you want to be forgiven for what you want to do to him?"

"I would never," said Connie. "It's just that it's on my mind, and I'm supposed to talk about what's on my mind."

"I think you're supposed to talk about anything that will help the family, and anything that's true and good to say about Ariel."

Connie's face was stiff.

"I'm sorry," said Polly, "but I think the last thing you want to talk about is who might be at fault."

"Mr. Susak is going to make him come to the memorial, and I'm going to watch his face. I told Mr. Susak I'd quit watching the kids if he didn't tell me why Graham moved here, and he said Graham hit and killed a girl crossing a street. I guess they were going to charge him with negligent homicide but it didn't stick."

Polly watched Helen float on her back. "When did this happen?"

"Six months ago. He gets his license back today or tomorrow."

"Maybe he'll finally leave," said Polly. "He should leave."

"You know Harry wants to kill him," said Connie. "And Drake, of course."

"People don't go around killing people," said Polly.

Polly didn't know that Ariel's life preserver had been found the night before. As it happened, the person who found it in a willow tangle on an island downstream from Pine Creek was subsequently arrested at a fishing access site for smoking marijuana. Already, in 2002, this wasn't an arrest most police were eager to bother with, but Cy was forced into it. He'd been dealing with a fender bender at the Mayor's Landing take-out when a young man named Shane Bobbin pulled up, his raft haloed in smoke. Shane, waving a red Stearns preserver in the air, swallowed his joint as Cy watched.

Shane Bobbin said he'd found this preserver high in a thicket on the island where Graham said he'd frolicked with Ariel. Cy did not listen to specifics and assumed that the preserver was marooned by high spring water from an accident the summer before, like the poor Yellowstone Park drowning victim's leg. Shane pointed out that the preserver was unbleached by the sun, without a year's worth of wind-borne dust or bird shit or leaves. He planned to keep it—it was at least a $50 model—but the blotch of blood near the neck killed the urge. So it was timely that he'd run into Cy. In a way.

Cy bagged the preserver, which fit the description of the one Vinnie bought for Ariel, and arrested Shane for possession. Cy knew he'd been remiss: He hadn't followed up on Connie's or the family's comments about Graham. He didn't entirely trust Harry's assessment about the bruise or cut on Ariel's face or arm or the marks on her hand or wrist, despite Harry's considerable training. No one understood the power of the river. People always wanted an explanation, and they always wanted someone to blame. But an accident was an accident. Blame God, thought Cy. Blame a long roll down the river. Even now, the blood, the cut and bruised face—maybe she'd fallen. Why expect the boy to remember everything?

In the morning, Cy reconsidered after another call from the Delgados, who insisted again that their daughter had not been in love with Graham, and as far as they could tell never dated him. Ariel sometimes went out after work, but unless she was with the Berrigans or Connie or Drake, she was always home by 7:00 or 8:00. Cy tracked down some of the rafters, and one now mentioned hearing Graham razz Ariel about her fear of the water, holding the preserver above her head, teasing. They didn't seem like a couple.

Cy sought out Connie at the pool, soon after Polly shot off into her full, rich day, and Connie said her bit again: Graham was a murderer. She went on about Ariel's fear of water and missing shorts. Cy was relieved when his radio went off, telling him about an altercation at the corner of Second and Park.

By coincidence, the attorney assigned to represent Shane Bobbin at the morning's hearing was Vinnie Susak. Vinnie listened to Shane's story, recommended he plead not guilty, and left the courthouse at 8:15 a.m. He walked into Graham's building and dragged Graham out of his bedroom and down his shitty soiled hall and stairs, screaming that Graham was going to visit the Delgados and apologize. The elderly neighbors called the police, and when Cy reached Vinnie and Graham, they were on the sidewalk across from Peake's, with Ned in the middle, and Vinnie saying he was going to use his prosthesis to beat his nephew to death if he didn't do the right thing.

Vinnie refused to explain his rage to Cy, who sent him off and followed Graham to his apartment—a squalid, airless hole—to ask about the preserver and the bloodstain. He listened to the basic story—Graham loved Ariel, and they'd kept it a secret because her parents wouldn't understand—and new explanations: Ariel threw the preserver into the brush to prove a point, but before that Graham remembered her falling on the beach, though he couldn't remember blood. It was when they'd first gotten out, when people were still around—hadn't anyone mentioned it? Everyone was drinking. Graham had wanted the others to go away.

Cy left, unhappy. He needed the autopsy results, but he knew the medical examiner's office in Missoula was short-staffed.

Ned, arriving home, gave Polly a dramatic account of the fight and absolutely no information on causation. Vinnie and Nora would not be coming to Maude's party; Vinnie would require a quiet cabin in the woods after the memorial.

Meanwhile, Polly and Ned needed to get on with the day. They set up the roasting box in the backyard, and Polly put the brisket for the memorial into the bottom oven to reheat. Before the box was opened and Ned carved the pig, they'd go full gout: the mixed blessing of the oysters, piles of cold shrimp from the Gulf with different sauces, *gougères*, fat stinky cheeses. She'd baked the tarts—apricot and plum, one gooseberry in a nod to the

Swedes—early to make way for the backup pork shoulders, potato gratins, and roasted tinfoil-wrapped packages of beets to be tossed with green beans and aioli, which would offend a certain contingent. She made an especially lively chimichurri for the same reason. Sam trimmed beans and Helen looked for bugs in the flat of blackberries they'd serve with their own raspberries and the real cake Polly had ordered, a tower of vanilla and ganache with the numeral *90* in a nicely archaic font.

Chairs out, tables out, and then Polly was left with the things she'd avoided. The family tree Sam was supposed to bring to school in the fall was problematic for a number of reasons. Sam muttered about "roots," and Polly knew his teacher probably wanted some shallow yet earnest examination of immigration, not the magpie nest that had gone into making him. She gave him a fancy notebook and printed out some prototypes, but the first loop-de-loops Sam came up with looked like a family vine in the style of Escher. Another attempt reminded her of the trees Rita splashed onto the wall in Stony Brook, before she'd been hauled off to the bin. Dryads, with vine-like limbs.

Sam expressed despair over this snarl of names, and they all trooped out to the alley house. Sam and Polly watched Jane draw a beautiful tree, a marvel of clarity and design. Contents would come from Maude, and what Maude didn't know, the extra layers of complexity—who, why, secrets—real secrets, as opposed to garbage—would come out or not at the party.

But back in the house, Maude was still singing in the bathtub. Helen sat by the door, memorizing the words. Sam didn't mind disappearing into his room, and Polly let the project drift away again, too. It took Drake to move things along. Maude, he said, talking through the bathroom door, the photos are all you've talked about for weeks, and yet you avoid looking at them. If it's too hard, let's leave them out.

Maude exited the bathtub, foraged for food in the refrigerator and made her way into the dining room. For the next two hours she moved back and forth from the photo pile to Polly, Jane, Merle, the children, even Ned, sliding through different lives with anyone who would listen. Eventually everyone left the dining room, leaving Maude alone with her dead.

"Is this too much?" asked Maude.

"No," said Polly. "You've had ninety years of being photogenic." She called for Drake, who was out on the porch, trying to come up with the right words for the memorial. He came inside and stood patiently while Maude dithered again, and when she reached a pause, he grabbed the stack and headed to the copy shop.

Try to tell a story of a family in photographs, thought Polly. Just try. When the boards were done, the largest of a hundred photos would show Maude with her father, sitting on the same porch. You could see Dee's shadow as she held the camera, and Maude's legs were moving and blurred. Maude's father was thin and the smile he was giving was all for the photographer. A second photo, probably earlier, showed the couple—had he been Dee's husband, yet? Maude claimed they'd "lived in sin" for some time—sitting on the lawn with friends, tiny new trees staked behind them and the frame of a new building, the greenhouse that had burned before Maude was even born, the source of Helen's broken glass and maybe Helen's pretty rock. And a third photo, taken on a Los Angeles beach in the early twenties, Maude and her brothers splashing in the surf and Papa and Dee on either side of small Asta, swinging her above the water. They'd been in their forties then, and Dee had looked pretty good, but Papa had been a long, cool drink of water.

Maude held up a last picture, a young Papa on a sun-blasted burial mound. "He was something," she said. "All this pretty wild hair, and brown skin from digs, and absolutely no interest in bullshit. Even later, my college friends would come home and stare at him, which I imagine he loved, but it was always all about Mother. He was certainly perfect with me, and it was only when I was older that I wondered just how imperfect he'd been before her."

"What do you think?" asked Polly.

"Quite," said Maude. "Quite wonderfully imperfect. The letters from the English actresses—Mama would burn them at the dinner table while he smiled. He'd say, 'All practice for you, dear.' "

Everyone had a hidden life.

Being a funeral lady gave you a shield: You could always be busy, always run for a tray if your heart burst; you were less likely to say the wrong thing. Usually you needed to attain a certain age, but Polly and Josie and Nora reached this status young, after old-guard training and by repetitive effort, working on vast quantities of food, making sure other people knew what to bring, the when and where and the cleanup.

This time, there wasn't much to do. Polly loaded her brisket into the car, picked up Nora (potato salad) and Josie (beans, inevitably underdone). At Josie's, they had a glass of wine and looked at the dress, wrapped in plastic on a hanger, that Ariel wouldn't be wearing. This was not a day for sobriety. They talked about the fight between Graham and Vinnie, but Vinnie had told Nora he'd explain later, and Nora, annoyingly, hadn't pushed. She was sorry she'd be missing the party, but it was good to get Vinnie out of town. Graham's stay hadn't been good for their marriage. She wished he'd head off into the sunset.

Nora always gripped the door handle when Polly was driving.

They stopped for other hot dishes in the ovens at the Elks Club and brought it all down to the park, where tables were laid out around a gazebo. Part of the mission was to keep people from eating immediately, before everyone arrived. Polly always underestimated the speed and gluttony of people avoiding thoughts of death.

The Delgados, having to survive the worst thing possible, didn't care. They hugged people and thanked people and wept. Ariel's stepfather picked up Helen and whirled her and told her that Ariel said she was the smartest girl on the planet, that she'd grow up and solve all the world's problems.

"How can they talk?" said Ned. "I wouldn't be able to talk. I can't talk."

Drake, who stayed close to them, barely opened his mouth. The phrase *at a loss* flitted through Polly's brain. Ned had met her there with the kids and Maude, who had known generations of Ariel's family. Jane and Merle felt they hadn't known Ariel well, and they didn't think it proper to show up. This diffidence didn't seem to affect most of the people in the park, who were embracing mass mourning with fervor. Polly wondered how many of them had really known Ariel well enough to act this way, though that was an undercurrent for any death. People were possessive, people talked of closeness and remade and recast relationships. Your own version of Ariel mattered the most.

A string quartet played—Ariel had been a cellist—and people drank beer and wine and sodas. Polly and Nora and Josie refilled and combined trays of food and plucked out drunken bees and bits of leaves.

Vinnie and Graham arrived late. Vinnie was flushed, and at a distance it was hard to see Graham's new layer of bruises. He stayed a half step behind his uncle and stopped twenty feet away from the family, marooned, while Vinnie and Nora greeted them. In the family group, everyone but Connie and Ariel's grandfather looked away. The grandfather followed Vinnie back and spoke to Graham briefly before he turned away cold-faced, shaking his head to the family.

Polly thought of how little it might bother her if they all circled Graham with rocks. But that wasn't true; it would bother her immensely.

The minister spoke, and members of the family read Bible passages and tributes. After Ariel's stepfather sat down, the microphone was opened to others—Ariel's friends, some teachers, the people she ran with. Ned spoke, and read notes from Polly and Josie and Drake. When Connie read about forgiveness, the Delgados looked uneasy.

Graham, through it all, stared at the ground. His face was puffy, maybe from crying. Everyone was stealing looks at him, wondering.

When it was Harry's turn, he talked about Ariel as a child, as they all had, but he moved on to his hopes that she would eat life up, have great loves, give great love. He talked about how badly they had all, always, wanted to protect her.

Extinguish my eyes, I'll go on seeing you.
Seal my ears, I'll go on hearing you.

Harry folded his wrinkled piece of paper. Polly focused on plumes of clouds and fought the hot heavy feeling again.

Many waters cannot quench love,
no flood can sweep it away.

When Polly looked again, Graham and Vinnie were gone.

A half hour later she hustled everyone to the car. Maude was in no hurry; Maude said they had plenty of time before the party, without acknowledging that she was doing nothing to make it happen. The proximate problem was the blue-black wedge of cloud approaching from the west. Polly pointed it out, without making a dent on Maude's agenda, and in the end Ned and Drake, seeing her panic, left to cover at least the tomatoes.

Polly decided to be indifferent, in a return of yesterday's thinking during the rose massacre. Why would she give a flying fuck about her tomatoes when Ariel was dead? Though she did, as she watched the evil black meringue of clouds decide where to open up. The faces around her, odd in the storm lighting, were oblivious to the change in the air, and mostly, she thought, to grief, but the vegetal smell of shrieking chlorophyll from the storm's progress reached her before the hail did. It didn't matter anymore: death, a deluge, destruction. She and Josie held trays over Maude's and Sam's and Helen's heads so that they could reach the car in an onslaught of ice, the skies opening up for Ariel.

They all sat together in the roar, waiting for the windshield to shatter. Maude rattled on about how a hailstorm reliably made her mother say the *F* word, then did an imitation of Dee yelling, "Fuck, fuck, fuck!"

"Fuck fuck fuck," said Helen.

Once the storm stopped, Polly drove on little balls of ice without caring about Helen swearing. Her delivery was perfect. Maude rebounded.

"What do you think of that boy, the one who lived?"

"Graham? Not much," said Polly.

"I think he's off. Sociopathic."

"Well," said Polly. "You're the expert. I've only recently become a textbook case."

"That's beneath you," snapped Maude. "I'm serious."

She was right, which made Polly slam the car door and walk inside her house without looking back at her passengers or at the garden. She was staring into her open refrigerator, wondering what to do next, when she realized she'd lost Josie and Maude and her children at the gate. She ran out expecting someone's tears, or a broken body, but she found Maude talking to Helen and Sam by the brick wall that ran along the alley.

"When I was little," said Maude, "I used to climb this wall with my father. When he first met my mother, he'd sneak over it so that the neighbors wouldn't see that he was spending time with her alone. He'd chiseled these recesses into it, and he showed me how to climb it so that I could sneak in when I felt like being naughty. Which I did do, when I was older, apologizing to him in my head."

Sam and Helen waited. "Shall I show you where to put your feet?" said Maude.

"Let me," said Polly hurriedly.

This was the oldest, strongest part of the wall, and she could see four slight recesses. It was kind of wonderful, thinking of a young man sliding his foot in the same shallow slots a hundred years earlier, all for lust and love. Polly hoisted her generous body up to the top of the cold wet bricks and loitered, looking at her hail-blasted yard, imagining Dee at twenty-five, waiting on the porch for a visitor. Why hadn't Maude brought this up on any earlier trip?

Polly lost her lettuce and basil and approximately a thousand rose and clematis blossoms. Otherwise the damage was cosmetic, though cosmetic just as dozens of judgmental relatives landed in her yard. When Sam and Helen grew bored of ice piles, Polly gave them a triple allowance to pick up the tattered leaves and branches that covered the grass, the gouged, under-ripe fruit. The children ate smashed raspberries and strawberries and flopped around, pretending they were drunk. Polly helped Maude up the stairs for her nap, and every place she touched, the bone was clear to fingertips: ulna, scapula, humerus. Polly could remember the same sense with Dee, leaning in for a kiss with fat child hands on old shoulders. Though not with Papa, who never seemed fragile.

She eased Maude into the bed in the office, then plucked a photograph from her bulletin board, one she hadn't bothered to take downstairs.

The tables were set before Maude came down again and belatedly insisted on a seating chart. Merle helped Helen and Sam collect dozens of flat rocks by the river and Sam wrote names with Sharpies. The rocks served the dual role of weighing down the tablecloths and helping Sam with the family tree. He followed Maude around, placing them where commanded, scribbling in his book and on the sticky notes Polly gave him for overflows. Polly thought the tree now looked like an image of the brain's neural pathways, like the bee-on-acid pattern of her own daily path through the house.

Maude rattled on, linking rock names to the tree. "Who's fallen, who's still attached," she said. "Look at how high I am, and yet I'm holding on."

From the corner of her eye, Polly watched Helen look worried.

"Maude is magic," Helen said, drawing her version of a tree. It looked like a maze and was covered by red apples, purple plums, yellow pears. She asked Polly what she wanted to be, and Polly said a plum. Helen made Sam a lemon and laughed at her own joke.

Polly gave Sam a list of helpful questions.

Ask For:
1. full name

2. birthplace and birth and death dates

3. profession

4. parents/siblings/children

Maude, with her first cocktail, added other possibilities, and the tree gradually filled with short, cryptic notes like *ask about his second marriage* or *ask her when she was born and then say are you sure?* Maude was careful to go back through and cross out suggestions that would cause suffering or trouble, like *Ask about 4F status*, and she told Sam that if anyone was offended, he was to blame her, and she'd blame Harry.

Polly put on a dress, tried another, ripped through the closet for a half hour while her family hid. She rarely managed to look crisp, or gauzy, for that matter, and she knew some of these people would watch her for signs and symptoms. Ned and Jane and Merle would worry that she'd forget names, and she would worry about them worrying about her, but once the party started, none of it would matter, at least as long as she was dealing with food. She could do this, dented head or no.

It began well. The surviving children of Papa's brothers arrived early, because this was the sort of people they were. Perhaps they could help set up chairs, chop something, butter the buns, pop the wine? Maude arrayed herself in the best chair, in the right amount of shade, the least wind, for her impressive receiving line, the better to relax and judge. Or maybe it was sweeter than that: Polly saw divorces and slack bodies and a consistent pattern of noses of character. But Maude saw babies, and the beloved dead who'd been their parents and grandparents.

They'd asked Graham to come an hour before the guests to set up the oyster station and the bar. Polly had a fancy new Kevlar glove, just in case Graham wasn't truly a dab hand. He came late, landing in the midst of Polly making this first round of drinks—an early run on vodka and gin— but he set up quickly, almost impressively. She peered at his new bruises and showed him the glove and some rags and the bowl with several dozen scrubbed oysters; she gave him his choice of knives and said she'd help him get started with the first platter. And then she watched in horror as he began to hack in all the wrong places.

"Watch me," said Polly, wriggling a tip in. Normally she'd have loved nothing more than having the problem of two hundred oysters, to sit in the yard with a knife and a bottle of Sancerre or Muscadet and a bowl of ice and a trash can until she tipped over or vomited. Graham chipped away at a hinge. "Did they have some different method where you worked?"

"I was a busboy."

He managed to open one. Polly ripped it out of his hand and flicked bits of shell off the mangled flesh. "Your resume said you ran the oyster bar."

"No," said Graham. "It didn't. It's okay, though. I know your memory isn't so hot."

Huh, thought Polly. "Okay, watch me again," she said, and then stepped back and let him go. "You're chewing them up," she said, "and you're losing all the liquor. And look at all that shell. That's why you check each one before you tray."

He threw the oyster into the trash can.

"Never," said Polly. "You'll get it. Watch me again."

"No."

No? Old Polly, who would have said get your fucking ass out of my restaurant, stirred. "Try it again, Graham."

He tried again, slowly, resentfully.

"All right," said Polly. "Go get backup ice, then. Use my car. The other fifty people are going to be here in ten minutes, wanting to eat."

"People will see me at the store. People from the memorial."

"Yes, and they're going to stare at you as long as you're in this town," said Polly. "Why not go back to Seattle? Don't your friends miss you?"

She said this deliberately, cruelly. She believed no one missed him, and that he missed no one. "Learn to shuck a fucking oyster. It's a simple skill. I'll go get the ice."

"Should you be driving?" Graham asked.

It was the second time he'd tried that line. His lower lip didn't move as he said it, and she thought of how odd this was before she leaned toward him. "I'm not the one who hit and killed a girl," said Polly. "And I know Ariel wasn't in love with you. I know you made that up. Did you hurt her?"

"Give it up, Poll," said Ned, behind her. "Graham, save yourself and do some work."

How long had he been there, or Helen, wailing and tugging on her dress, holding the old alarm clock? The potatoes needed to come out. Polly backed away and the party as a whole came into focus, another thirty arrivals generating a large noise. Why should a drowning stop their happiness, when everyone died anyway?

Jane and Drake helped at the bar and Josie darted around with shrimp and cheeses. Polly dealt with potatoes and poured herself a glass of wine and shucked. Across the yard, Merle tilted his head and smiled patiently at a story from a deaf man. Polly wanted him to live forever.

Cy stewed all day, right through Ariel's memorial and two hail-related car accidents, before he drove up to the Poor Farm and unburdened himself to Harry.

Graham, who had arrived late to help dig—Harry noted his puffy face, and did not inquire—was gone by then, off to help with Maude's party. Harry, listening to Cy's story, was perfectly aware that Shane was a dealer. He was aware of other things, too, having talked them over with Shari Swenson, having led Cy through a preliminary talk on speakerphone with the state lab. Harry thought things over as he drove back to town, showered and dressed for his grandmother's party, and headed for the jail.

Shane, a local kid, said there was no way the preserver had been left in the thicket to dry. It was at least thirty feet into dense underbrush—he'd scratched himself up getting it. Someone had thrown it, but it wouldn't have been Ariel, who'd been a year behind him in grade school. She was strong, but not strong enough to throw the jacket that high and far.

When Harry arrived at the party, a maddening hour late, Polly ran to him through the open gate between the front and back yards, intending to have him help with the whole oyster shit show, get Maude off gimlets and on to something lighter, run interference in family squabbles. Harry nodded but walked on, and in hindsight, he had the look of a bad fairy arriving in a Brothers Grimm story. He crooked his finger to Graham through the open gate in the six-foot wood fence, and Graham, possibly thinking he was getting sprung, put down a mauled oyster and walked through. The gate swung shut and a moment later shook. Polly ran to open it and they all watched Harry punch Graham a second time and Graham rake at Harry's hand with the oyster knife. Harry howled and hit Graham again. Blood everywhere, blood flying out of Harry's hand and Graham's nose as Harry threw Graham back into the yard, hard. Ned pinned Graham's arm, and Polly stepped onto Graham's outstretched hand with the back of her right heel.

Drake picked the knife up and shut the gate, cocooning them in a private coliseum.

The crowd was surprised by all of it, attentive and ready for more, but the thrill was gone for Polly, because Harry kept repeating, "You threw her jacket away, you cruel, controlling fuck. Did you hit her? Why was there blood on it?" He stood over Graham. "What happened to her hands?"

"She caught the kayak rope. I tried to pull her in," said Graham, climbing to his feet.

More blood flooded down Harry's arm as he smacked Graham to the ground again. Harry was no bigger than Graham; it was all coordination, a cat on a drunken rabbit. "How? I thought you were in the fucking water. You said you both fell in."

"I went in after I tried to pull her in. I threw her the rope. I tried to pull her in."

"Why didn't you tell us?"

"Because I wasn't strong enough. Because I failed. Would you want to admit that?" He spat it out through a bloody mouth.

"I wouldn't want to admit anything that goes on in your fucking insect mind," said Harry. "What happened to her face? What happened earlier? What happened on the island?"

"We fucked."

Harry kicked him, then knelt next to him and whispered in his ear. Graham hissed something back and Harry put his bleeding hand over Graham's mouth and held it there until Graham started choking, blowing blood out of his nose.

"I talked to your uncle. You knew that girl you ran over in Seattle, didn't you? You fucking meant to hit her, didn't you?"

Ned wrenched Harry backward.

"I'll give you a ride home," Drake said to Graham.

"I want a ride to the hospital," said Graham.

"Get in my fucking car," said Drake.

"What did Ari say to make you angry?" screamed Harry. "'No'?"

In the kitchen, Polly helped Josie clean and stitch and wrap Harry's hand. Josie kept a kit in her truck; she'd been an EMT when Harry met her. Harry said he hoped Maude's birthday wasn't ruined. Maude, briefly joining the semicircle around Harry, said he'd made it exciting and sped off again to report on the wound, completely misunderstanding the mood of the kitchen.

"Please explain," said Polly, cleaning the oyster knife.

"He threw the preserver into the brush, and there was blood on it. The injuries on her face—I think she was alive long enough for a bruise and a scab to form," said Harry. "Her back, too. The lab agrees, informally. Maybe they'll be able to say for sure with the autopsy."

Polly thought of what she'd seen in the willows, all of the stones in the river and all the damage they could do. It stunned her, in hindsight, that anything—Ariel, a cottonwood branch—made it through the river without ripping into pieces. "No one saw her fall before they put in?"

"No," said Harry, watching a needle going in and out of his hand. "I think he hit her. Maybe more." He started to cry.

Ned opened Champagne and they toasted Maude, who, as everyone joked, had always been bloodthirsty. People were jolly, back to full roar; they all loved a little blood, and they loved Harry, chip off a three-generation block. He had Papa's middle name and he'd chosen Papa's profession.

People crowded around the photo boards and argued, birds talking at a feeder, all at once. At first, there was an annoying sameness to the conversations, braggadocio and lumpen bluster blending with mundanities: the weather then, the weather now, old affairs, unwelcome changes, their own legends. Maude made some things up, early on, which got them rolling, and she introduced everyone to Drake, who was her party trick. He was an excuse, and he embraced it. As far as Drake could tell, the whole family was simultaneously fucked up and mildly glorious. Bored old people debating a truly batshit past, getting a last word in, nattering about roadhouses in the thirties and forties, about younger drunks driving off cliffs and causing fireballs that caused conflagrations, about Italian prisoners of war and derailed trains. They'd fucked and gambled across the country, some of them across Europe, done horrible, memorable things: Polly could shut her eyes and see exploding rattlesnake dens, burning booze warehouses, a half dozen World War II stories, a gambler's body in a borrow pit. They told these stories while giggling like teenagers, wheezing and wiping their eyes.

Polly watched Sam listen and work the crowd. He wanted the strangest thing each person could remember—easier as people continued to drink—and he wrote these down as if he were taking orders, moving down the line of picnic tables. Helen followed Sam with colored pens for a while before she disappeared under the tables with the other children. When Ned carved the pig, Polly saw her dart away with some skin.

Polly hid twice during the party. The first time, she wound up in the garden, looking for aphids on the new tips of the plum tree, sliding back into green privacy. She was peering at the party like a child, like a bird from a bush, when Ned found her. "If you climb it, try not to fall," he said. "It's almost over. You don't need to run."

Half an hour later, Polly was laughing with long-suffering Merle, snickering over misbehavior during previous parties, when her glitchy peripheral vision caught Ned moving toward the house, as if on some important task. She found him upstairs, lying on the bed, staring at the ceiling. Ned had more levels of exhaustion than anyone she knew. He was a mille-feuille, a layered pastry; maybe she'd try baking one for him. Grief, resentment, the isolation of being alone within this large extended family. She took off her dress.

Later, she watched him roll a joint. Polly thought about how good the air felt moving over her body, how lucky she was to be alive and lying naked in a bed next to someone she liked. He was so dark from the days on the river, and his fingers were brown against pink nails. She thought of Papa rolling a cigarette faster than whatever Merle's friends could roll, everyone laughing at his dexterity, his amusement at their shock.

"I love you," said Ned. "What are they doing now?"

Polly sidled up to the window and peered down. "They're all fine."

"How's Jane?"

"Listening. Bemused."

"Harry says the wound on Ari's head could have been made by a paddle," said Ned.

"Another rock in the river," she said. She put her dress back on and headed down.

But an hour later, she'd mostly stopped noticing what people were doing—drinking, throwing napkins at each other, looking for canes—and began to deflate again, wind down like a drunken toddler.

"Slow down on the wine," said Ned, setting up the badminton net.

Saint Ned. You could watch his face change from a soulful, listening Irishman into a WASP autocrat, a shift in eyebrows and attention and jaw.

"They aren't thinking of her," said Polly. "Everyone's forgetting Ariel."

"No," he said. "But we haven't, and it's almost over."

When the cake came out, everyone sang badly, and Maude told more stories. Polly thought she wanted the party not only because she was the queen for the night, but so that these people, survivors and descendants, might understand her glory years before boring decades of good deeds and children, because she loved the way people admired the photos of her laughing and gorgeous and young. A definition of true death was that it happened when the last person who remembered you died, and maybe this is what panicked Maude. With this party she was forcing people to see her disappearing dead, her mother and father, sister and brothers, lovers, world. Maude was the last person to keep her father—dead at forty-four—alive, and with a completely different span, Polly might be the last to keep Papa and Dee alive, just as Helen and Sam might remember Maude.

What resounded, through the years? Ariel, Asta. All the peripheral shit faded, but it was fun in the meantime. Late in the evening, Maude started telling stories again. She had a funny habit of throwing her chin up when she was fibbing, and most of the family knew the trait.

"Murderous Swedes!" she yelled.

Polly wished she'd heard the story. Everyone laughed, but it wasn't really a joke.

Polly moved through remnants after everyone went to bed, after almost everything was cleaned up. She collected stray glasses from the lawn, made a pile of sweaters and purses by the door, emptied the dish drain, ate someone's forgotten serving of tart.

When she lost steam, she sat at one end of the heaped dining room table and read Sam's stack of family tree notes. Out of an innate sense of fairness, he'd tried to say something interesting about everyone, but some of the stories were sadder because of their brevity. Asta had been the best dancer, Papa's little brother had been brain-damaged in a fight but loved to sing. The cousins had all fought or served as nurses, in World War II, if they weren't home with babies.

At some point, as people became more incoherent, Sam had veered from biography to the life of the mind and asked people what most scared them. A wrinkled sheet with answers was tucked into the notebook. Jane, whose thesis had compared the world's apocalypse stories, was terrified by floods. Merle, whose paternal grandfather had seen a horse blow into a tree, feared tornados. Jane said Dee had been obsessed with earthquakes, and that Papa had fretted whenever a child was by a high window. Ned was sure insects would inherit the earth, and had nightmares about jellyfish. Harry imagined the ground collapsing under his feet.

They were all disaster people. Other answers:

Maude—being blind

Hans—freezing to death

Drake—looking in a mirror and seeing no face. Or falling.

Josie—nurses

Helen—Dad disappearing

Mom—deep still water

Sam—

He wasn't sure yet. Not waking up?

Polly poured one last glass of wine and looked harder at a box of snapshots Jane had put aside, mostly color from the fifties and sixties, going into the picture one more time to look at the grubby carpets and pretty furniture, the air filled with dust motes and smoke and the smell of long-lost dogs and people who took baths, not showers. Looking at the photos, Polly smelled bleach and vinegar, Ivory soap. Dee had used Murphy Oil Soap, which smelled like waxflower, and Polly did, too. Rita and Jane hugging—Polly had no memory of such a thing happening, but there they were, and it was later in the summer of 1968, because Rita's arm was bandaged. Lemon and

Merle posed by the new fence, Dee at her potting wheel, Jane at her desk. And photos—blurred and tipsy—from a party Jane and Merle had given that summer while Papa and Dee were in the city. Polly studied the profile of a man standing near Rita, who seemed so familiar. He troubled her.

14

Summer 1968

Dee and Papa hoped to go to Europe that spring but canceled because of the student riots. Now they simply planned two nights in the city—the usual trip to the doctor and dinner with friends from London—and Jane and Merle secretly, giddily, decided to have a party. She'd finished her thesis; he'd been offered a good research position at NYU.

They hid fragile things, bought cheese and salami and gallons of wine, and dragged chairs out of the basement and into the yard. People Polly had never met arrived. Rita showed up after a weeklong disappearance, but she was calm, and her agent brought along a Parisian gallery owner, a stocky American man with a booming voice and light-blue eyes, who reminded Polly of her school's bust of Beethoven. When people came inside, Polly and Edmund skittered to the banister; when people needed to use the upstairs bathroom, or came up to see the map painting, they hid in their rooms. From their windows, they watched groups walk to the greenhouse to see the other canvases, and through their floor grates they watched the gallery owner talk about Rita's art and put his arm around her. He looked up as if he knew they were there, and they recoiled.

Eventually, they climbed onto the grape arbor, something that made them feel as if they'd walked into a spy movie. They stayed there, shaded by the vines, spitting grape skins and seeds at the oblivious drunks, taking in details with Merle's binoculars. No one noticed them; no one ever looked at the edge of anything.

By 9:00 or 10:00, the mood waffled. Merle, who was relatively alert, made Edmund and Polly sandwiches and asked them to keep the drunks away from Dee and Papa's rooms. They grabbed Lemon and May and drew large signs for the bedroom doors: *Verboten!* They thought this was very funny, but beyond the door, they felt the tenor of the party swing. They played checkers with Dee's jewelry, rings versus earrings, while arguments began below the open window. The man who looked like Beethoven kept talking to Jane, and Merle didn't like it; they could hear him ask what the man thought he was doing. The man bellowed for Rita and the agent, and off they went.

In the morning, a minefield of comatose adults blocked the path to the front door. Someone had thrown up in the bathtub, and incense had burned off a plate and scorched the marble table yellow. Edmund picked up a blue worry-bead roach and put it in his pocket. Rita's room was empty. Edmund, in a good mood, wondered if she'd ever return.

Everyone was gone when Dee and Papa got home the next afternoon, and the place was almost clean. Polly watched Dee look around, seeing mostly invisible things. Edmund followed her up the stairs dragging her suitcase, and Jane stuck to the kitchen, destroying the last bits of evidence.

Papa asked Merle to make him a drink and come outside, and soon Polly saw that Merle was crying. But why? Nothing was broken, and it didn't seem as if Papa was angry. They sat quietly, Merle wiping at his face, petting the worried dog, and sipping a drink.

The big party for Papa in late August would be a combination of a birthday and retirement celebration, held at the place with the hedges where they'd gone for Edmund's birthday. Papa's brothers and his sister Inge and Perdita's sister Odile were flying in from Montana. Dee's children were all coming from California.

Dee said she was behind on everything—she'd failed to spring clean, and now she was in danger of not summer cleaning. She gave Edmund and Polly each a dollar and they stripped all the bedding; she ran both washers, the old and the new, and bullied Merle into hanging extra lines and hauling a third broken machine with a mangle outside. When the sheets and blankets were all on the line, Polly and Edmund ran between the waving linen as if it were a maze. By the time it dried, they'd lost interest and floated off toward the Sound. Jane made the beds, and for once Rita helped, before she retreated to the greenhouse to paint a hillside of sheets, which would one day sell for $50,000.

Dee had done too much, and the next day, the day before everyone arrived, Polly heard her calling and ran down the hall to the bedroom. Dee said she was just a little weak, and could Polly go find Papa for her? Tell him she needed him.

Polly ran down to the beach, waving at Papa to come out of the water, and he broke into a run, a stricken look on his gaunt face. A half hour later Jane helped him get Dee into the car, to see the doctor to find medicine to get her through the week. After they drove away, Merle marveled at the fact Dee could move at all. Jane asked him not to talk about it.

The next morning, Dee was in the kitchen, waiting for her children and other relatives to arrive, saying she felt fine. They came bearing presents—

books, puzzles, calligraphy sets—for Edmund, too. The uncles doled out $5 bills. Odile and Inge brought Edmund and Polly small cameras and a roll of film, which was gone within fifteen minutes. Maude brought them fancy chocolates.

Papa's brothers visited the city every year to argue and look at art and drink too much—old, skinny, hawk-faced men who were given to silly giggles, who liked to talk about how badly they'd behaved when they were young. Papa was the oldest, and Papa had always been in charge. Merle and Arnold shucked dozens of oysters, and the brothers offered Edmund and Polly money to eat oysters and clams, to suck on crab legs, to try the tomalley in lobster carapaces. They all drank too much wine, even Dee, whom they called the Runaway. She cooked feasts on the first and second nights but got a little snappish, and sometimes she snuck toward her greenhouse, not an easy thing to do these days. Papa bought a tin of caviar by way of apology for the circus of guests, and Dee ate most of it alone in the corner of the kitchen before anyone else knew it existed.

On the third night, the family went into Manhattan. Polly had just gotten her glasses, and the city became a spiky and glittery hive rather than a gray mound. They stayed in a hotel near the park. Polly was Eloise: She fluffed everything, bounced, peered through open doors and underneath furniture. Edmund was fascinated by the mechanics of the place, the elevator men, the dumbwaiters, the mystery of where all the people in uniform came from. They raced around the halls but at dinner they were seated apart at far corners of the long table, left to watch the waiters and women in fancy dresses, the movement of candlelight on chandeliers.

Dee was barely able to stand after the meal. Back in the rooms, Polly saw Papa giving her an injection, her arm wrapped around his neck.

On the morning of the party, Papa and Merle and Dee's sons left early to pick up the booze and wine and food, taking Edmund along. Jane and her aunts argued in the kitchen. Upstairs, Polly heard Maude's voice in Dee's room.

"Time to get out of bed, Mom."

Polly walked down the hall. "She needs her coffee," she said.

"Well, get it then, please," said Maude.

Polly made sure the tray was perfect. She found a vase for nasturtiums from the pot on the porch while Maude told everyone else in the kitchen that they were crazy to be doing their own cooking, that everyone in the family had always been insane. She let Polly carry the tray as they headed upstairs and down the long hall. Nothing moved in Rita's ocean that morning, and the only thing moving in Dee's bed was her face, a smile and her eyes looking at the flower and the steaming coffee.

"Out of bed, Mom," said Maude, gentle now. "I'll brush your hair. One more party."

"One last party," said Dee.

Papa would not wear his suit. He wore what he always wore—gray trousers, a white shirt open at the neck, sleeves rolled up. On days at home, his clothes were older or mended. A suit was saved for teaching, for dinner out with Dee, for friends' funerals, and normally for something like this. But not for something on the beach, he said to Dee.

They took a first load of food down in the midafternoon and brought Lemon. The wine and Champagne and beer were on ice and the tables were set up, tablecloths bunching in the wind. The children and the aunts and uncles all walked down to the water—it was hot and wavier than usual, almost like an ocean-side beach. Polly and Edmund tagged along with Odile and Inge as they waded in and sat back in the sand, looking at the old ladies' oddly identical horned feet, brown-gray and white-gray, the crippled hands with matching opal rings.

"We are both October babies," said Odile, piling sand on her toes. "So we gave these to each other."

They all waved to Arnold and Maude, out on Papa's boat. Arnold had rowed down from the house in case anyone wanted a ride during the party. Now, at low tide, they all helped him drag it up on the beach.

What had Polly imagined, what had she seen that day with her sharp new eyes, her tortoiseshell glasses? A hundred people, dressed for summer but in all the variety of the period. In a photo from that day, Maude wore a low-cut linen shirt and cigarette pants. She looked like the cover of a John D. MacDonald paperback. Jane wore something turquoise blue, short and sleeveless, and Polly watched her paint her toenails a deep blood-red.

Merle didn't think the Porters, the owner's children, were around, and so Polly and Edmund ran up the steps and into the woods toward the larger estate. There was nothing as beautiful as the old stables, painted with moons and stars. If only the horses were still there. When they heard voices, they bolted back down to the lawn, panicked.

"Beware," said Dee, nodding toward the Porters, who had appeared at the top of the path. "Try the labyrinth."

Dee knew they loved that word. In the maze, they'd stashed a hamper with food and sodas, towels and comic books, underused suntan lotion, a leaky float ring. Dee gave them an umbrella—a parasol—for the sun, and "the better to hide you." They set up camp in the farthest corner of the maze, the corner closest to the beach, with a gap in the yews that gave a view of the water. By going back and forth, they knew that no one could see this corner or patch of beach from the party lawn, but they could (with Merle's binoculars, taken from the glove box of the car) see the path up to the stables. The Porters never came closer than the top step on the hill, but Polly and Edmund used them as an excuse for squirrelly behavior. They took to their camp in the hedge; they took to the water. They ran west to the boat; they made a map of the party grounds with other hiding places and the food locations. The water was warm, and they walked out as far as they could touch and stayed still, waiting for fish, using a single broken scuba mask to watch fry swarm and nibble at their skinny shins. They took turns holding each other upside down to see the bottom, to try to see a scallop's eyes, to try to see a clam move. A larger shadow would send them shrieking back to shore, which always brought a pissed-off adult down to the beach.

The house and lawn filled up, and the brothers opened Champagne. As the food came out, Edmund and Polly raced around, pilfering shrimp, choosing which people to spy on and taking notes. *Tall, stripes, Nazi.* Or: *Yellow tie and polka dot lady kissed by fountain.* People gave speeches, the words drifting across the lawn and through the hedge, marooned of meaning. Halfway through a final car arrived, carrying Rita and her agent and the stocky gallery owner who had been to the wild party, the one when Dee and Papa were in the city. They listened politely to the speeches, and then walked to the drinks table. The gallery owner accepted a glass and held it away from Rita, shaking his head to the bartender; she hopped playfully, and he shook his head again.

Rita stormed away, making for the Sound. She veered around the hedge, dropped her purse and shoes in the sand, and walked straight into the water.

Edmund blasted through the hedge after her and grabbed her hand. Rita swung and hit him in the face, hard, and he fell backward. Merle ran into the water and carried Rita out with his good arm while she kicked at him. He crouched with her on the beach as she calmed down.

Edmund wiped his bloody nose with a beach towel. Polly pulled him up to the party to explain, to have Jane or Dee fix things.

"How on earth did she get here?" asked Dee, who was in a chair with her eyeglasses on, reading Papa's cards.

"Rita came with that man," said Polly.

Dee only glanced. "Who is he?" she asked.

"He has a showroom in Paris," said Jane. "He's an art dealer. We met him a couple of weeks ago, and Merle took a real dislike to him. But he might get Rita's work sold. He's sort of a good-looking man, or maybe he once was."

"Well, he's porcine now," said Dee.

"Leonine," said Jane. "But pretty eyes."

"Yes," said Dee. "He does look like he'd eat his own babies." Now she was truly looking. "But what was the name, dear?"

"Ivor Dewitt," said Jane. "How's that for pompous?"

She wasn't watching Dee, but Polly and Edmund were, and Dee looked as if she was in pain. Edmund sidled close.

"Honey," she said, touching his hair. "Can you get Papa for me, please?"

And so Edmund ran off while Polly watched Merle, soaking wet, lead Rita back up to the man. They spoke and the man finished his Champagne and put his arm around Rita's waist. Papa was next to Dee now, bending down, listening to her whisper. She pointed, and he looked for a long moment. Then he walked across the lawn.

"Have you met?" asked Merle.

"We have," said Papa. "Let's take a walk, Mr. Dewitt. Let's talk on the beach."

They headed down, bending around the maze, trailed by Rita. Polly ran after them, dodging through the maze. She knew Papa hated the man. Wrath—that part of Papa, the half-understood part, sliding out in the way he walked. They talked, Papa pacing around, before Dewitt walked back to the party. Papa spoke to Jane and Merle and Arnold, and they all smoked a cigarette; Papa put his arm around Jane and walked off with her in the other direction.

The episode was over, but Edmund returned to say Maude was taking Dee home. They could hear nothing but music from the party, voices, waves. Croquet on the lawn, a bonfire in a bronze bowl on the terrace. The lights that were strung in the trees on the perimeter of the lawn were turned on, making the rest of the grounds, the beach and maze, seem darker than they were. They ran up to the lawn for cake and played croquet and they were watching Jane dance—Jane was drinking too much wine—when Polly found her way between chairs blocked by Dewitt, who said, "Hello, little girl. Little Schuster girl."

Polly said nothing. The man was drunk. Everyone was, but he grabbed her arm with one hand and her face with the other. He tilted it, bending close and studying her.

"Let go of her," said Edmund.

The hand hurt her face. The man blinked his strange eyes and looked amused, but now Papa was walking toward them.

"Mr. Dewitt," he said. "Let's have another talk."

Dewitt let Polly go, and Edmund pulled her into the maze. At the far end, at the corner, they heard: "It will clear our heads," said Papa. "Unless yours is too muzzy."

"My head is clear," said Dewitt. "But I'm happy to row you, old man."

The men pushed the boat out, even though it was almost dark, while Lemon barked from the beach. People were still dancing, and Edmund and Polly could see Rita's hair flash in the light of the bonfire. Lemon, guard dog, finally stopped running and lay down at the entrance to the maze. Polly and Edmund tried cards, playing with Dee's fancy deck and a flashlight. All the faces were wild-eyed in the beam: They held up opposing jacks, growled, and giggled. Eventually they gave up on the dying flashlight and realized they could still see everything but color. They looked ghostly to each other and they curled up together in the blanket next to Lemon, trying to forget Jane's scary stories.

They were down to arguing about stars, tired and beginning to be cold, when they heard splashing. The sound terrified Polly, but Edmund jumped up and pushed through the hedge and they watched Papa drag himself out of the waves and stand dripping, shiny against the dark water in the half-moon light.

Old god, almost-dead god. He walked toward them. "I'm so cold. Give me that blanket, sweethearts."

"Where is that man?" asked Polly.

"Who?" asked Papa. He seemed surprised; maybe he was as drunk as everyone else.

"The man you don't like," said Polly. "Mr. Dewitt."

Papa snorted and followed Edmund and Polly through the hedge. He wrapped himself up and looked around their squalid camp.

"Did he throw you out of the boat?" asked Polly.

"No one throws me out of a boat," said Papa. "I'll admit I didn't like him, and he was drunk, and so I left him alone."

"What about the boat?" Edmund looked stricken.

"He'll return it. I showed him where to tie up. There's plenty of light out there. Don't tell anyone. Dee wouldn't be happy that I took a swim during my own party. Where is she?"

"Maude took Dee and the aunties home," said Polly.

"I'll take you to them, then," said Papa. "It's late, and now I've gotten your blanket wet. Gather your things." He took the palm of his massive hand and covered the top of Polly's head, swiveling gently so that he messed up her hair, pushing down so that she giggled and fell to her knees, batting at his legs. He did the same thing to Edmund, who shrieked as he dropped.

They took Arnold's convertible and Polly ran her finger on the goose bumps on Papa's skin while he made dramatic sounds of suffering about the cold. Edmund waved his arms around to stay warm and Lemon barked. At the house, Maude and the aunts were drinking around the table. None of them seemed surprised to see Papa wet.

Maude said, "Don't bother saying anything."

Polly and Edmund were whipped up to their small pallets, the cushions on either side of Jane and Merle's bed. They were asleep within minutes.

But in the morning, thoughts of the lost boat tortured Edmund. He cleared his throat and coughed until Polly woke. Merle was snoring and Jane's head was hidden by pillows. From Polly's side cushions, she watched Edmund's hand, disembodied on the far side, theatrically point to the door.

They crept down the stairs. The counters were covered with half-finished cases of wine and food. They picked up handfuls—grapes, ham, cheesy Italian bread—and jammed them in their mouths. Edmund's eye was black from Rita's blow, and both of them were sunburnt. Even Lemon was tired and they prodded her up. She trotted along with them on the path like a dog that knew how to heel.

The tide was just beginning to go out, and the wind of the night before had died to nothing, and the Sound was flat and mirrored. They walked far down the beach, Polly humoring Edmund, who would not stop fretting about the rowboat, and when they came around the point they saw it immediately, dragging its anchor and twenty feet out in shallow water. Edmund gave a howl and splashed out to grab it, moving faster than Polly, who saw the thing on the beach. Edmund didn't notice the body until he was towing the boat back in, almost to the shore, and when he stopped the boat bumped into him, and some loose metal trim on the side cut his leg.

A man lay facedown on the wet sand. They should have felt dread, but Polly wouldn't remember it that way. They were so tired, and the world, strange for a long time, had lately been especially unreliable. They walked slowly to the body and around it, as if they were circling a museum exhibit. Ivor Dewitt's one visible eye was open and half-filled with sand; no detail had ever been deader. Pretty violet-tinted jellyfish were marooned on his twisted white shirt, on his gray back, making him look like an iridescent sponge. A tangle of brown seaweed bound his legs together.

Blood from the cut in Edmund's leg ran into the sand. Two hermit crabs scuttled from the body toward the pooling blood and he kicked them away. He told Polly later he was sure the crabs and jellyfish would attach to him and burrow in, change the way his body was made.

Part Three

15

Saturday, July 6, 2002

These strange long nights. How long could she keep this up? These were memories, not dreams.

After Maude's party, moments from Papa's party played on a brutal loop. The cold black air, the smell of the hedge, a splash and a sigh. Polly saw the women waiting around the kitchen table, the mess on the counters still not cleared. The wet old man, Maude tragic and angry, with smeared mascara and a lit cigarette, Odile surrounding Polly and Edmund as if she were a blanket. Smoke and the curtains gusting, everyone bleary and afraid, everyone sad all over again. Papa saying, Say nothing. Or had he? Polly could feel him behind them on the stairs, softly closing the bedroom door to be alone with Dee.

Polly could see so many things: the rowboat with two men bobbing into the water, the tall ancient figure staggering out, the dead man on the beach in the morning light. But she could not see the order of all of it together, the meaning of the men in the boat and the death.

———

The state lab was theoretically closed on Saturday, but the medical examiner called Cy anyway and confirmed damage to both Ariel's hands and her right wrist, consistent with someone trying to hang on to a nylon rope by wrapping it around a wrist. They confirmed that a cut and bruise on her cheekbone occurred far enough in advance of death to bruise. There were other injuries that didn't fit well with river damage: bruising and cuts on Ariel's back that might also be antemortem, a contusion on her bicep that didn't quite align with a sweeper branch, along with a slicing cut on the right side of her head. She had vaginal abrasions, and a tampon was found pressed against her cervix. Her blood alcohol level was minuscule—perhaps a beer—and toxicology hadn't come back for other substances. There was water in her lungs. Ariel had drowned, though another head injury—this one entirely consistent with river rock, fresh-cracked during winter or high water—would have rendered her unconscious and might ultimately have killed her on dry land.

Nothing, Harry explained, was conclusive. Ariel might have fallen and cut her face; she might have chosen to have rough sex on sharp gravel, without mentioning a tampon. She might have chosen not to wear her life preserver. The blow to her arm and the narrow blow to the side of her head could have been Graham's branch, though both made no sense.

When Cy brought Graham in, Graham spoke of wild sex, of no complaints from Ariel, no mention of her period. He would never have slept with a woman having her period, and it was disgusting that she hadn't told him.

We did it twice, he said. Then we cuddled. We climbed back in and the branch happened. I lost my paddle and barely stayed on the kayak, and when I saw her I threw the rope. She caught it, and I started to pull, and I saw her head hit the rock. Her face went blank and she let go and I watched the rope unwind from her wrist. I jumped in to find her, and almost drowned myself.

Harry said that you could pull apart Graham's versions of the story—he'd been swept out with her in the beginning; he'd been able to stay in the kayak and tried and failed to save her—but there was no way to know what really happened, or at least what Harry and Cy believed happened: Graham tried, and when she turned him down, he'd thrown the preserver in a thicket and beaten and raped her. At some point, together again in the kayak, he struck her arm and her head with his paddle, knocking her into the water. The wounds on Ariel's arm and head were consistent with the edge of a paddle. Their futile search for a branch on the east side of the river—there had been no branch. There had been Graham, losing his temper a second time after whatever had happened on the island, or perhaps Graham, thinking about how Ariel would accuse him of rape. Or maybe she only failed to feed some fantasy with a loving, postcoital look.

"He kept her on that island for a long time," said Harry. "He said he waited to be rescued, but really it was Ariel who waited."

A girl says no, I don't want to. Or: No, I don't want you. I don't love you. Or the final shot: I love someone else.

Polly saw the paddle slicing through the air.

Cy let Graham go without charging him, though he would bring him in for questioning every day for a week. There was nothing to charge him with. Cy talked to prosecutors in Park and other counties, to a lawyer for the statewide battered women's network, and to the FBI, but no one knew of a successful prosecution on such grounds, not for manslaughter or rape or murder. They could question Graham again and again, but it was hard to see how it would change. The evidence just wasn't there.

There's always a true story, whether or not anyone knows it. Ariel would have tried to be nice about it with Graham, thought Polly. She might have said that it wasn't about him, just that she loved someone else. He must have tried—asked?—as soon as they'd gotten to the island, before she took the preserver off. She said no and he hit her, took her down, and a few minutes later she would have been trying to think her way out of the situation, with a bleeding face, a bruised back and vulva. She could get into the kayak with him, or he would do more. She must have thought there was a chance of surviving if she climbed into the kayak in front of him; she must have believed she would at least get home. She had no good choice, but she chose wrong.

Polly thought about older things, too, other moments that ended in the river, other men who thought the world would and should go their way, men who struck and regretted or who were only made angrier by their own guilt, who would rather have someone die than let the world know they'd done the wrong thing. Throw in a little shock, a little cowardice: A girl was better off dead.

There shouldn't have been anything wrong with Ariel climbing into that kayak, Polly thought, on a beautiful river with friends. You can't go through life expecting someone like Graham.

Don't think, Polly said to Ned and to herself. Leave all of it twisting on the ground until you know where to put it. The other people in the house, not having heard Ned on the phone, were floating with relief. The party was over, and the detritus was in no rush. The yard was littered with bits of wrapping paper and ribbon, spiral cake candles looking like bright worms in the grass—Polly thought they were squirming for a moment—napkins and drink cups. The tablecloths were akimbo or against the fence; there was an east wind, and they would have to postpone Maude's float down the river.

Polly took Sam to soccer practice, the first session before the fall rec season, and it was a relief to sit on the grass alone. No one approached her—she was older than the other mothers and tainted by Ariel and grief—and for an hour she thought of nothing but the awkwardness of boys, the jumble of sticklike shins and knobby knees. Half the kids picked their nose during every huddle with the coach, but Sam was uncoiling, running and kicking, becoming more of a physical being, though he would never be a jock. He still read obsessively, and he was openhearted, with no obvious chips and a rich, perverse sense of humor. In the midst of the weirdness that spring and summer, he and Helen reached a kind of balance. They sized things up together, we two against the world.

Polly and Ned had both loved and been surprised by Sam's boyness. When Helen arrived, part of Polly's exhausted brain watched Ned react. He covered her tiny bedroom with posters of color—a Goethe wheel and a Runge ball, shades of blues and greens, yellows and peach and orange— and a beautiful print of the alphabet in ten different scripts. His daughter would not be limited to pink and purple. Her crib mobile was made of sea creatures; her stuffed animals were carnivores. Her pajamas were stripes, her flower prints were bold, her china-headed doll had an indigo dress and delicate hands. When Helen turned three, her presents were six-guns and a cowboy hat and a pirate ship and a plastic saber; for Christmas she'd gotten a tool set and a doctor's kit. That spring, Ned perched her on a stool over the car engine while he worked on it, and let her demolish the old wind-up alarm with real tools while he cooked Easter dinner. He got Sam to teach Helen to hit a T-ball and play marbles, and he taught Sam to sew and cook. And when he felt bad for taking Sam's future relatively for granted, he took him alone for the first week of the trip they made to Ireland.

Ned worked it. He was going to stave off both the modern girl's and the old girl's world as long as he could, and either as a result or by nature, Helen, though not a brat, was obedient without being obeisant, figuring out how to handle the inevitable—tasks, unpleasantnesses like doctors and swim lessons or picking up her room—without drama but without full agreement. Her lip already curled. Polly hoped to somehow make enough money to go on a world tour starting with Helen's thirteenth birthday, some Möbius strip of distraction. Jane's way of getting Polly through that period had been to have another three children, and Polly wasn't going to go that route.

On a camping trip to the Sunlight Basin the year before, Vinnie had watched Helen spin around the campsite, dancing with a plastic tiger.

"She's a doll," said Vinnie.

"Don't call her a doll," snapped Ned. "Maybe a treasure, or a jewel. I don't want her to be anyone's fucking doll."

It was hard to be a girl. It was hard to be anything.

Maude asked to eat at home again. She wanted to sit in the yard and study the mountains, which hadn't changed a bit since her childhood, and she wanted to think of her mother in the garden while she watched Helen in her mud pile. It was so soothing, she said. Dee would be so happy to know this.

Ned grilled lamb. Polly watched Maude from the kitchen while she made a salad, thinking that they needed to get her to a doctor, because something was going on, beyond being ninety. Then the scene through the window dropped away. The world turned green, as if it were made of water, and she saw a door. Polly ran down the hall and through the map, circling mountains and leaping over rivers, tricked into looking in all the wrong places while something awful was happening that she should prevent, while Dee called to her from downstairs—something was burning, and now everyone was yelling.

The smoke alarm sounded. Polly gave Ned a big smile as he jerked the oven door open.

"You're tired," he said, throwing pistachio cinders into the alley; Polly had been toasting them for the salad. "It's been a while. Don't fret."

Liar. Polly shooed magpies away until she was sure they wouldn't burn their beaks or their feet on the smoking nuts.

"Where'd you go?" asked Ned.

"Into the map," she said. "Rita's map."

After dinner, Sam brought out his family tree again, but Jane and Merle were off with friends, and Maude and Josie and Harry were leaving to visit Harry's mother, who was just back from seeing a new grandchild. How lovely to have babies born, said Maude to Josie.

Sam, miffed, pointed to the empty circle above Jane's name. "Your grandmother can fill that in," Maude told Sam.

"Can she?" asked Polly.

"Of course she can," said Maude. "Just because she doesn't talk about it doesn't mean she doesn't know."

"Is he alive?"

"I believe you know the answer to that question," said Maude. Harry was helping her to the door, and looked back at Polly, shaking his head in confusion.

Where to begin a story? Polly had hauled her childhood along through life without examination. She'd relied on it being there if she needed to find it, but she disliked navel-gazing, even before she needed to pretend her head felt just fine. Biographies bored her, and she connected most bouts of self-examination with depression.

But the past had become much more interesting since the accident, once she worried she was losing the ability to bring it back, once she caught herself having the urge to make things up. She needed to find a balance between what she'd remembered, what she'd imagined, what she'd forgotten to consider, and what had been knocked out of her when she bounced on the pavement. And it started with Jane's blue lovely eyes—no one else in the family had those eyes—and Jane's invisible mother.

Understanding Asta, over time: Polly's first version was a soft-featured girl on Jane's bedside table, a dead girl who was darker and older than Evie in the paired portraits of Polly's childhood. Both were laughing, both were dead in accidents, both still made people cry decades later. The second version of Asta, after they left New York for Michigan: understanding that Jane never knew her mother, couldn't remember her, and felt that Dee, who'd raised her, was her real mother. The third, as a teenager on a trip to Livingston: understanding that Asta died when her car went off the road and into the river when Jane was not quite two. And as a teenager, the fourth and central question: Who was Jane's father? An openly out-of-wedlock baby in 1939 was no average thing. Polly asked for years and was dismissed.

The fifth, this last week: that Asta hadn't been alone, and the sixth, that she'd drowned. The seventh, yesterday: The man was drunk, survived, and left Asta to die.

The eighth was Polly understanding that she might already know the end of the story.

Ned was on the phone, pacing in the garden. Polly knew he was talking to Drake, and she guessed it was about Graham. She was offended that he kept the conversation private, that everyone kept secrets from her. She got the kids to bed and tried to order her thoughts by sorting Drake's backlog of manuscripts, listening for Harry's car and the return of Maude. She missed hearing it, somehow, and it was almost nine before she smelled tobacco and looked outside to see Maude and Harry smoking surreptitious cigarettes in the garden, while Helen was back to her golem game in the corner. Ned and Sam were reading on the front porch, a stealth location to avoid a Maude inquisition.

"Don't tell Josie," said Harry, handing Maude the ashtray.

"Will you tell me the truth, Maude?" asked Polly.

Maude looked at the moon, looked at Harry, asked for a titch of sherry, asked for another cigarette, and spoke.

Asta fell in love with a college man (there was an archaic phrase, thought Polly, and Maude delivered it with sarcasm) at a weekend party in Providence, and for a few months the world was a lovely place. A good-looking, rich, intelligent boy. He proposed and Asta brought him home that summer, but that fall, after she found out she was pregnant, he stopped answering his phone. When she took the train to Providence to see him, he cried and blamed his parents for backing out of the engagement, then got drunk and called her a slut in front of his fraternity brothers. A proctor led her out of the dormitory. Asta went back to Bryn Mawr and stayed in her room for a week, until a friend talked to the school authorities. She bolted from Philadelphia for New York and Papa found her two weeks later in a hotel.

By then it was too late to do anything about the pregnancy and he brought Asta home, all of them moving around town with a distinct lack of shame that people came to admire. Dee gave a baby shower, and everyone came. People loved Asta and people hated to see her wronged. Jane was born, and things were more or less fine until the man reappeared.

The ninth version of the story: The boy Asta was with when she died in the river had been Jane's father. Though he abandoned Asta when he learned she was pregnant, he returned two years later to see her—no one knew why, or why she'd agreed—while Dee and Papa were visiting Maude in California. He knocked on the door of the house, this house, ignored the baby that Asta handed to Odile and Inge as she left, and took her off for a drive in a green Ford. The next morning, she was found drowned in the car in the river, and the boy was gone.

And that was that? Of course not. Maude and Papa and Dee drove north from California for a day and a night and saw Asta's body. She had a black eye and a healing split lip from a beating that must have happened earlier in the day, and they found that though she'd suffered a blow to the head, she'd died of drowning. The water wasn't that deep—the boy fled and left her to die. And so it wasn't just that he'd caused the accident. Seeing her lovely face after the agony of drowning—Maude said it pushed Papa around a corner, forever. He hired a private detective, but the boy enlisted, shipping out days before the detective reached his parents' house. Pearl Harbor was timely for him.

The bats were herding mosquitos again, listening. Harry leaned back in the lawn chair with his eyes closed.

"Jesus," he said. "You'd never get over wanting to kill him."

"It was her bad luck to have met him, and none of her fault," said Maude. "Papa and Mother felt that if they'd made other choices, she'd be alive. Maybe if they'd stayed in California, or in Europe, this stuck-up Ivy League brat, this piece of inbred crap, wouldn't have eaten her up and dropped her like trash."

They couldn't bear to stay near the icy river. They couldn't run away with Jane to Europe because of the war, and they went down to Tucson and rented a house in the Sam Hughes neighborhood. Papa volunteered on a dig of Hohokam irrigation systems and they took trips to Mexico. He checked with a friend in Washington every few months, hoping the boy would be killed by the Germans, the Japanese, in friendly fire, anything, but he stayed in Paris and never came back, even when his parents died. Maude and her cousins thought of trying to find him after the war, but one of them was always pregnant, and ultimately all of them had too much to lose.

Jane remembered hummingbirds and beautiful flowers, and like Polly, she remembered train rides across the country. But eventually Papa and Dee connected both Arizona and Montana, places where they'd survived their daughter, with pain, and so they bought the place in Stony Brook and went back and forth to postwar Europe. Papa poured himself into work, teaching half the year and going on digs to all the reachable places ripped open by the war. He wanted to soak into the old world like blood. They still came back to Montana for summers for a few years, but the place was ash to them. Dee turned her back on her garden. After 1960, when her friend Margaret died, they never returned.

"What was his name?" asked Polly.

"What does it matter?"

"It matters to me. He was my grandfather."

Maude watched her. "Ivor Dewitt. Fancy family. He became an art dealer."

"Why didn't he marry Asta?" asked Polly, who thought she managed to keep her face blank. "She was beautiful, Papa had money."

Maude stubbed out her cigarette and rattled her ice cubes. "When he visited us in Montana, after they were engaged, he was quite irritable, and we think he looked around at the town and the house and just thought we were a little too scrubby and mysterious, not up to snuff. Perdita's patchy family background—who knows? Some people do cruel things for no reason at all."

Maude went to bed and Harry drove home. When Jane returned, Polly walked over to the alley house and they talked about whether it might rain for Maude's float, and if so, what to do—a matinee?

"Are you all right?" said Jane. "You look odd."

"I'm thinking," said Polly. "Believe it or not."

Ned was still hiding on the front porch with a book, a halo of bugs surrounding the wall light. Polly floated around, making a list, cleaning up stray bits, and waved peacefully when he headed upstairs.

Polly of the blinking mind. The man at the party, the man on the beach—she'd never forgotten him, but she'd been blind to the context, never even talking with Ned about it. Until now, the cause and effect, the *why* of the bad man—the two bad men—getting into the boat, was what Jane as a student called an onion story, an artichoke story. It confused, and Polly shied away. Now she needed confirmation, but the blinking thought felt red, not green—there was a point to Jane's willful ignorance. Polly shouldn't think any memory was true, ever, especially after wine, especially when she was tired. Ivor was one of those turn-of-the-century names that might seem like a one-off, but nothing in the world ever really was, and why would her memory be right about the last name? Maybe it had been Dewar, Dworkin. She'd been eight.

Still, she saw Papa's grim face, white against the green hedges of that old estate, water dripping off his clothes. She went down to the dining room table for the photo she'd pulled off the board earlier, an old man rinsing himself with a hose after a swim, grinning at laughing children, the children they'd been. He was so old but so strong, the long muscles on his arms withered but still defined, every motion still sure and coordinated. Had he felt relief when he let the boat go and swam back to shore?

Upstairs, in bed, Ned looked up from a cookbook. In times like these he stuck with nonfiction. "Are you coming soon?"

"I won't be long," said Polly. "I'll be quiet."

"Are you all right?"

Everyone was asking that; her pride in a poker face was dented. "I'm fine," said Polly. "I'll explain later. I promise."

Before her accident he might have been impatient. At the computer, tucked on the cramped landing to make way for Maude, Polly wasted time reading about another Ivor—Novello—before she finally searched the *New York Times* for an obituary. If the Dewitts were that sort of family, that sort of paper might show a trace. Polly watched her shitty dusty curtains blow in the first cool nighttime gust to breach the heat of the landing, the dial-up connection laboring along.

The screen snapped into focus: Ivor Madison Dewitt, gallery owner and ex-pat, who'd spent his postwar years (after serving in noncombat positions, as the *Times* somewhat bitchily pointed out) in Paris. Married three times, no children, born 1917, dead August 30, 1968, of drowning, near Stony Brook. No photo, but Polly could see his face, the sand in his open eye.

Things Polly had seen, without really seeing: the way Papa touched Dee, the way her parents danced, Ivor teasing Rita with a glass, the things on Papa's desk that didn't glitter, objects that were subtler but still strange—a small hammer, a ruler, a collection of eyeglasses, a stone bird's foot, a ribbon with a lock of dark hair, a quote from Hart Crane that he'd copied out in his European hand: *Because it is bitter, and it is my heart.*

And one man wading out of the Sound, after two had gone out in a boat. Polly didn't think he'd asked the people in the kitchen to be quiet when he drove them home. That was their decision.

She peered around the corner—Ned's light was on, but he was asleep with the cookbook on his chest.

The last version of the story of Asta: Papa sidestepped violence for almost thirty years, but when a man offers his throat to you, you fall back to the habit of revenge. You know how to do it; you know you're good at it. The men in the boat rowed out over the still water, speaking quietly, knowing incrementally what was about to happen. For Ivor Dewitt, disbelief, because why should he have worried about getting into a boat with an ancient academic? Ivor couldn't have imagined that this old, old man would row them out of sight, knock him into the water with an oar, and hold him under until he drowned.

Polly typed in Papa's name, wondering why she'd never done this before, and when she finished reading his obituary, she went to wake Ned. They'd already really known. They just hadn't understood that the man Papa killed was Jane's father, Polly's grandfather.

16

The End of the World, 1968

The afternoon after the party, after finding the dead man on the beach, while the uncles, unimpressed with the body, were off seeking lobster, and the aunts were on a walk, and Dee and Papa were having a nap, the police arrived and Jane sent Polly upstairs to fetch Papa.

Papa and Dee always looked serene when they slept. His arm was under her head, and he opened his eyes before Polly could say anything, and put a finger to his lips, and slid away from his wife carefully, so that she didn't wake. Dee had not been able to get up that morning.

Downstairs, Jane made Polly stay with her in the kitchen and Papa took the police into the front room. They heard him say that he'd gone with Mr. Dewitt to the beach to talk, after breaking up the argument with his son-in-law. Merle Schuster was a possessive man with a beautiful wife. Papa managed to cool the situation when Mr. Dewitt, seeing the boat, mentioned he'd been a rower in college, and Papa unwisely allowed him to take it, if only to keep the peace. He went out with Mr. Dewitt just long enough to show him a trick or two about how the boat handled, and warn about tides, and to show him where he kept it anchored.

Maude brought in coffee, and when the police asked if she'd dealt with Mr. Dewitt, she said he'd been a complete boor. But he was an important gallery owner, and helpful for Mrs. Ward's career. An uninvited, drunken, difficult guest, but nevertheless a guest.

It was odd, said the police, and Papa agreed. But when a drunk wants your boat, and says he rowed for Brown, and you'd rather not continue talking to him, you let him go. Mr. Dewitt was in a bad mood, and he was putting Papa in one, making him miss his own party. Understandably, he wanted to head back in, and when Mr. Dewitt wanted to continue his boat ride, Papa asked to be brought near shore. There was still some light, and if someone saw him wet, it's because he became wet in the course of getting out of his boat. He drove the children home and changed before he returned, and if he had not mentioned this at the outset, it's fair to say that he was not proud of having driven children after so many cocktails, wet, and that he was annoyed by the whole irksome episode. They could check with Mr. Galante, the poet, or Mr. Schuster—he'd seen them on his return. And of course all the people who were still awake at the house when he brought the children home. He hadn't seen Mr. Dewitt again until the children found his body. An awful thing for them to see. He didn't know how Mr. Dewitt managed to drown, but the man was a drunk, out of shape, used to calm rivers, not blustery waves.

As Papa showed them out, he said, I'm ninety, sirs. I'm flattered that you think me capable of murder. He moved like a very old man when he opened the door and shook their hands.

The next day, a Sunday, the relatives said goodbye. Maude was virtually liquid, her eyes coursing with tears. Everyone took to a corner. Polly read all of *The Horse and His Boy* and Edmund read two new Hardy Boys mysteries from Maude. Papa stayed in his study but with the door open, pacing about, so that he was framed against the window at the end of the hall whenever Polly came out of her room. Dee managed to get out of bed and wrote letters in the kitchen, warm in the sunlight, letter after letter. She said her treatment always made her feel ill for a few days.

Monday was a blur, the first day of school. It was better going with Edmund, but Polly still worried about her clothes, about pencils, notebooks, which door to enter. Dee was up and cooking when they got off the bus— chicken and biscuits, because she said a full potpie was beyond her. Edmund chopped carrots and parsley and Dee applauded his precision. Polly chopped an onion, complaining, and set the timer for batches of biscuits. Papa spent the day cleaning out his office at Columbia and gave them each gifts: Roman coins, a bone whistle and beads, glass bowls. When Jane and Merle came home and they ate dinner, the world was almost normal.

Papa carried Dee up to bed that night. He wouldn't let Merle help, though he was nice about it. On Tuesday, Papa and Dee went to the city for a doctor's appointment and brought back Chinese duck and sauce and thin pancakes. After Papa carried Dee back upstairs, she sent Polly and Edmund to find boxes in the attic, things she wanted to see again. They forgot what they were doing while sorting through compasses and photographs and rock specimens, pricking their fingers on the spinning wheel and pretending to change into one of Papa's statues. Then they heard the thumping cane, and hurried down, and spent the rest of the evening with Dee, Polly sitting in bed next to her while Edmund played solitaire on the floor, May sometimes knocking cards into the wrong pile. Polly helped sort through jewelry cases and photos while Dee fretted that she should have gotten this chore done when Maude and the aunts were in town. There was not enough time in the world, Dee said while they tried to match earrings, find every pearl from a broken string. Try to never be bored. She told them stories, wandering in time and between people, about all the places she'd been and they should visit, cities and oceans she'd seen with her father, Walton—unbalanced but in a different way than Rita—and others with Maude's sweet father Lewis before he died young, of malaria. She'd had two great loves; she'd had such luck.

Mostly, she talked about Papa, her sweet Henning, her oldest friend, twenty years of knowing each other through many hard things even before they married. After they'd each been widowed, Dee took the train to Los Angeles—he was forever meeting her at a train—and he drove her around town in his fancy car, took her to dinner and to gardens and gave her too much wine. She always called him Hen, a silly name for a scary man, and he always called her Dulcy but that night he teased her with Dulcinea, her full name. It meant sweetness but it was a name for tilting at windmills, meant for a windy place, and when they drove to his beach cottage that night and went swimming in the ocean, it was as if the water were a magic potion. The world changed, and they were in love. That was all, and it was everything.

She snapped her weak, knotted fingers for emphasis, just a whisper of a sound.

"Shazam," said Edmund, putting down the cards and climbing up on the bed.

"Abracadabra," said Dee, kissing Edmund. "Life is good," she said. "Try not to forget that."

Nothing seemed wrong, or more wrong than usual, but that night, through the bedroom wall, Polly heard the wavery edge of Jane's voice as she talked to Merle: "Something's going on. They aren't telling the truth about the doctor."

On Wednesday, Papa and Dee planned to be in the city again, and said they'd be gone until dinner. Jane was in class until 5:00. Merle was supposed to meet a plumber at 3:00 at the house. Once again, he welcomed an excuse to skip teaching, and said he'd be home when Polly and Edmund got off the bus at 3:30. Papa got up early to make a better breakfast, a Swede spread. He peeled their soft-boiled eggs, spread raspberry jam on their toast, and gave them $5 of belated school-starting money. They kissed Dee, in bed with coffee, and bopped off in relative happiness.

But the plumber called Merle at the college office to cancel, and with a rare free afternoon, Merle shopped for a good bottle of wine and a big bag of clams, in hopes that Dee would be up to cooking, because though Jane tried, she wasn't Dee yet. He stopped at a bookstore and bought a novel by John Fowles, and he didn't forget the children, exactly, but he did forget to check his watch. He was still walking to his car in the village, laden with bags, as they climbed off the bus at the house.

Polly poured herself some milk, found the cookies, spread out the envelopes and magazines from the mailbox. Edmund covered an apple with peanut butter. Polly wondered what Dee and Papa would do in the city, besides visit the doctor. She thought of the old men on the sidewalk, with their endless chess game.

Edmund was already in his room, arranging his notebooks, coming up with some grand plan for his glorious fourth-grade year, when Polly saw that Papa and Dee hadn't taken the car. She ran upstairs to their room, because of course they'd overslept from their nap. And because the note on the door had been left for someone tall—Merle—she didn't see it. She knocked and went in, and they were as always when they slept, young looking, curled up together, his arm under her head. May lay at the foot of the bed, watching Polly, who crept closer and waited for someone to move.

She called for Edmund, who came to the doorway but no further.

17

The Beginning
of the World, 1968

The beginning of the world: According to Jane, it was a mother, a baby's skin reaching the air, the air itself.

Water, said Papa. Skin and air are not the beginning of the world, just the beginning of the story.

The beginning of Papa: a village in southern Sweden in 1878, in a farmhouse five miles from the ocean. He'd loved his mother, been terrified of his father.

The beginning of Dee: an orchard town on Lake Erie in the spring of 1880. She'd loved everyone always, she said, even when she'd left them. She'd had more than one life, too.

Polly and Edmund, listening to Papa and Dee in the car on the way to the Met in 1968, wandering through halls of ruined worlds. Everything was larger because they were smaller back then, passing objects that were once people, explanations of the world, the night and day and winter and summer: eggs, monsters, fire spurting out of mountains, a woman walking out of the sea, an old god biting off a child's head. So many stories were about the mother or father dying, and the child left alone. It doesn't happen so much anymore, said Dee, but when it does, you must remember you are surrounded by other people. She didn't admit that they might not be the people you'd choose.

Polly believed then, and she was more or less right, that Papa and Dee willed this to happen, floated off into the air, turned to smoke and memory. Like a fairy tale, like a myth, they'd lain down together and stopped, changed nature, become air. Magic, despite the ambulance, the police, Jane sobbing, people talking about enough morphine to take out a five-ring circus. Dee's pancreatic cancer meant she was down to weeks and would be in increasing pain; Papa would not abandon her to a hospital and had no interest in being on the planet without her. He had at points in the past failed her, but not now.

Everything seemed to disappear with them, the whole nature of the house and its sounds and smells and meaning. Polly could not comprehend that Papa and Dee were not in the corner of her eye, behind a door, that they weren't the breeze that moved through a room or the footsteps on the ceiling. Sometimes she thought she saw them in the hall or on a sidewalk, dissolving in the sunlight, close enough to touch her. And when they couldn't, her grief was as fresh and as physical as walking out of a warm room into a cold one. This time, she knew no one was hiding. They were gone, and the only way to keep them was to store them in her mind.

In the long, bleak confusion that followed their deaths, no one paid much attention to Edmund and Polly. Arnold took them to a movie that first night, while the bodies were being taken away, and cried through the whole thing. Papa had been his oldest friend through love and murder and poetry, cases of wine, years of arguments about gods and art.

No one made Polly or Edmund go to school. No one made them do anything or talked about any of it. And even earlier, after the body on the beach, only Dee had tried to help. Put your memories in a box, she said, good and bad, and pull them out when you need them, or can bear them. Or keep them hidden away, but know that it's up to you.

Maude came back, along with Papa's brother Ansel. Rita, who vanished after the party, returned several times and took most of her canvases out of the greenhouse. Papa and Dee came back, in a way: They were in the last pretty jars Dee made, trapped by Merle's cork stoppers.

On a Monday a week later, Polly and Edmund got up together and dressed and went off to school on their own. Polly wrote Edmund's excuse note, and Edmund wrote hers, and they both used the handwriting they'd learned from Dee and Papa. At night they could hear Merle and Jane talking about moving back to Michigan, to be in a different place. Really it was just the same as five years earlier, running away after Evie's and Frank's deaths. Polly remembered thinking this, and being angry, but she doubted it would make a difference if she argued. Rita's brother arrived from Boston. He was nothing like Rita and he clearly didn't approve of her, or believe in her madness, but Edmund, who refused to stay in a hotel with him, talked about running away. He'd found Papa's keys to the apartment in the city. No one would expect them to go there. The old men on the sidewalk would help them. They could take one of the diamonds from Dee's jewelry box and a bag of her late plums to eat, and then they'd come up with a new place and a new plan.

But before Edmund could convince her to disappear with the key, before Polly could argue with her parents, they took Edmund away: Rita and her silent, resentful brother, a brown car, bound for some unimaginable place. Polly couldn't look at his face as he walked down the stairs and the sidewalk, guess his despair, think about the fact that he might have believed that she and her family lived on in the house he'd loved on Christian Avenue, as if he'd never been there.

Rita wouldn't kill herself until he was ten.

18

Sunday, July 7, 2002

Polly poured a huge whiskey before she went to bed, a big brown Ned-sized drink, and fell into dreams, literally. A whole night of teetering on edges: She was in the attic, watching Papa help Dee out of the car, she was falling from a horse, seeing the underside of leaves as Edmund looked down at her, she was lying on leaves watching a sky shedding snowflakes, she was at her bedroom window, watching Dee and three children make a pile of icicles.

Ned was having his own dream, doglike twitches and muttering. The wind made the house creak and Polly pulled an extra blanket over both of them and drifted away again. She was small, lying on a beach next to Dee, who was young and wearing a bathing suit and telling Polly important things while Papa swam in the background. The sense of falling started again—waves made the ground erode under Polly's body, but Dee held on.

When Ned woke up to an empty bed, he walked downstairs to find the door open and Polly in a blanket at the picnic table.

"Poll?"

"I'm just saying hello to Dee," said Polly. "She's only here for a minute."

"Give her my love," said Ned.

The earworm of the morning, thanks to Maude, who was humming in the bathtub:

> *Bobby Shafto's gone to sea*
> *silver buckles on his knee.*
> *He'll come back and marry me,*
> *pretty Bobby Shafto.*

Polly paused by the bathroom door a half hour later. If Maude couldn't get out of the tub, or fell, would she call for help? And if she fell, how long would it take her to recover, to be able to get on a plane? Polly felt a little cold around the gills. She bent closer to the door and heard:

> *I'm just wild about Harry, and Harry's wild about me . . .*

Maude splashed. "I can hear you looming out there," she said. "And I'm quite all right."

Polly retreated. She was passing the stairwell window when a thunk startled her. A ball hadn't shattered the glass. She looked down at Ned, smiling, and Sam, stricken and clutching a tennis racquet.

"Hey, Rapunzel," said Ned.

"Hey, what?" said Polly.

"Push down your hair."

Sam thought this was very funny.

> *Maude doc appointment*
> *Maude rebook flight?*

dinner—Szechuan?
float

There was no getting around the original list: Maude wanted to go on a float; she thought they'd see some birds. What sorts of snacks should they pack? And should they bring wine, or something more assertive? The mind reeled at the possibilities.

Polly headed off to walk the dogs and stop at the restaurant for supplies. In the alley, she paused politely: two rabbits having a standoff, neither of them budging. She honked and they shot into her garden. She hated them, gently, as she drove on to the restaurant, wondering at any deeper meaning.

She was foraging for ice and something edible when Graham entered the kitchen and stood next to her. Polly did not quite scream. She did, however, think, Look, an actual murderer. He seemed larger—was that a trick of his new title, or was it because he was wearing shorts and a T-shirt, and more of him was revealed? The river injuries were fading, but Harry's marks were iridescent: purple and yellow, a tinge of green. Now the scrapes on his face and throat looked different to her, as if they might have been made by a woman's nails, and she wondered if his scabbed knees had less to do with saving himself than from raping another human on the shingle.

"You owe me money," said Graham. "Eleven hours, plus your party."

She noticed he was holding car keys, and through the window she saw a running Jeep. "Of course," said Polly.

He followed her into the kitchen, as always, a little too close. Polly waved to an arriving pastry chef. She hated that she was relieved to see someone. "Are you happy to be driving again?"

"Sure."

"You saved up?"

"My father promised."

"What, if you stayed out of trouble?"

He shrugged; he wanted her to speed up.

"In Seattle, you knew the girl you hit, didn't you?" said Polly. "People said you were upset, that it was traumatic."

"I didn't know her very well," said Graham. He was wary. "Of course it was traumatic."

"It's strange that you happened to hit someone you knew at all," said Polly. "Maybe she turned you down, too?"

"No one's ever turned me down," said Graham.

Polly found the check and put it down on the counter rather than handing it to him. "You killed a girl with a car, you killed a girl on the water. I'm hoping you'll be hit by a fucking train."

"That's not true. And you're crazy. Everyone knows you can't think straight."

Polly watched him, waiting him out, while a deep flush covered his face, darkened the marks.

"It's not true," he said again.

"I don't believe you," said Polly.

Graham lifted a stool and smashed it onto the floor, picked up the check, and walked out. Polly told the pastry chef not to worry about it.

Polly took the dogs to the river, climbed down the bank, and stayed there by the water, in the sunlight, while the dogs splashed and sniffed and her heart slowed. She looked around for a place to lie down, but it wasn't that kind of stretch. She flipped a rock, Helen style, and stared down at some sort of larva, gray and shiny and wriggling.

The dogs shot by after a small furred animal, and a smell of musk floated past. Maybe a mink, but not a skunk, thank god. Invisible animals scrabbling around her, all the things she didn't usually notice screaming to be seen, when all she could see were dead girls leaving their swing sets, ponies, dance floors, velvet chairs or dirt-poor houses for twirling cars, for spinning rivers, for appointments with shitty humans. If you were a girl, so much of life was down to luck, walking home at the wrong time, with the wrong man behind you. It came down to your mother picking the wrong second husband, to errors of trust, to bad timing.

None of it had happened to Polly. One man in the hallway of the Thompson Street apartment building when she was four, the Porter girl at the beach estate, one time when she almost didn't lie to get out of a strange-eyed date's car in high school. His eyes reminded her of veering away from Rita's eyes, and maybe she'd veered away from crazy all her life afterward, maybe knowing Rita had made her just wary enough.

But mostly Polly had been lucky, and she knew it. Never the wrong person on the stairs, in a car, in a boat, in her bed, someone she'd welcome as sane, someone who would slip his humanity. Instead Polly had sweet boys, randy boys, smart boys, run-of-the-mill feckless boys. There were some shits, but she had good friends, cousins, teachers, brothers, lovers. It wasn't fair, but it was a relief. She recognized her good fortune.

Her memories were waking up like her eyes. One bad man brings another to mind. Polly faced west, to where Ariel had been, to where the bridge had been and Asta had last breathed air. It didn't seem to matter that it had been sixty-one years ago, any more than the thought of Ariel was easier on the sixth rather than the first day.

She climbed back up to the path. A stroller approached, and Jane's dog once again barked. It didn't jar Polly out of her state. Back in the car, on the way home, she wondered how anyone could miss the snakeskin on the road, the thin new screen of smoke in the air from Oregon fires, the man watching from the window across the street when she came to a stop. Why could she see these things and not the car coming from the left?

She braked in time. No one had to know.

They set off in a convoy, shuttled the cars, and put in at Loch Leven. They'd brought too much food for a picnic. Polly and Ned and the kids took their drift boat, Jane rode with Maude in Drake's raft, and Merle paddled defiantly in a single kayak, one arm making up for the other, going faster than anyone else. Josie and Harry used a double kayak, and at one point when they trailed the others, Ned nodded, and Polly looked to see Harry swing his paddle experimentally at Josie, who was tilting, maybe trying to see how far she could lean without losing her balance. They were going to keep breaking their minds and hearts over Graham's guilt.

The silence and isolation of the river was a relief. There wasn't much you could do on the planet more beautiful than riding the surface of the water through this landscape. The water was moving, you were moving, the world had a combined hush and roar. Swallows and a golden eagle, ducks and herons. When they passed an old washing machine jutting out between 1930s cars, Polly pointed to the mangle and tried to explain to Sam and Helen. They followed Drake down a chute to a better channel, pulling to reach a beach on the far end of the island where Graham said he'd stopped with Ariel on that last day. Drake knew his stuff; people from his former life would have been stunned.

Into the boat, out of the boat. Maude said, "Somewhere inside, I am spring. But I'm never doing this again, except in ash form."

They all swam, except for Maude, who sat in a folding chair in shallow water and wiggled her old toes. A sandbar upstream created a wide, calm pool, and Jane and Polly could stand waist-deep and tow the children around by their preservers, though Helen could probably swim better than Polly now. They dipped their faces underwater together and opened their eyes to see Sam swim beneath their arms. The others made for a deeper, larger pool twenty yards away, and Polly watched Drake check the depth and take running jumps.

Ned followed Drake once, then twice. Polly waited to see his head again, and when she waited too long, her blood began to pound. But there he was, crawling out of the river downstream, dripping, seeing the look on her face and trotting toward her, telling her everything was fine. "See the day, Polly. It's beautiful."

"Where's Harry?" asked Maude.

"Looking for things," said Josie.

Cornflower-blue shorts, ripped off a girl with Titian red hair, thought Polly. When Harry returned, shaking his head, Drake disappeared. Eventually Polly worried and followed him around the bend of the island.

She found him sitting near the water, holding a plastic bag with Ariel's shorts. There was blood at the crotch, and Drake was crying. Polly sat there for a while with him.

"Finding them won't make a difference," said Drake.

"Probably not," said Polly.

When they got back to the others, they tucked the bag into Ned's dry sack while Maude called for Polly, wondering where on earth she'd hidden the ginger cookies.

Back on the water, Jane and Maude, at the front of the raft, talked about their mirror memories of traveling, being taken to college, being nursed, being advised, being kept safe. They had duplicate memories, too, of a yearly raging fight between Papa and Dee, usually around the time the garden froze, Papa teasing, reminding Dee that she could do nothing about winter—"*Dulce and decorum est.* You're short on decorum, my dear"—and Dee saying he was such an ass.

"And the stories," said Maude. "His stories, testing which was real and which was more terrifying. I'm shocked that none of us were bed wetters."

But Jane had done it, too, and she told them she'd tried her scary stories on Rita—a fable about dead babies, an Italian story about paintings waking—until Dee found out and worried about Rita's reaction and told Jane to stop. But Jane had always wondered if Dee had been doing some of the same thing, making the world wake up in a way that was wonderful only if you could bear it.

She had, they agreed.

"You know," said Maude, "I was so jealous. You had Mother and Hen all to yourselves. I wanted them to go on forever, and it's only now that I'm beginning to understand why they didn't mind leaving. Somehow it just starts feeling like the right thing to do."

No one said anything for a moment. Ned was in the drift boat with the kids, all of them giggling, and Merle was off alone in the kayak again, letting it spin on a quiet, wide stretch. Drake let the raft drift.

"Maude," he said.

"I'm fine," she said. "I am content. I was thinking of your sociopath just now. It's funny how you keep meeting the same people, decade after decade."

"If this was a movie, he'd die," said Drake. "But I doubt he's long for this world."

"Horrible people live forever," said Polly.

"Not always."

"Mostly," said Polly.

He smiled and she watched his mind go.

At home, Helen was back to her mud creatures. She'd found a new piece of old glass from the long-lost greenhouse. It was wavy, attached to a blackened piece of glazing, and only then did Polly remember the tiny lump of diamond she'd tucked in the windowsill bowl. There was no explanation for Dee storing diamonds with her tomatoes, but maybe they should look for more, get Harry and his archaeological sifting screens into the garden and all take a trip to Rome or Thailand or something somewhere pricey.

Helen was writing letters with the hose in the air now, flushing birds. It was supposed to rain and the whole yard would look like Helen's body, slick pale clay that dried and turned to dust and would eventually coat every surface in Polly's house. Dee's Long Island garden and Jane's garden in Michigan had been built on ancient sand dunes, ground quartz and coral dreaming green ocean thoughts. Polly's mud dreamed nothing, but in the garden, digging, her bicycle lobotomy was meaningless, icing on the cake. Polly put her water glass down to weed, knowing she would find it again next week. Here you didn't fret about garter snakes or daddy longlegs; almost nothing survived here, including the hissing hornworms of her memory of Frank's garden. Polly had seen only one in Montana, crawling across the street as she drove to the grocery. She'd been pregnant with Helen, and Sam had watched quietly as she got out to stare at the thing, backed up, ran over the worm, and climbed out again to check the result.

Sam would remember that. How Polly loved him, how she would always be ready to die for him. When she was pregnant with Helen she'd worried about having to share him, him having to share her, but how could anyone pick a favorite child? This wasn't lovers, apples or oranges, favorite novels. It was air or water.

All the bad men, all the made monsters. Sam wasn't going to be one, and Helen wasn't going to fall to one.

Helen wasn't going to fall to anything—she was shrieking at the cat for stalking a magpie, dragging the poor animal back onto a blanket to watch more of the mud magic show. When the rain began, they flipped a coin, and Helen picked the movie: *Sleeping Beauty*. Sam sneered until Polly said she and Ned had both liked it at the same age. She lay under them on the couch, thinking of spindles, thinking of standing by an old sewing machine, Edmund saying touch your finger. Try it. It might change us.

Had he meant: Transform? Take us out of this place, make us someone else, make the world go away? She should see if he remembered.

19

Her Oldest Friend, 1987

In 1968, Polly's first life ended. By the fall she lost the old people, lost her friend, her house, her school, lost almost everything about the way life had been, and she'd begun a different, more hesitant childhood. She and Merle and Jane were alone together in a farmhouse in a small town in Michigan, and by Halloween Polly was waiting for a school bus to a place where she knew no one, guts gone liquid with fear. Utterly lonely.

The farmhouse they'd rented for $50 a month was surrounded by ponds, barns, orchards. She couldn't remember anything of that winter but snowdrifts and asking Jane if she'd tried to find Edmund. In the spring new things were everywhere: fresh-hatched toads, strawberries, bird eggs. Polly draped herself over branches, watching the sky or reading horse books; she ran behind the crop duster when it sprayed sweet-smelling DDT. When the cherries were ripe, the pickers showed up in old cars, huge families packing into concrete bungalows, sleeping on thin mattresses covered with stained striped ticking. She followed them as they picked, because all the children did. She didn't understand the jokes, but the Mexican families, having appraised the renters' clothes and car with some sympathy, were kind to her.

Jane wrote to Rita's brother in Boston, and he replied that his sister was hospitalized but improving, Edmund was fine, everyone was eager to forget this unfortunate period. Jane's next letters were returned, with no forwarding address.

And so Edmund disappeared. Eight months together; nothing like a brother, but nothing like the boys she liked at school, and nothing left but a blurry photo from that first day at the beach, his face in profile, and Rita's painting, which showed their minds, not their bodies. It was as if he had never existed, and when she tried to think of him a few months later on his birthday, she could not see his face or hear his voice.

And then everything about daily life changed again: Jane and Merle produced three more children, and the times before and after New York were divided by a wall of babies, pets, car breakdowns, blizzards. It's hard to be a self-involved teenager in the midst of a swarm; this sudden bloom was probably the best thing Jane could have done for her daughter. Eventually Polly's sadness was convenient, a wallow after a lonely day at school, when she'd lie in bed and imagine she could see Dee make her slow evasive way to the greenhouse, or hear Papa moving through the kitchen, humming or whistling, snapping his fingers. The worst moments came from a sense that she was letting go of things she should keep.

When Polly thought of Edmund in the next few years, he'd become one of the lost people, someone who'd vanished as absolutely as Evie and Frank, Papa and Dee. Edmund wasn't the only abandoned child of that time, and by high school, many of her friends would be ruined, while others would bounce through.

After college, Polly moved to New York. She found a job in the pastry department at Dean & DeLuca, then small but glorious on Prince Street; she aspired to a job in cheese or meat. She ate coffee beans and berries all day, trading sweets for slices of pâté and salami, sable and vacherin, and she weighed barely a hundred pounds. Caterings blurred together in a succession of white carpets and cupboards, and larger parties were like going to war. This was at the dawn of actually trying to make food taste good at huge events: vans filled with lilacs and mock orange, vats of cream, always several mental breakdowns to monitor. And it was the dawn of AIDS, Polly moving through the boys who didn't know they were dying yet, none of them understanding how deeply they'd later wish they'd loved even these low-wage hours, any hour, just one more day.

After two years, sick of food and drama, she crawled through a series of magazine offices with her English degree clamped in her teeth, pumped up her typing skills with an egg timer, and found a job as an assistant, and then a script editor. She gave up words again when she finally had a good salary and joined her friend Jimmy in opening a place down on Hudson. Polly would handle the bar menu.

One of their customers was a writer named Mark. She'd met him when he'd been hired to write a piece for one of the magazines, which he turned in late. Neither had been impressed with the other, and he hadn't asked her out until he'd seen her slide past the line at Great Jones at 2:00 a.m. He made love competently and energetically, but entirely in his own head, watching. She'd seen him peering down his long flat stomach at his erection with more obvious admiration than she managed. In his novels, he made striking observations without real curiosity, and certainly without empathy, and that would eventually leave him without much of a career when the novelty wore off.

But Polly was unkind. Mark had all the right pieces around a flawed, sulky core. She liked his friends, liked the glow—the second novel was getting advance talk—and she was so bruised by the attempt to open the restaurant that she rolled along, mostly smiling, even when Mark introduced her as Papa's granddaughter. Great-granddaughter, she'd say, looking the other way, reaching for a glass.

"Well, he raised you," Mark would snap. "*The Arc of the Mind*, you know, *Myths and Variations*. Dated now, but revolutionary in the day."

They, she thought. They raised me. And not really; they were gone before she was nine. Though it was true that they had changed everything in the world.

She and Jimmy began serving to friends while the kitchen was still Visqueened, wires exposed, drywall not yet taped. On this particular afternoon, an eighteen-year-old actor named Drake had been in for scraps and stayed too long, and now Polly was catching up, moving too quickly between a crap stove and a jerry-rigged hot plate, stirring lemon curd while she told Jimmy a story about the kid's affair with a producer's daughter, the hours he'd spent hiding naked in a dumbwaiter at the Dakota.

Polly laughed at her own story and water from the double boiler splashed onto the hot plate wiring. The shock threw her against the industrial shelving five feet away as if the room had tilted and she'd fallen out a window, as if someone had yanked her into a crevasse.

"Oh, Evie," she said from the floor. "What a surprise."

But it was Barry the cheese seller bending over her with a different kind of soft eyes; he'd just arrived with a delivery of illicit raw milk cheeses. Polly felt slow-muscled but clear, dreamy and lucid, like a flu victim on cool sheets after a fever breaks. From the level of alarm—Jimmy was keening—she wondered if her hair had changed color, if her ears were bleeding, if she'd peed her pants. She wondered if she were dead, but when she started to cry the tears were convulsive, almost ecstatic.

But Barry was calm.

"I fall all the time," said Polly.

"I'm sure you do," he said. "But you actually flew this time."

She was up and back at the bar by then, after speeding through her prep. She'd never felt better in her life. She loved this combination of serving and cooking, performance art without fussiness. It was a warm day in April, and women outside were forcing summer in short skirts, their pale legs mottled with the effort. Barry, who'd been in twice before, was tall, with curly brown hair and a long, lumpy, Celtic face that would probably droop later in life. He'd been monosyllabic on earlier deliveries until he had a glass of something, and she'd caught him watching her, but he seemed curious, not creepy. He simply seemed to like her, and this was endearing compared to Mark, who now was leaning on a weary arm and lecturing him on psychology. Mark was writing a novel about a shrink, and he'd spent the last month testing his theories on Polly.

Still, she felt good, clean and strange after the shock. "I'm remembering things I haven't in years," she said. "I had a theory when I was a kid that people didn't die, they just found a new life and started over in a different place, as children. My aunt and grandfather were killed in an accident, and I thought I would find them."

"A dream, darling," said Mark. "Not a memory." He thought her family had encouraged an unhealthy fantasy life. She'd told him very little, but now she wished she'd told him nothing.

"No," Polly said. She had a theory, and the whole world was a story, and every story she'd ever heard had a point. "I can track it back. I remember remembering."

"What she isn't mentioning is that her whole family is strange," Mark said to Barry. "Maybe they reinforced this."

"You've never met my family, Mark."

That snapping sound in the background was a last vestige of affection, puffing away like a dandelion, popping like a lightbulb element, henceforth unfathomable. Polly had been on her way to this point, but now she achieved several stages in a matter of seconds. She couldn't believe she'd slept with him; she couldn't believe she'd touched him.

"Did you ever feel like you'd found them?" Barry asked.

"Once, in the Village," she said. She stood still, singed brain seeing Jane ironing with starch, hearing the hiss and crackle and smell while Walter Cronkite or Chet Huntley talked about death. A casket, more weeping, beautiful horses towing a box with a body through crowds. How would magic be done with so many people watching?

"Tell me about it," said Barry.

Back then, when cooking hadn't accelerated into annual cassoulet parties and a hundred pissy, redundant blog entries on how to make ricotta, you could still stun a human with simple things, real mozzarella or an honest tomato or a good butter crust, fresh sardines at 25 cents a pound from Queens, $1 one-clawed lobsters from Chinatown. The next day, Polly chopped green olives with a not quite Swedish version of cured salmon—cured the way Dee had cured it for Papa, not too sweet—with good olive oil and chives; she made chickpea fritters with red onion and drizzled them with an aioli made with the syrup from preserved lemons. She'd stuffed squid and stewed it in a fresh red sauce, à la Dee; she would slice it and serve it over a pile of orecchiette, topped with chopped basil. For the following day, she planned a duck thigh—soft inside, crackling outside, topped with bread crumbs and a sauce with sharp cider and mustard—and Jane's anchovy-dosed meatloaf (anchovies had been Dee's secret ingredient; the past was never quite past), caramelized on the outside and served with ribbons of *conserva*. Maybe a jarring note of scallops with a lime and red chiles—none of these things necessarily went together. The surviving lemon curd folded with meringue, studded with fresh berries for today, a macaroon with palm sugar tomorrow.

On this second night, Polly again noticed Barry's discomfort when he first entered, when he first looked at her, and she did not know if she should try to surmount it. She brought the dishes out one at a time, wanting to see his expression. The seduction might have seemed feminine, but the whole approach was essentially macho, a boy dare, less a tease (anything placed in a mouth is beyond a tease) than a challenge: Try this, little boy. Try to keep a straight face when you put this in your mouth. Try to say it's nothing. Try to resist.

"Open your mouth and shut your eyes," she said. She was nervous, because there was no one else in the bar, no buffer to awkwardness. She waited, and she fell into love.

Barry dabbed a finger into the squid and sauce and smiled at her as he put the finger in his mouth. "This is wonderful."

He looked different today, better. His hair looked darker and thicker, and the bruiser look to his nose now seemed comforting and lived-in.

"It was my great-grandmother's recipe," Polly said, and then wondered at the way his face closed down. Did he doubt her, too?

"You were lucky," he said. The line dangled, but he changed the topic. There was a show at the Met he wanted to see. Would she ever want to meet up on her day off?

She said she would, and that she would show him some things her great-grandfather had found in Scythia before World War I, still on display.

The next afternoon, when she had to leave early for a catering, she left a note for Jimmy: *Give Barry a slice of focaccia.*

"You mean Berry, as in Berrigan?" said Jimmy. "His real name's Ned."

He didn't notice when she started calling him Ned. Maybe she'd never called him anything out loud before, but the next night at the bar she asked questions. Why cheese? Why not farming? Pork, bees, apples. Why not law? (She had at some point sussed out the fact that Ned had gone to law school.)

He made a face and laughed. Jimmy had brought in a bowl of tiny wild strawberries and she popped one in Ned's mouth. He smiled while he ate it, and she leaned over and kissed him, and he kissed her back and then pulled away.

His face was flushed, and now Polly flushed, too. She should have waited; she should not have assumed he felt that way. She filled their wine-glasses and went back to scribbling down a list of recipes. Why not fishing? she asked, floundering back to the conversation, trying to pretend the kiss hadn't happened.

Ned shook his head. He stabbed away at the food—a potpie like no other, a spinach salad with pistachios. "What was the world like, when you were looking for your dead people?" he asked. "What did you see? The daily things."

At three, riding on Merle's young brown back while he swam, looking up at the tops of her grandfather's tomatoes, the whirring sound of Evie shuffling cards. Or at eight, the green parrot from below, flapping away from the hissing cat, the dogwood tree dropping petals, the map.

"A map," she finished.

"I have always loved maps," he said, wiping up crumbs with her bar cloth. He had graceful, smooth-muscled arms, with a line of moles above one wrist.

"What do you remember, from that age?" asked Polly.

"Everything," he said. "But let's start with a girl. I had a friend, a good friend."

Something was happening, and she took in the whorl in his hair, the shape of his mouth, her mind slowing down. "You grew up in Ireland?"

"Not until I was eight. My father died in the war, and my mother was insane."

He emptied his wine and fiddled with his napkin. When he looked up Polly's ears were roaring. She thought of Dee's hands in Edmund's hair, Edmund drawing on a sidewalk with the same arm, Edmund ripping at her as she climbed a tree, Edmund under the porch while they listened to Jane's sad voice, watching each other's eyes and maybe knowing in that moment that everything might go away.

"But you knew that," said Ned. "Polly, I should have told you sooner."

Polly was a crumbled, weeping mess. Jimmy let her close early, and she and Ned walked down to Bayard for dumplings, and then to a bar on Crosby Street, and then to more and later food on Varick. He told her that he'd heard her name when friends were talking about a new place that spring, a few months after he'd arrived in the city from Dublin. He'd headed to the restaurant to see her, to confront her about the way they'd all abandoned him, to explain he'd taken his aunt and uncle's name because he needed to give up everything about his life before the age of ten, to get away from the loss of Rita, Papa and Dee, and, of course, her. He wanted to walk in and witness the moment she recognized him, watch guilt flood over her face, but the shock of seeing her, the shock at realizing he might not have been able to recognize her without some foreknowledge, took him to silence, and dawning familiarity kept him there. His anger cracked off while he watched her move in the chaos behind the bar, and a blast of love followed, something like what he'd felt as a child but also fascination, and lust. If it had seemed like the old longing—Polly as lost family, lost childhood—he might have retreated, creeped out by his own motives. But he felt none of that, or resentment anymore. He just wanted to be with her.

And so he sold her cheeses, and held his tongue. He was sorry he hadn't come out with it, but the longer he waited, the harder it was to imagine explaining. He didn't want to lose her again and he did not know how to get past this moment, this horrible confusion of affections. He called his uncle and told him and said she was always my friend, not my sister. How could it be wrong to feel this way?

Ned's uncle said that it depended on Polly, who at this point was next to Ned as they worked through a nightclub crowd on a sidewalk. He touched her shoulder and then her hip to steer her through and she felt like his hand burned her skin.

They looped around each other for hours, and she waited until he was asleep, facedown and stretched out in the warm apartment, to look at the scars on his shoulder, the kind a cat's claws might make, the raised scar on the back of his leg, the kind of tear the bent metal of an old boat might make, if a boy had tried to tow it toward a beach and a waiting girl and a dead man.

She'd put a fan on, and when she heard rustling paper she sat up: On the far wall, a large map of the New York coast, really just shoreline and islands and a world of blue ocean, was missing one tack, and the loose corner shuddered.

Ned opened one eye.

"It looks alive," Polly said.

"It is alive," said Ned.

They were twenty-seven now, but his face was younger with his eyes closed. Nineteen years later, but how could she not have known?

20

Sunday, July 7, 2002

Ned remembered different things than Polly: a fear of burning astronauts, the funeral train, the riots in Chicago, things Polly had somehow lost. The soft suffering sounds Dee made when she thought no one could hear her, the way Jane danced when she did the dishes and didn't know someone was watching her. He remembered Merle buying the "Hey Jude" single and thinking that the song, with its effort to comfort, was somehow for him. He remembered the things Papa said just to him, those days at the Sound when they went swimming together, about how Ned could live through all of this. He remembered being saved, even though with the loss of Papa and Dee he would be lost again.

The unknowables, always. Ned thought Tommy had had cold-colored gray eyes, but according to Jane, they were green, like Sam's. Maybe that part of Ned's mind had gone to black and white, except for the parrots and the stained glass. The only thing he could remember his father saying, other than "eat your dinner" and "because I said so," was that yes, Tommy had seen and heard bombs, and he'd told Ned he'd learned that if you screamed during an explosion, it kept your eardrums from blowing.

Some things neither of them were sure about.

"Were they magic?" asked Polly.

"Oh yes," said Merle.

"Did the cards move?"

"Probably. I'd forgotten about you going on about that, Dee making you look at the faces. When you had a fever, you made me shuffle endlessly."

"Did the feathers move?"

"They did after May finally killed Dwight. We managed not to tell you that."

"What do you really remember of that time?" she asked Ned, a few months in, when she'd gotten back from Montana and asked if he'd move and he had to decide whether to make that leap of faith. "What is strongest?"

"I remember love," he said. "And wonder. So much was so hard afterward, too, but they saved me."

Late on the afternoon of the float, after the rain and movie ended, Ned found Polly in the garden. He didn't ask where she'd been this time.

"Oh god," she said. "What time is it? We're down to Chinese on Maude's list."

He sat down in the next chair and leaned back. Polly knew he was thinking of the last Chinese feast, the toxic cloud of smoke when she walked away from the pan of hot chile oil. Or maybe he was thinking of the previous week, which felt like a lifetime away now: a column of flaming oil, the souls of battered squash blossoms ascending, shrieking their way toward the ceiling. Polly snapped out of it to find Ned lowering the wok lid to snuff the flames.

"You've outdone yourself," he said. "But why be upset when we like to cook together?"

The new normal. Tonight, though, he said, "We could just order some fucking pizzas."

"What a good idea," said Polly.

You never knew when she would just agree. The new, constructive Polly let Ned talk Maude and the others into takeout and stayed in the garden with her notebook to make a list of tasks that she thought she could and could not do well anymore. It was a nice clean feeling. She put an arrow by what might improve and a question mark for things she might be too cocky about.

> *Can do: organizing day generally, laying out Drake's series plot, turning off ovens.*
> *Not so good: attention while driving, attention while cooking, patience, open flames and hot oil.*

And so on. No longer grace in motion in the kitchen, no longer second nature. Ned said he wouldn't worry about her if she wouldn't worry about him. She looked up and could see him through the window, moving around the kitchen, laughing at something Jane or Merle was saying. Her love, her oldest friend.

They finally cleaned off the dining room table for the meal. Over their heads Maude thumped around, packing for her morning flight. She refused to stay to see a local doctor. Merle and Ned were belatedly taking an interest in the photos that hadn't been displayed, the ones that weren't about Maude: their own childhoods and families, the other lives of the house, left behind in the messy boxes. The smiling aunts Inge and Odile, posed in front of the porch—if Polly looked out her bedroom window, they would have been standing directly below, and she'd have seen their coiled silver hair and smelled their lily of the valley perfume. Merle as a bedridden child and a tanned, fit teenager on a dock, the withered arm hidden by a towel. Scrabbly shots of Polly and her toddler sister and brothers, the surprises, sitting on a draft horse. Ned leggy and sixteen next to a tower at Glendalough, Ned and his uncle and Rita, taken the day before she walked into the ocean at Sandy-mount; Ned and Polly lying on the grass in Prospect Park. When Polly had mailed this last one home to Michigan with the news of their meeting, a bomb went off. Merle opened his first bottle of wine in a decade, and Jane took to her bed. It was all somehow funny in hindsight, but that first visit to Michigan—Merle and Ned arguing, Polly and Jane arguing—had been fraught.

When she and Ned first slept together, and for the next several months, it shocked Polly, over and over. When he wasn't in her presence, she'd start feeling woozy and nostalgic, thinking of them as children, thinking of the strangeness of it all. When they were together, he wasn't that boy, and she wasn't that girl. They were new.

It took a long time for Merle and Jane to leave the guilt behind. There were constant small scenes. "Just let us go then," said Ned, pulling Polly out the door on the third day of their visit. They went swimming and found a place in the dunes in the hot wind, and nothing would ever be that good again, pleasure that ripped at your heart and skin and bones.

Now Merle and Ned snickered over a photo from that visit, the two of them surly by a barbecue, Polly's younger siblings circling them, confused by the subtext but waiting for a fight. These days Ned and Merle could handle talking about Rita, they could talk about Tommy, and they could even handle Maude stumping downstairs, demanding a gimlet, saying one last time that it was a wonder that they'd all survived. She looked through the evidence of that survival once Ned delivered her drink: photographs from the wedding, from the trip to Spain, from bleaker moments during renovation. Polly pregnant, Sam as a newborn, the three of them in Ireland with Ned's aunt and uncle, Helen still screaming in her fourth month of colic, Polly's sister, Millie, caught sitting on Drake's lap.

Drake's researcher had found footage from Papa's retirement party in 1968, and he'd printed out some stills for them. Polly could make out the hedge, and it seemed so ratty. No one could lose herself in such a maze. She could see the rowboat down by the shore, closer than she remembered, and it all looked very domesticated. They—Edmund Thomas Ward Berrigan and Apollonia Asta Schuster—were mostly blurs. Polly was visible leaning in behind Dee, whispering in Jane's ear, Jane with beautiful legs and sandaled painted toes, and Edmund stood behind them, waiting for the answer to whatever question Polly had asked: When will the cake be served, can we let Lemon out of the car again, why do you think it's too late to swim? Tonight she thought of the brief good moment it had been, rather than disappearance—the beach, the salty stink mixing with the bonfire, the crowd on the lawn moving around beautiful Jane in the turquoise shift, while the doomed man and doomed Rita, the other beauty, walked toward the edge of the water. Borderlands, liminal spaces: Papa had written a great essay on that, too, about the tilting moment in so many stories.

Polly looked up and Ned was watching her—no message, just watching.

Maybe the wall had moved, maybe the air in the glass had said something. Maybe that witch really had bitten the dog's tail off. Love and wonder; everything goes missing but everything lives on, at least for a while, in the small kingdom of your head.

Things Polly couldn't know, even with the best mind on the planet: That Thomas Ward really had lain on a garden path in a quiet yard in Hue, with ants marching by as he died; that for some reason he hadn't felt pain, or fear, and the last thing he saw was a beetle climbing and bending a blade of grass. That Polly would develop a script for Drake that would finally work, and she would make silly money with him and see Italy with her family and get food poisoning in the Rome airport. That Josie and Harry, who would end up eloping to Fort Benton after their third wedding date was derailed, would have thirty years together. That Merle would start writing poetry again, and Jane would like it. That the man and girl Polly had watched in the city when she was little—the people she thought were Frank and Evie—had thought they recognized her somehow, too. That Graham would die a few months later as a passenger in a car accident, lost on a bad turn to the

Columbia River. That when Jane, who had always known what Ivor had done to her mother, realized who he was that night at the party, and Papa had asked if she wanted him left alone, she said she wanted him dead. That Maude wouldn't make the trip the next year or go to the tribute in New York; she would fall and hit her head in late September and die a few hours later without waking up.

That there was no way around any of this.

After dinner, Polly went out to the garden. Jane would think she was having a spell but really she was watching the bats as she let herself go back to a moment in Stony Brook. Maybe it had been in June, while Rita was in the bin, maybe a day in July, rainy just like today. They were in the attic, arguing about how to put together Dee's spinning wheel—Dee had tried to learn weaving during the months after she'd shattered her leg. Jane had taken them to *Sleeping Beauty* the day before, to get them away from Rita, and watched them sneer at the fear in the faces of the less worldly children around them. This had been one of the stories Jane had tested on them, admittedly not a myth about flood but about another wall of nature, a garden and thorns.

"Touch it," said Edmund in the attic. "See if it changes us."

The creak of the wheel. "You try," said Polly.

"All right," said Edmund. "Now switch dreams."

Rain was thudding down on wet grass, browning dogwood blossoms, discarded toys, the towels Jane had left on the line weighing down the cheap cord so that the laundry dipped to the grass, to the mud and whatever else. The cat darted toward the house, tail like a baseball bat, making for the broken basement window. The witch's parrot swooped after it, playing hawk.

Nothing happened. They turned to the pieces of glass, stowed up here after the greenhouse was cleaned out for Rita. Red—would it smell like blood if they smacked it open? It would not. Polly chose yellow, and they thought they smelled sulfur. It wasn't like either of them to destroy old things; they were far too superstitious. Maybe they thought they could grind the glass into some special paint for Rita. Maybe they thought they were freeing ghosts. They decided on a last color, the deep blue. Another crunch, and a gust through the window blew the lamp over. In the kitchen, it scattered the flour around Dulcy's dough, and she laughed, and in Henning's study, it swept a map of France off the wall, and they could hear him swear and then hum on his way down the hall to make more coffee, to see how she was feeling.

"I don't think we should break the blue pieces again," Polly said.

"No," said Edmund.

Decades later, in the Montana wind, Polly thought about the mostly lost order of things, the hidden worlds in her brain, where everyone was still alive, the smell of Dee cooking, the wars of the face cards, the succession of plants on the path to the Sound. But the shifting creatures in the hallway map gradually gave way to the clank of Ned playing alchemist in their kitchen right now, to Sam running by or whatever spell Helen was casting in her mud kingdom.

The way Polly had hoped the world would always be was maybe not far from what it had become. She kept her eyes shut to see people she loved for a few more minutes, to move once again down the long hall past Rita's moving map of the world, a river filling the overwhelming ocean. Then she gave up and opened them to the new green of the old yard.

ACKNOWLEDGMENTS

I'd like to thank Stephen Potenberg and the rest of my family and friends for their patience, love, and support, and for the thousand small things I've borrowed from all of them and hidden in this book. Thanks go to Martha Crewe and Janice Kimmel, for finding mistakes that are invisible to the normal eye, and to Teresa "Lilly" White, who provided forensic knowledge and humor. Sharon Dynak and all the wonderful people at the Ucross Foundation gave me a beautiful place and the luxury of time to finish this book and start another.

My deepest thanks to Dara Hyde of Hill Nadell Literary Agency, for her friendship and her wisdom and her ability to lead me out of swamps.

Working with Megan Fishmann, Jennifer Kovitz, and the other fine people at Counterpoint and Catapult is a joy. And while it's trite to say "I couldn't have written this book without . . ." it can also be true: My editor, Dan Smetanka, is a genius. You're right, Dan. Thank you.

© Melanie Maganias Nashan

JAMIE HARRISON, who has lived in Montana with her family for more than thirty years, has worked as a caterer, a gardener, and an editor. She is the author of five previous novels—the Jules Clement series of mysteries and *The Widow Nash*, a finalist for the High Plains Book Award and the winner of the Mountains & Plains Independent Booksellers Association Reading the West Book Award. Find out more at jamieharrisonbooks.com.